ASHLEY FONTAINNE

a novel

RMSW PRESS

Copyright © by Ashley Fontainne 2014

Publisher: RMSW Press, LLC

ISBN-13: 978-0692354346

ISBN-10: 0692354346

Cover and interior design: Ashley Fontainne

Photo credit: Taylor Bellott http://www.tbellottgallery.com

Editor: Jeff LaFerney

Dedication

For my Mother,

Joanna Lee Doster, Donna Thompson, Betty Dravis and Donna Lickteig.

My heartfelt thanks to each of you for all

the support and encouragement given.

Contents

Other works

Novels
Empty Shell
The Lie – soon to be the feature film FORESEEN
www.foreseenmovie.com
Number Seventy-Five – soon to be a feature film
www.number75themovie.com
Eviscerating the Snake Trilogy:
Accountable to None
Zero Balance
Adjusting Journal Entries
Poetry and Short Story Collection
Ramblings of a Mad Southern Woman
Coming soon
The Magnolia Series – co-authored with Lillian
Hansen
Blood Ties
Blood Loss
Blood Stain

CHAPTER ONE

My name is Sheryl Ilene Newcomb. And yes, my initials are S.I.N. A funny little piece of whimsical humor my parents found amusing when I arrived. Mom and Dad were two high school sweethearts who adored their guns, their beer, and their self-appointed titles of King and Queen of the Rebellious Rednecks. The day I was born, they didn't think anyone in the town would have the mental acuity to put two and two together to discover their little inside joke. Shame on the pathetic excuses who called themselves teachers in this dreary city because Mom and Dad had been right: no one caught on to their little attempt at humor.

Then, it turned out to be true. Looking back with wiser eyes now, my family and I concluded that the events leading up to my transformation started the summer I turned nine. But the day we realized there was a problem, and no turning back, was a week before I started my senior year at Junction City High. The day the fangs and claws appeared and the monster inside of me emerged. When mutilated corpses appeared near a pile of brush down by Caney Creek, everything changed.

That day I changed—forever—because evil woke up and growled, its ominous rumblings heard by every living thing in Locasia County, Mississippi.

CHAPTER TWO

It was all over—for now. The ending completed, and the living nightmare of what happened in our sleepy little town nothing more than a permanent stain embedded in my mind and body. I stared at the words on the page, the white paper covered in bright blue ink. The empty pages behind it waited, impatient for me to add more. They sat in mocking silence on the desk in front of me. A twinge of apprehension slithered up my back.

What am I doing?

During the last three months, I thought I'd done a decent job of stopping the memories. None of what happened was something anyone could be prepared to endure. No longer did the vile sounds and unbelievable images pop up during the middle of the day. I felt a sense of pride I stopped them without the use of medication. With the support of my mom and dad and the Lord above, I worked daily to bury the horrific events.

I shivered at the disturbing recollections. When the crystal clear images of the final battle exploded inside my head, they turned my slender torso into a shivering pile of goose bumps. I was unable to stop the screams of agony and anger when my mind replayed the events at night. Physical and mental anguish would slam into my body and soul as I fought not only the animal inside of me, but the one that stared at me from inside my mind.

The eerie visions of the final confrontation were as terrifying in my mind's eye as the actual day they occurred. Dark, jade-green eyes lit from within bored through my own with their anticipatory killing stare. The growl from its furry throat would seem as loud in my memories as it did when it happened. The flexed muscles of the creature jerked in its readiness to shred me down to a bloody pile of mush. The bright moon's rays shimmered off of its stark white fangs. One swipe of the enormous paw or bite from the strong jaws would end it all. My cries of sorrow erupted at night when the images of the dismembered corpses appeared inside my mind. They were seared into my memory banks. I hadn't experienced a moment of heart-stopping, frozen-to-one-spot freakouts in two months during the daytime. I whittled them down to only haunting my dreams at night.

Progress, plain and simple.

A sound caught my attention, so I lifted my stare from the ruled, white paper on the desk and looked out my bedroom window. My sharp, one-eyed gaze glanced over to the pool and settled on the old, rusty swing at the edge of our backyard. I recalled with a slight smile the day last week when I took my first step out of the house and sat outside for almost an hour. The warmth of the sun and the gentle urges of my mother's voice lured me into the water—at least the shallow end. I considered it a big leap in my recovery progress since I had developed a strong distaste for water. I had sat on the bottom step, the cool water barely up to my shins, and fought the urge to run back inside and lock myself inside my bedroom. The task of quelling my paralyzing fears had taken every ounce of mental strength to overcome. It was beyond weird at my age, but I felt safe in my adolescent bedroom. It was my territory. But I also knew it would become my prison if I didn't learn to live outside its four walls again. Like a normal, sane person lives.

A quiet snicker from my lips bounced off the walls of my room. Sanity. Normalcy. Those ships sailed away *eons* ago, pulled under the dark waters of the mighty Mississippi River, never to be seen again.

The cold pencil in my right hand was my only weapon now—and I hoped all I would ever need again. My other, formidable weapons I kept well hidden after I learned to control them. Well, not actually control but coexist with them.

I took a long, hard look at the slender pencil and gave myself a mental kick for my decision to relive it all. Only yesterday, I had made the complete transition between the house and the backyard without a hitch or any assistance or prodding from my parents. My doctor and physical therapist, Dr. Joanna Montray, told us when she visited yesterday, I was making significant progress toward recovery. I recalled the air of bemusement from the good doctor while she took my vitals. Dr. Montray stopped asking weeks ago why we refused to let the wounds be cared for at the hospital. The answer was always the same. Silence. As Dr. Montray's warm fingers poked and prodded my old injuries, she had seemed pleased my limp was less pronounced and the numerous scars had become a light pink rather than blaring red.

I refused to show any outward emotion when Dr. Montray announced in her calm, gentle way that my eye would never recover. She followed her statement with assurance that the left eye had fully taken over duties from the useless right one. Unable to blink enough to keep my eyeball wet, the black eye patch would need to stay in place a while longer. The only smidgeon of comfort was it didn't need to be removed.

I already lost enough.

Dr. Montray seemed happy when she discovered me outside in the backyard by the pool and commented on the benefits of the sun. It would help the healing process she'd said with genuine enthusiasm. Vitamin D from the warm rays would accelerate my recovery. But as Dr. Montray examined me, I sensed her uneasiness at being so close to me. My broken bones had already healed in record time. My shattered pelvis and right leg should have taken months to mend.

Instead, they took less than three weeks.

The doctor's hands quaked with a slight tremble, yet her movements were skilled and quick while she gave me the world's fastest exam. With irritation, I smiled and nodded in agreement, even though what I really wanted to do was burst out into a wild cackle. Seriously? Recovery? None of us would ever be the same.

Ever.

Mom must have sensed the doctor's thoughts or something because she intervened and maneuvered Dr. Montray toward the front door. Of course, Mom knew the truth and played along in the deceitful storyline she helped to concoct. The Newcomb clan told the police, medical staff, reporters, and anyone who dared ask about what had happened, our little contrived tale. The whole town bought our story, but that was only because their minds had been manipulated. Only my little family knew the entire truth, and we sure weren't going to let it out. No one would believe us anyway, even if we did decide to open our mouths.

Thinking about the doctor's visit yesterday agitated me. I slammed the pencil down on the old oak desk with too much force. A small crack appeared where my fist connected. I shoved aside the memories of the good doctor's visit and sought out other musings to stew upon.

A few days after I regained consciousness from the final showdown, it was discussed in hushed tones inside the relative safety of our kitchen what we should do next. The topic on the table was if the family should pack up a few bags and split town. We had plenty of reasons to leave and few to stay, but we reached the decision to remain. In some weird, creepy way, staying in what the entire family knew as home was comforting. Gratifying might be a better way to describe it. It was, after all, my territory, forever marked with the stain of not only my blood, but the blood of those I loved. My contribution to the conversation, and what I believe swayed my parents to stay, was since I fought the battle and won, why would I give up the spoils of war? Six generations of Newcomb's had owned the land, and the ones who lived and died there before us worked it as sharecroppers before they became land owners. Like it or not, the soil ran deep and gave as much life to us as our blood did, so we stayed.

My valiant speech, full of pride and determination, was not the truth. We all knew it, yet no one brought the real subject up. We wouldn't leave because it was my duty, my hereditary destiny, to remain.

To catch a better view out the window, I cocked my head. The sounds of children playing outside at recess at McCarson Elementary had caught my attention earlier. Miles away from my house, it was still eerie to me to hear things from such a distance. I shook the thought away and tried to find some contentment and comfort in the meticulous backyard, groomed to perfection by my mother, or the four walls of our small house—walls which hid me away from the rest of the world and helped muffle my screams of anguish at night. It was the same framing and basic design as it had been when Pop-pop built it in 1925. The house was one of a handful that hadn't been washed away in the flood of 1927, and it sported updated plumbing and electrical work. When other families moved back into town, they must have all thought Pop-pop did a great job on the design because the homes that lined our block looked almost identical. The town's layout was probably an exact replica of every other small, southern town in the Delta region.

But for me, nothing was the same.

Junction City, Mississippi, was still full of gossipy women. Ones who flitted about, their mouths eager to drop the latest juicy stories into the prickling ears of whomever would hold still long enough to listen. The bored wives of the town's mayor, police chief, and two lawyers were the worst of the bunch. How many times I had overheard them at the diner, pretending to whisper to each other, but really, speaking loud enough that most of the customers would hear the latest news? All of their hen parties were conducted while they slurped down dessert to add to the wide load they already carried. An ant couldn't walk across a blade of crisp grass with a crumb of cake on its back without it becoming a topic of discussion. God knows they had a lot to chirp about after the events of the last few months. Their tongues would explode from being overworked. The murders, fires, and massive explosion would keep them gabbing well into their graves. Their tongues might give out before their chubby bodies expired.

Some of the younger folks, like me, had whined about poor cell phone reception and slower-than-cold-molasses Internet speed. Last summer, a few of us combined our talents. We put together a slick presentation for the board members of the Quorum Court, requesting newer, faster equipment. We had it all worked out—fancy charts full of financial figures of the costs and benefits to the community. It was just a simple matter of getting the phone company to come in and install a new tower and lines. Easy as baking an apple pie, we said. The expenditure would benefit all of the residents of the county, including all students and our ability to study and learn online at a faster pace.

For school and studying purposes, of course. None of us had kept a straight face when that little lie popped out, and our request was denied. Dane had laughed and said that a faster form of communication was not necessary since we had the lightning fast tongues of the local Gossip Queens.

Friday night football games, and the players gifted with athletic ability, still ruled the school and the town. Even though our basketball team, led by Dane, won the state basketball championship last year, football reigned supreme. It seemed the town was drawn to the violent, bone-crushing tackles and acrobatic catches by the players. Football brought out the beast in everyone, and basketball simply did not.

The six block radius which made up the downtown section shut down every Sunday, except for the two restaurants, one of which my family owned. Both opened precisely after church ended. Preston's Gas-N-Go, another business in its fifth generation of family ownership, was the only place to get your fuel, including diesel for all the farmers. During harvest season, the line of vehicles waiting to get gas would sometimes be twenty deep.

If you wanted something from Wilson's Sundries, you'd better get it before the store closed at 11:59 pm on the dot each Saturday. If, God forbid, your kid was sick and needed medicine, you ran out of tampons, sore throat lozenges, chips or snacks, or had a hankering for chocolate, you were out of luck. That is, unless you wanted to drive over forty miles to the nearest Walmart or hospital in Greenville.

Each year, trampy cheerleaders bounced around the downtown area in short skirts and skintight tops. They blinked their heavily painted eyelids at the shopkeepers to pledge donations for the school. Well, really for the football team, but that was an unspoken understanding. And each year, the store owners caved to the pressure and hurled cash at the girls, even if their money drawers were running on fumes. It was good practice for the girls for later in life while they worked stripper poles at the casinos in Greenville or Helena.

I smirked at the memory of the last time I had been a part of the fleecing because I made sure some of the money went to the basketball team. Yesterday, while I sat in the very same spot, I watched the newest batch of young meat strut up and down Main Street, led by the new head cheerleader, Savannah. She had taken my place at the helm of the Junction City Cheering Cats. Even after everything that happened, the lives lost and the survivors damaged beyond repair, vanity still trumped sorrow.

Bitter and harsh, but the truth hurts. And I had every right to think such things because before my transformation, I had been one of those gals. I had no qualms about parading around the streets like I owned the place. That type of behavior was ingrained in young females since the dawn of time. The outcome of displaying sexual availability was always the same—to find a mate. It ensured the next generation would be produced. The only thing that changed with each new crop of teenagers was the way they conducted themselves. My generation had no moral hangups and embraced our sexuality with fervor.

I had been a tad different than the rest of my small peer group. I only wielded my budding sexuality as a teaser, a tantalizing glimpse, in front of the locals. The only person I let experience the full package was my boyfriend, Dane. None of the other country bumpkins piqued my interest in the slightest. Oh, I had my fair share of crushes when I first hit puberty, but they were innocent and harmless. My first real date had been with Dane Witherspoon V, and once we held hands while walking down the main part of town, I was hooked.

Some of my friends didn't just play the part—they lived it. They gave the Gossip Queens at the diner lots to talk about when one cheerleader, Tami Rogers, became the proud parent of a bouncing baby boy in her sophomore year. The father, Drexel Kilgore Jr., was the son of the biggest rice farmer in the county. According to the wagging tongues, Drexel Jr. didn't exactly *go* for girls. Rumors spread about a few others who went down to

Greenville to take care of unpleasant and unwanted situations. Dr. Montray was the only physician in town, and she didn't offer that type service. I overheard my parents discuss it one night after dinner years ago, right after Dr. Montray set up her practice. They both agreed it was a strong stance for the young doctor to take. I think they sort of admired her grit and determination to uphold what she saw was her duty—save lives, not take them.

Most of my former friends hopped from the back of one pickup truck bed to another during our high school years. Once they learned power rested on their chest and between their legs, they used it. Daily. Like every other woman had done when her hips widened, her rump spread, and her boobs appeared since the dawn of time. Hell, Tami Kilgore (nee Rogers) lived the high life at the Kilgore place because of her skills, her offspring the newest heir to the Kilgore fortune.

Well, she *used* to live there. Now, Drexel and his parents were raising little Drex alone. What pieces of Tami left big enough to gather and bury were crammed inside a pink casket six feet under in Ridgemond Cemetery, Tami's plan to reign as the "Queen Bee of Locasia County" ripped to shreds.

Right along with her innards.

No stripper pole for me, though. I had big plans which included a move to Memphis with Dane. We had it all worked out. Graduation, summer break in Panama City, then on to the excitement of living in a big city, away from the backwoods muck pile we'd been raised in. Dane's stellar basketball skills landed him a full scholarship with the Tigers, and my knack for science won my acceptance to the same school—though not on a full ride. After the first year of living in the freshman dorms, Dane and I would move

in with my cousin, Corinne, in her two bedroom apartment. Corinne offered us the opportunity to stay rent free
until we graduated. It was a sweet deal because I would get
to keep part of the tip share while I cooked three nights
each week at Corinne's restaurant. My parents agreed to
help with financial aid, excited their only child would be a
college graduate—the first in our family.

Best laid plans...

I raised my misty eye from my backyard. I looked past
the tops of the little houses lining the streets beyond the
central part of town. My gaze landed on the blackened
patch of earth known as Cohestra Industries. The place
used to take up over twenty acres, parking lot included.
Nothing was left except the grain silos and the smaller
outbuildings. The silos stood next to each other like two
orphaned children in front of the soot-covered debris of
their childhood home.

A surge of energy prickled in my skin. The hairs on the
back of my neck stood erect as my hackles raised. My fingers gripped the table with such force, my thick nails dug
into the hard wood. A low rumble rose from deep within.
My chair shook from the vibrations. The guttural growl
reverberated inside the walls of my chest. It was one thing
to recall the night in my head, but looking at the charred
leftovers of the real thing was quite another. The strong
pull of the evil inside, buried under the piles of rubble,
made me gasp in pain. I blinked and moved my gaze away,
focusing on the Newcomb's Diner sign about six miles
from town.

In ignorant bliss, generations of townspeople born and
raised inside the confines of Locasia County lived quiet
lives. In the heart of the Mississippi Delta country, the
roots to the founding fathers ran deep and long, like the

namesake mighty river. The entire region lived, breathed, and died farming. Mostly rice but a few cotton and sugar cane fields remained. Unlike the rest of the region, our county was profitable—and relatively crime free. Over the years, some adventurous souls slipped through the cracks and escaped. Unwilling to live around the stubborn, old fashioned etiquette and pace of the place, they wanted the fast lane lifestyles only found in the bigger cities—like I intended to do. But those escapees were few and far between. Most stayed because their roots, like my own, tethered them to the fertile soil.

Once the first breath was drawn in the town, the tie was sealed. Forever.

Guess I haven't been fair with my portrayal of Junction City. As with all places where humans live, it was peppered with people with hearts full of hate, but also those with hearts of love. Kind souls like crazy Nana, sweet Meemaw, Mom, and Dad. Of course I felt that way about them, for they were family, so it didn't seem fair to include them. But folks like Papa Joe and Shirlene—both of them worked at the diner ever since I could remember. Papa Joe cooked and Shirlene waited tables for over thirty years. They were real, down-home people full of warmth and kindness. Most people in Junction City would literally give you the shirt off their backs if you needed it or a warm meal and an interested ear to listen to your grievances. The majority of our community was full of good people.

But when weighed against the few evil ones, it didn't matter.

I took a deep breath and focused my attention back to my original plan. The fear of being outside had finally been conquered, so it was time to confront the last hurdle looming in front of me. In one of our last conversations,

Papa Joe said I needed to pass the truth along to the next generation. Prepare the next guardian. It was part of my duty. Plus, I had to dislodge the memories and remove them from my dreams before I went completely bonkers. Well, not dreams. The appropriate word for the broken sleep, ear-splitting screams, and sweat-soaked sheets would be night terrors.

Mom brought home a new typewriter yesterday. Her rationale was if I started to write things down, they would leave my head and vanish into the air. Or stick to the pages and be trapped forever. I had not told her about Papa Joe's admonitions to keep the next generation informed. I smiled at the memory, Mom's face so full of love and worry after she set the ancient thing on my desk. I still wasn't used to the snow-white hair on her head and had snickered a bit at the messy mass of curls that stuck up every which way. I pecked at the dirty, old keys a while last night, but soon realized I would never get the hang of using it—there was no backspace key. So I decided to use pencil and paper.

I planned to write about ancient evil, so I may as well do it old-school style.

With shaky fingers, I picked the pencil back up and hovered over the blank pages. The decision of where to start first seemed difficult. The beginning would be the most appropriate spot, since most stories start out that way. But I wasn't entirely sure when everything changed—at least in my life. The history of what I had become, and why, I understood from countless hours spent listening to Papa Joe. His sweet, rhythmic voice explained with the utmost patience the ancient ways and answered my multitude of disbelieving questions with ease. He never flinched, never balked at my rude responses

and some of the hateful things I'd said to him in the beginning.

God, how I miss him.

To exorcise the awful memories, to try and dislodge
the painful thoughts from my mind, I shouldn't start out
by lying. I knew the moment things changed for me. A
tremor of fear made my heart beat faster. Was I really
doing the right thing by letting the wickedness from my
head escape, knowing it still lingered in the town? In all
the years, the story had never been written down, only
passed orally from one generation to the next. Mom worried about that too, which was why she bought me a typewriter rather than a computer. Once the words were freed
from my mind, she wanted me to burn them, chapter by
chapter, so no copy would be around. That way, nothing
would be left but a small pile of ashes—gray, lifeless ashes
to be spread out over the blackened embers of what had
been the wicked heart of Junction City before it burned to
the ground.

Mom hoped the soot of my mind-altering fear would
be the adhesive that kept the lid sealed shut on the evil
that nearly killed me...and the entire town.

I would let Mom continue that line of thinking for a
while. After all, she had to heal as well. So did Dad, for
that matter. I wasn't ready to drop the next bombshell on
either of them yet because if I told them the *real* reason I
was writing, they would flip their proverbial lids.

I gripped the pencil harder, the sweat beginning to
bead on my brow, and began where I should.

At the beginning.

CHAPTER THREE

PART ONE – THE PREVIOUS ELEVEN YEARS

I woke up from deep, innocent slumber with a strange sensation I had never experienced before. The hairs on my nine-year-old arms stood on end, my bare limbs covered with small little bumps. I brought my hand to my eyes and rubbed the crusted sleep stuck to my lashes. A sense of uneasiness settled over me. I was fully alert although I didn't know why.

With the aid of the nightlight in the corner, I looked around the room, searching for my cat, Tinker. Maybe he was prowling around my room. I figured he knocked something over, which must have been the reason I woke up. I eased out from under the covers and slid to the edge of the high bed, quietly calling his name. "Tinker...Tinker...here kitty kitty."

I waited, straining to hear any noise, only to be greeted with the silence of the night. A cold breeze swept over my pajamas, causing a shiver to race down my spine. My body twitched in response. My eyes focused on the bedroom door. It had been closed when I went to bed less than fifteen minutes before, but now it was ajar.

I froze, my eyes locked in terror. A shadow covered the door. A huge, bulky man stood there. One arm raised, he held what looked like a knife. My mind tried to grasp it all, my heart thumping wildly in my chest. I drew in a ragged breath and tried to comfort my thoughts. I must still be dreaming. With shaking fingers, I pinched my arm, hoping it would make me wake up. All it did was make me all the more aware I was awake.

Never taking my eyes off the shadowy figure, I inched my way backward and slid off the bed. I crouched down, using the bed as a shield and peeked back over the fluffy comforter. The figure hadn't moved. I stared in silence a few more minutes as my fear began to dissipate with each passing moment. The Shadow-Man wasn't coming after me. It was motionless. I shook my head and laughed out loud, mocking my silliness for being so frightened.

I decided the shadow must be coming from the nightlight. Confidence growing, I stood up and strode over to the corner where it was plugged in. I waved my hands in front of it, knowing I would soon find what was making the scary-looking thing appear on my door. While I waved my hands, the air turned cold once again, and my breath came out like it did when snow covered the ground. My heart lost its spirited glow of success. The shadow was not affected at all by my arms.

The head turned and looked my way.

Fear pulsed through me and exploded out in one giant eruption. I screamed at the top of my lungs. "Mooooooooommmmmmm!"

The shrill scream from my lips filled the house. I

crushed my eyes shut to the vision in front of me, willing the shadow to disappear from my mind. Suddenly, warm hands latched onto my shoulders and shook me violently from side to side. My screams ended after my brain shut down all bodily systems, except for my bladder. The hot liquid pooled around my feet after running down my legs.

"Honey, what's wrong? Wake up...wake up! It's ok. I'm here now!" chirped my mother as she shook my little shoulders. "You're only dreaming!"

The sound of her sweet voice broke the paralyzing terror in my mind, and my eyes flew open. I shot a glance over to the door where the Shadow-Man loomed before. He was gone, banished by the overhead light and the presence of my mom.

"Mom, it was awful! The man, the big shadow man, he...he...he had a knife and was lookin' at me!" I managed to eke out, my voice a hoarse whisper. I collapsed into Mom's gentle arms, sobbing.

"What man, honey? Oh, you were just dreamin'. It was only a nightmare, baby," Mom cooed in her quiet voice, gently stroking my hair. "Sssshhhh...it's all right now."

"No, Mom, he was real! I saw him! I even pinched myself, and I was awake! He was right there at the door!" I whimpered through my tears, pointing at the bedroom door.

Mom turned her head and followed my shaking hand, and upon seeing nothing, she lifted me up off the floor. "Come on, sweetie. Let's get you cleaned up. It was just a bad dream, that's all. See? Nothin' is there...just your door. No bogeyman, I promise."

"He was there, Mom, I swear! And he moved! He was watchin' me. I woke up feelin' funny and then it got really cold, and I saw my breath! Please, please let me sleep with you and Daddy!" I whined all the way into the bathroom.

"Baby, let's get you cleaned up, and then we can go have a secret, nighttime snack, okay? You'll be fine once your tummy is full."

Before Mom shut the bathroom door, I glanced back over her shoulder into my room, eyeing the bedroom door sharply. That's when I noticed the little white stray cat I named Tinker was in the room. His back arched, ears flattened back against his head and teeth exposed, as he hissed at the door.

"There now...all full! That's my girl," Mom said. She rinsed out the hot cocoa from my empty cup. "I told you a midnight snack would do the trick!"

I had tried desperately to prolong my snack, chewing slowly and sipping the hot chocolate for so long that it turned into cold chocolate milk. I had begged Mom the whole time to let me sleep anywhere but my own room, all for nothing. For some strange reason, Mom was adamant that I go back to my own room to sleep—something about conquering my fears. Well, I didn't want to conquer them (whatever that word meant). I wanted to never sleep in my room again. Ever. Mom tried to convince me during our snack time it was a dream.

I knew better.

Even Tinker knew.

"Mom, Tinker saw him too! He was hissin' and growlin' at the door!" I whined, hoping she would give in.

"Sheryl, you had a nightmare, baby. A dream. It didn't

really happen. As I said earlier, dreams are just the mind workin' overtime at night, makin' a big movie out of bits and pieces of the memories in your head. Sometimes those movie images don't make sense. They come in random patterns that don't have any meanin'. But sometimes, they form a movie that you can follow and can seem so real, especially using stored images of familiar things, like your room. What you saw was in your head. For goodness sake girl, your eyes were closed and you were still sleepin' when I came in there!"

Mom took my hand and started out toward my room.

"But Moommmy..." I moaned, trying in vain to pull her back toward the kitchen. "It was real. I can't stay in there. I just can't!"

"Sheryl Ilene Newcomb! I have tried to be patient with you, but this is enough! Look," she said, stopping in front of the door, "there is nothin' here. Just your door...same as it always was." Mom rubbed her hands along the lines of the door. She grabbed my hands and placed them on the door, forcing me to feel it with her. "There, see? Only wood, baby. That's all. Nothin' else. Now, enough with this nonsense. It's time for bed."

My body shook as she guided my hands along the surface of the wood. It was slippery and cold—nothing at all like wood was supposed to feel. I opened my mouth to protest, wanting to ask why it felt like ice, but I realized Mom didn't notice it.

Only I did.

I inhaled and let out a long sigh. Mom didn't believe me, and wouldn't, no matter what I said or did. I was doomed. Mom wasn't going to budge, forcing me to sleep in my room—a place I was terrified of—all alone with nothing except my fear to keep me company.

I looked quickly around my room, searching for something, anything, I could use as some sort of protection from the Shadow-Man. "Mom, can Tinker sleep with me?" I begged, my eyes boring into hers, hoping she would grant my request.

"Fine, but don't tell your father. You know what he thinks about Tinker sleepin' in your bed. He's a stray and your father worries about him bitin' you. Plus, all that cat fur will be impossible to get out of your hair in the mornin'," she said while she tucked me in under the fluffy pink comforter. "I'll go get him and bring him right back. Remember though, he won't stay if you leave the door open. Cats are nocturnal creatures, and he'll soon want to go out and prowl around."

I cringed at the idea of being trapped in the room. But somehow, I had the idea that Tinker, with his huge white feet full of very sharp claws, would protect me from the Shadow-Man. Maybe he would warn me with a loud hiss if the Shadow-Man showed up while I slept. If I ever slept again.

After she walked out of the room, I squeezed my eyes shut and wrapped my arms around my chest. I buried my head under the protection of the warm comforter. Out of sight, out of mind. That's what Nana always said. I clung to the hope that my kitty-guardian would save me.

Mom talked in soft whispers to Tinker as she came down the hall. Tinker had a really loud, deep purr that would usually make me giggle when I heard it, but tonight, it sounded more like a roar. A terrifying growl, which was exactly what I needed to keep me safe in the dark. Tinker the Terminator was what he needed to be—a strong lion to be my constant companion and keep me from harm.

"Okay, Tinky, you stay here and keep Miss Sheryl

warm tonight...and no gettin' up and wanderin' into my room or any hairballs for me to find in the mornin'!" Mom quipped. She handed Tinker over, and I buried him under my comforter. His soft fur tickled my arms as he nuzzled into my chest. I let out a small breath of relief when he started to purr.

"You'll be a good boy, won't you Tinky?" I said, stroking his blocky head.

"Good night, sweetie. Sleep well. I love you," Mom said. She swiped her warm lips across my damp forehead.

"Night, Mom," I squeaked from under the covers.

After Mom closed the door behind her, I closed my eyes and began talking to Tinker. I rubbed his silky coat with stronger strokes. Sweat beads formed on my brow, making my hairline wet. The harder I rubbed, the louder he purred. The rumbles sounded like he was growling, and I prayed that his growls would keep away the Shadow-Man.

I wasn't sure how long it had been, but at some point during the night, I stopped petting Tinker after my hands and body began to relax and my arms grew tired. My constant chatter with Tinker became soft murmurs and eventually subsided when I began to drift off to sleep.

Tinker, however, remained awake, like he understood his duty to watch over me. His purrs had been reduced to low grumbles as my petting grew less and less. Right before I crossed the line over into sleep, I felt him poke his head out from under the comforter. He was on top of my chest, his body rigid and his claws digging into my skin. His blocky head stared at my door. Panic jolted me awake when I took in the first breath of the freezing cold air.

Tinker laid his ears back and bared his teeth for the second time that evening. An ominous growl rumbled in his chest with enough force to make my body shake. His brilliant green eyes narrowed into miniscule slits as his gaze moved to my right, away from the door. I knew, without looking, what stood beside my bed. Frozen in fear, I couldn't even whimper. Hot tears cascaded down my cheeks as I sensed the entity beside me. Though petrified, I couldn't stop my eyes from following Tinker's. I didn't need to hold my breath because my chest was unable to move to give me air.

Before I grasped the horror that the Shadow-Man stood next to me, I realized why I couldn't breathe.

The four-pound little stray was gone. From my toes to my neck, a heavy weight covered my body. I blinked back the tears of fear, my thoughts no longer on the shadowy figure by the edge of my bed. Instead, I stared in utter shock at the basketball-sized head full of enormous teeth and fangs which were longer than my fingers. White, heavy wisps of steam exited from his huge mouth, the skin pulled away from his gums in a silent snarl. Every muscle in his giant torso was taut and tense, ready to pounce. Rough, sandpaperlike fur had replaced his silken coat and made the skin on my bare legs, arms, and neck itch. His eyes were no longer green. They had turned into a bright gold, so intense they glowed in the darkness of my room, along with the brilliant white of his coat. His whiskers were thick and sharp as they glanced across my cheek. Heat rolled off him in waves, and I grimaced at the strange, sweet aroma coming from his coat and mouth.

Lost in confusion, I figured I was trapped in a vivid dream—one where my little furry stray was bigger than the neighbor's Great Dane, Beowulf. I had forgotten all about the Shadow-Man. Tinker, or what had been Tinker, had not forgotten. Any doubt about being asleep vanished as pain ripped through my chest. The claws were like sharp, hot daggers as the cat's mammoth paws dug in, followed by a sound I had never heard before. It was almost like a woman screaming at the top of her lungs but much more frightening—the roar so loud it made my ears ring. My heart skipped several beats when the growl followed. The bed shook, and I heard pictures fall off my wall and crash on the floor.

It was all too much for me to take in. My mind and body went limp. Terror from the monster beside my bed and the one on top of me consumed all reasonable thoughts from my brain. I wanted to scream out for my mom, willing her to answer my silent pleas for help. Instead, all I heard was unfamiliar voices, full of power and might, say:

"*Give her to me, Nahu'ala.*"

"*Be gone, Hattak'katos. You are too late—the child is already mine.*"

CHAPTER FOUR

"Mom, can I have another piece of bacon?"

"Of course, sweetie. Comin' right up. My, but what an appetite you have this mornin'! You must be excited about cheerleadin' class today."

"I am. Can't wait to show everyone I can do the splits! But Mom, uh, would you make it less crispy this time?"

"Sheryl!"

"Sorry, Daddy, but the last ones were too crunchy."

"Since when did that ever bother you before?" Dad shot back.

I shrugged my shoulders. "I don't know. Since now?"

"My, my. Aren't you a bossy little thing today? Guess your dream last night made you wake up on the wrong side of bed. Either that or you have ants in your pants. Lawd, not even old enough to be on the squad and already actin' like a snotty cheerleader. Won't be no livin' with her if she makes the cut in middle school."

Daddy reached over my plate and grabbed the salt shaker. His words were harsher than the look on his face. In his early morning funk, his big fingers knocked the grape jelly bowl off the table. It would have been a sticky mess to clean up had my hand not shot out and caught it before it hit the floor. Daddy grinned at me, the topic of my new preference for bacon long gone. Trouble would have started if he broke another one of Mom's favorite glass bowls. He gave me a quick *thank you* wink while he salted his eggs. "Jolene, she acts more and more like you every day. A real Dixie Diva in the making. And reflexes like a cat. That she gets from me. Wish you'd use those skills on the basketball court, punkin', instead all that energy you waste runnin'. And now this! Bouncin' on the sidelines, wavin' them pompoms at the crowd. It's a shame, I tell ya."

Mom swatted her spatula at Daddy's head, her heavy blonde curls bouncing behind her with the movement. They exchanged glances with each other, full of love and playfulness at their verbal sparring. I ignored them both and set the jelly dish back on the table. The argument about my chosen sport would never end until I caved and decided to play hoops when I was old enough to play for the team.

"Call me what you like, but you married me, knowin' full well I'm a handful. I want my daughter to speak her peace, even if it is for somethin' as trivial as how she likes her food cooked. Good practice for later on in life when menfolk try to control her. We are raisin' us a modern gal, not some wimpy girl afraid to voice her opinions. No siree. Now, one or two slices, honey?"

"Two, please. One for me and one for Tinker. I owe him a treat. He saved me last night."

"Now, there's some nice manners. And though I appreciate you usin' 'em, you aren't to give that walkin' hairball our bacon. He has his own food right over there." Daddy pointed to the small alcove at the other end of the kitchen. "It's bad enough he's eatin' in the house. I'll be damned if he eats our food, too."

"Jared...language?"

Daddy waived Mom's words away with his hand. "The only thing that critter did for you was bring dam...dang fleas into your bed."

"Daddy, he *saved* me last night. From the Shadow-Man. He was gonna kill me. Slice me up right there in my bed with his big knife."

Mom turned off the stove and brought a steaming plate of bacon and eggs to the table. Before Daddy said another word, she shot him a look. "Sheryl, I told you last night you just had a bad nightmare. You went right to sleep after I tucked you back in without another peep. I think part of that was because Tinker was in your room. Made you feel safe, sort of like a livin', breathin' teddy bear. The other part was that you were exhausted. And the reason you had a bad dream is your nana's fault."

"How is it Nana's fault?" I asked, trying not to giggle as Tinker wound his body around my legs under the table. I slipped him a piece of limp bacon from my plate while Mom and Daddy busied themselves with piling more food onto their own.

"She filled your head yesterday with all her silly stories, honey. But that's all they are. *Silly stories.* Shoot, I heard them so many times when I was a youngin', even I used to dream about them. And when I went back home after a visit at Nana's, your meemaw would tell me the exact same thing I'm tellin' you now—they are just the ramblin's of a woman who's gettin' old and confuses things in her head.

Nana has trouble tellin' the difference between what she reads or sees on TV and what's real. Always has, ever since the flood and she lost Pop-pop."

"Well, I believe her. I saw with my own eyes. Tinker turned into a big cat—bigger than Beowulf! He snarled and growled, and it scared away the Shadow-Man. Told him he couldn't have me because I was already his."

The sound of Daddy's fork as it landed on his plate was loud and made me jump. Tinker flung his body against the screen door in fright and shot out into the backyard, a piece of bacon clamped in his jaws as he ran. "Sheryl Ilene, that is enough back talkin' this mornin.' Eat your breakfast and then get yourself upstairs and ready for school. No more jabberin' about shadows and strays growin' into monsters. You and your imagination!"

I tried to hold back my tears. Daddy rarely snapped at me, and usually it was when I had done something to cause his anger to flare. I could tell from the tone in his voice and the look on his face he didn't believe me. But I knew I hadn't imagined things, and I had the marks to prove it.

For a second, I thought about showing them both the scratches on my chest. I sensed they wouldn't believe me, though. Mom didn't believe me last night. And I had been the only one to feel the icy cold of the wood on my door. Would they even be able to see the claw marks on my chest? If they could, they would probably think I scratched myself in my sleep. Instead of crying, I gobbled two pieces of bacon in one big bite and stood up. "Yes sir," I mumbled. Without raising my eyes to meet theirs, I walked over to the back door and pushed it open. Daddy was muttering under his breath about Nana and her crazy stories, scolding Mom for letting the old woman scare me on our visit to her house yesterday. I didn't pay him any attention because I knew Nana had nothing to do with last night. "Nahu'ala, here kitty. Come back inside."

The grumbled conversation between my parents ended when the sound of shattering glass filled the kitchen. I looked over my shoulder to see what fell on the floor, thinking Daddy knocked something else off the table. Mom's face turned white, her skin almost matching her light hair and white shirt. Her voice was thick with worry when she asked, "What did you just say?"

"I called for Tinker. I want him inside with me while I brush my teeth."

"You said Nahu'ala, not Tinker. Where...where did you hear that name? Did Nana say that name to you before?"

I shook my head no. With a cluck of my tongue and a snap of my fingers, I tried one more time to entice Tinker to come back. I scanned the back yard but didn't see him anywhere. The look on my mom's face made my stomach feel funny. I needed my furry friend to help calm my nerves.

"Sheryl, your momma asked..."

Daddy's comment was cut short when the cordless phone on the table rang. He wiped his mouth and stood up, snatching the phone to his ear with one quick scoop. In two strides, he was in the living room and out of earshot.

Mom still waited for my answer, and somehow I felt the strange urge to not say another word. A cold sensation inside of me, like invisible fingers, kept my mouth clamped shut. I let the screen door go and turned around to head upstairs to finish getting ready for school. I bounded up the stairs two at a time and hoped Mom wouldn't follow me. Once I reached the bathroom door, I heard her dainty footsteps coming up the stairs.

In a rush, I raced to the sink and grabbed my toothbrush, plopped a dab of paste on it and began brushing furiously. By the time Mom made it to the bathroom, my mouth was full of white, creamy foam. "Sheryl, you didn't answer my question earlier."

"Ansther what, Mooma?"

"Spit. Rinse. Turn around and look at me."

I saw her reflection in the mirror. She didn't look mad, and her tone wasn't angry either. But her voice was full of concern and something else I couldn't quite place. I spit the minty contents out and wiped my lips on the back of my hand. "No, Nana didn't tell me," I said, turning around to face her.

She knelt down in front of me, her bright blue eyes watery as they searched my face to see if I was lying to her or not. Her thick, curly hair framed her face and fell around her slender shoulders like a lion's mane. Normally, when I looked at her, all I would do was marvel at how pretty she was and wonder why Daddy said I was the spitting image of her. But seeing her shimmering tears caught me off guard. I felt the immediate sting of my own and forced them not to spill down my cheeks. "Sheryl, are you sure? Think. Think real hard on all the times Nana told you stories. Not even once?"

"No, Mom. I promise. I...I already told you. The Shadow-Man called him that last night. And I liked the name and the way it sounded. Guess I shoulda' kept it to myself."

Mom's hand trembled as she reached out to touch my forehead like she did when checking for a fever. Daddy was loudly talking on the phone downstairs, but neither of us paid much attention to him. Mom's worried gaze sent chills of alarm up my back. "The Shadow-Man called Tinker Nahu'ala? Did he say anything else?"

"No. But Tinker did."

"What..." she started, then cleared her throat before she continued, "did you hear next?"

"He said, 'Be gone, Hattak'katos. You are too late. The child is already mine.' But it sounded funny. Like I heard it in my head and not with my ears."

Mom's eyebrows crushed together and a look of confusion passed over her face. Her warm hand fell away from my forehead and down to the floor to steady her kneeling, wobbly legs. Heat from embarrassment flushed my cheeks, for I knew my words were the source of her distress. I wanted to kick myself for calling out the new name of my furry protector and wasn't exactly sure why I did to begin with. The name rolled easily off my tongue, though, and sent waves of comfort flowing through my body when spoken.

Unsure what I should say or do, I stood on the bright yellow bath mat in the middle of the floor and looked at Mom. With a few blinks of her eyes, she seemed to regain her composure. She stood up and wiped her slender fingers across her upper lip, removing the droplets of sweat that had formed there. She started to speak, but the sound of Daddy's heavy footsteps in the hallway and loud voice made her pause.

"*Jolene!* Where are...oh, there you are," Daddy barked. His eyes shifted between the two of us for a split second. He took a heavy breath and lowered his voice. "Jolene, honey. We need to talk."

The thin hairs on my arms and neck stood up in response to the electricity level in the room skyrocketing.

Daddy's face was red, and tears of his own welled up in his eyes. It was one thing to see Mom's tears, but Daddy's? The only other time I had seen him so upset was when his momma, Gramma Pat, passed away two years before.

"What's wrong, honey? Did somethin' happen at the restaurant? Oh, God, was it a fire? Someone hurt? It's not Papa Joe, is it?"

Daddy didn't answer Mom's rapid fire questions. He motioned with his head for her to follow him out into the hallway. As Mom walked out of the bathroom, Daddy's warm hand ruffled the top of my hair and he said, "Sheryl, finish gettin' ready. Mommy and Daddy need to talk. Hurry up now. Barb will be here any minute to walk to school with ya, and it ain't polite to make her wait."

I shot into my room, but then peeked around my bedroom doorframe. They made their way to the top of the staircase and stopped. I noticed Daddy's arm covered Mom's stiff shoulders with a protective grip. His lips were within inches of Mom's ear and his voice but a mere whisper. I strained to listen to what he said, but all I heard was the low rumble from his throat, the words unintelligible.

My bare feet moved without a sound over the polished hardwood floor as I stepped out of the bedroom and inched my way toward the bathroom. I was trying to follow Daddy's instructions and finish getting ready for school, but I sensed something was wrong. Daddy's words were coming faster now. Although Mom's back was turned to me, I knew I was right. Her shoulder's sagged and she leaned into his chest with her head bowed. Daddy's big arms wrapped around her, and she shuddered. I knew the news was not good.

"Oh, no. Oh, God. Poor Nana. I can't believe she's..."

Mom's words cut off with great sobs as she fell apart in

Daddy's strong arms. The minute I heard them, my body froze. My view of the hallway shifted, and suddenly, I wasn't inside our house anymore.

My head whipped from side to side as I tried to figure out where I was. Goosebumps spread over me and my feet felt strange. I looked down and discovered it was because I stood in wet mud. A small gasp escaped when I noticed I was naked and outside in the darkest part of the night. Moonlight streamed through the gnarled trees that surrounded me from every angle, illuminating the area like floodlights. The chill of the night air breezed across my bare skin, and the hair on my arms, legs, and torso stood erect. My nose twitched as it took in all the smells of the wet woods. The mold, the damp pine needles, the rotting leaves and mud under my feet hit me all at once. Then, I caught a whiff of something else. Something I had never smelled before yet seemed to instinctively know what it was.

Fear.

Terrified, I closed my eyes and willed myself to wake up. I had to be dreaming again. I clenched my hands together at my sides and tried to make my legs respond to my instructions to stand still, but they moved on their own. My eyes flew back open. My body wound seamlessly through the tangle of underbrush and vines, my steps sure and steady. The moon's silvery rays lit up the path, and I saw every detail of the forest, from the tiniest leaf to the farthest limb. My feet glided with ease, and my footfalls were silent. The odor was stronger now. My ears picked up the sounds of the forest—things impossible for me to hear. A squirrel high above me in the trees hunkered down in its nest for the night. The sound of scurrying feet to my left I somehow knew was a small field mouse scuttling through the leaves on its way to its warm den. I heard heavy, raspy breathing in front of me from some creature—type unknown but obviously large—judging by the respirations. I let go of the fear inside me, knowing I must be dreaming, and I embraced the warm power surging through my body.

Once I gave in and stopped trying to control my limbs, my pace quickened and I moved deeper into the forest. The scent was stronger now, accompanied by a strange sound. It took a few seconds for me to recognize it as whimpering. A woman's faint voice drifted across the air, and I sensed her pain and fear.

"Do as you wish, you foul, unholy creature. I ain't gonna tell you the location."

Horror pounded inside my head when I realized it was the voice of Nana. My legs pumped in a flat-out run. My feet barely touched the wet ground as I zigzagged through the forest toward her feeble voice. Anger licked a fire inside me, igniting the muscles of my entire body. The forest whizzed by in a blur as I charged through it. Her words were forceful, but I sensed the raw terror behind them. Hearing them infuriated me and filled me with blinding rage.

In seconds, I spotted a break in the tree line and Nana's frail body on top of a mound of damp grass to my right. Her favorite nightgown hung in tattered pieces, her gray head of hair loose, splayed out behind her like a white blanket. Her breath came in great gasps and her withered, wrinkled hands clutched something to her chest. She turned her head and looked at me, her cloudy eyes wild with fright. My leg muscles contracted and propelled me across the open area from the edge of the tree line. In one giant leap, I was right next to her. When I landed, my body shook with emotion.

She spoke again. "The torch has passed on, and I ain't needed no more. What you want from me, I ain't never gonna give. End it. I ain't afraid to die. I know where I'm goin' when I do, and you'll surely never step foot there!"

An inhuman, piercing scream ripped through the forest, the sound so loud the ground beneath us shook from the intensity. Fury pulsed through me as a roar burst from my lips. My mouth filled with hot, rust-flavored liquid and spilled out down my chin, soaking my neck with its sticky heat. Warm flesh gave way underneath my strong bite. The sound of it, as I tore pieces away from the body, made my heart pound with glee. Hunger for more overrode everything else. The scent of the rusty blood drove me mad with rage. My fingers dug deep into the exposed flesh, tearing and pulling chunks off of the writhing body.

Another shriek, louder than the one before it, rang out in the darkened woods. This time, it was full of pain and not anger.

And this time, it was human.

CHAPTER FIVE
- THREE DAYS
LATER

Questions about where I heard the name Nahu'ala were long forgotten, overshadowed by the passing of Nana. The strange vision I had in the hallway the day my family found out about her death stayed locked inside of me. I was unable to bring myself to tell anyone. Something inside my mind whispered to keep the disturbing images to myself. When I snapped back to reality and found myself in the hallway once more, my mouth locked tight. Mom didn't handle me mentioning the name Nahu'ala to her very well, so I didn't dare say a word about what I had seen in the forest. The thought of telling her the gruesome scenes left my mind as I watched her sob in Daddy's arms.

For the last three days, our tiny farmhouse had been filled with so many people I'd lost count after one hundred. The majority of the faces I recognized, but a few I did not. All of them had the same expression—compassion and shock. Food of all sorts piled up on every available nook and cranny in our small kitchen. The competing scents overwhelmed my nose so I steered clear of the area. After the second day, Mom politely asked the visitors to please take what they brought home because we would never eat it all before it spoiled.

My best friend Barb was allowed to stay with me to "keep me occupied." Her mother, Nanette Ransford, told her it was her job as she carried a pile of green bean casserole and fresh cornbread to the kitchen the first day after Nana's death. As my best friend, it was her job help me smile and keep me out from under the feet of my family while they grieved. Barb had turned three shades of red when she realized I overheard her mother's instructions from my spot by the open window. I jumped from my perch and helped lug the food in, and then Barb and I snuck out back to sit in the afternoon shade.

I didn't care what the reasons were for Barb being at my house. I was simply grateful she was there. She stuck to my side like a wad of gum embedded in a chunk of my hair. Her motormouth never stopped as she flitted from one topic to the next, determined to keep my head full of so many other thoughts I didn't have a chance to break down.

Meemaw had been at our house ever since the discovery of Nana's body. She was heartbroken and needed to be near her daughter and granddaughter. Normally, when the three generations of Kovlin women were in the same room, no one could get a word in edgewise. Meemaw, Mom, and I were all talkers, mouths always flapping. When Nana was with us and four generations occupied the same space, it was utter chaos.

But not anymore. The matriarch of our family would never be in the middle of marathon gabfests or whisper her outrageous tales of the past into my ears.

I came close to spilling to Barb what I saw the day Nana died only once during the three days. It was after listening to Daddy talk to Sheriff Gilmore the evening after Nana's death. Both of them thought I was inside with Barb, Mom, and Meemaw, but I wasn't. I hadn't slept much since Nana died. An hour or two here and there, but nothing solid or resembling real sleep. It terrified me to think I might have another weird dream or vision. Instead, I faked sleep until Barb crashed next to me and then snuck downstairs when I heard the sheriff's car pull up. Like a quiet church mouse, I listened from my perch on the bench under the living room window, hidden by the heavy drapes. Daddy and Sheriff Gilmore spoke in hushed tones on the front porch.

"I'm tellin' ya, Jared. Ain't never seen anythin' like it in my life. Poor ol' Ralph Wemscott ain't never gonna be the same. Swore off ever settin' foot in the woods again. Not even to hunt. Took forever to get a full statement from him. He kept stoppin' to puke."

There was a long pause before Daddy responded. "You don't think he...?"

"Oh, hell no! What happened to Ms. Beulah weren't done by no man, like I told ya yesterday. Besides, ol' Ralph is just a harmless drunk. You know that."

"Yeah, I know that. Just a hard pill to swallow, thinkin' we got ourselves a bear or wolf in the woods. Ain't had one around these parts in what, years?"

"Weren't no wolf. Bite marks were too big for a wolf's mouth. Claw marks were too...deep. Coroner is leanin' toward a panther or bear. My money's on a bear. Time was when the Delta was full of the black scourges, back 'fore them damned Injuns killed them all off. Least that's what my Pa told me 'cause I ain't never seen one, and I've hunted all over the woods for years. Ralph thinks it's a panther though. Said he heard screams in the forest while he was out huntin' that weren't made by a human. Hard to imagine it's either one, 'cause ya know, ain't a big predator been seen in these parts for decades. Then again, nature has a way of rebuildin', so I betcha that's what we's seein' here. Wish we coulda got some good prints, but we didn't. The rains that night left nothin' but a pile of mush around her. Don't make no sense no matter what thing got to her. Animals kill because they's hungry. But, Ms. Beulah wasn't...I mean...it just...killed her."

The sheriff's words trailed off, followed by a long moment of silence. My skin crawled at his words. Finally, Daddy responded. "Listen, Sheriff. I appreciate you lettin' me be the one to...ID her. Woulda sent Jolene or Ms. Gertie to the hospital from a stroke or heart attack if they'd done it. Almost did me, and she ain't my ma or grandma. And I saw the leftovers *after* she was, um, cleaned up. Can't imagine the horror Ralph witnessed when he found her. God, stumblin' on that musta' knocked a few years off him for sure. And probably sent him headfirst into the nearest bottle."

Sheriff Gilmore pulled out a can of dip, stuck a large pinch between his lips, then spat over the railing a few times. "Listen, Jared. We finished goin' through her house and didn't find nothin' that would explain just what in tarnation Ms. Beulah was doin' out down by the creek at night. It's damn near six miles from her house! We didn't find no evidence of someone harrasin' her, no sign anyone had been inside or broke into her place. Nothin' disturbed or signs of a struggle. Ned Simpkins checked with the phone company this mornin', and Ms. Beulah didn't get no phone calls in the last week 'cept from your house. So, I wanted to ask you: do Ms. Jolene or Ms. Gertie have any ideas? Say anythin' to you that might shine some light on why Ms. Beulah went out there—besides what they told me already?"

Daddy rubbed his head in frustration, wiping away a small bead of sweat before it trickled down into his eyes. "No. We're all just as stumped as you, Sheriff. Ain't like Ms. Beulah ever wandered before out like that, at least not that we knew about. Once we got Sheryl and Barb to bed, it's all the three of us talked about, off and on, 'til you drove up. We came up with diddly-squat. Course, I ain't been completely forthcomin' with the girls either—you know, about everythin'."

"You didn't tell Ms. Jolene and Ms. Gertie the truth?" Sheriff Gilmore queried.

Daddy wiped his brow again and eased down into the rocking chair to his left. "Of course not, Sheriff. How can I? You said it yourself. You don't rightly know exactly what kinda critter tore her to pieces. They's havin' enough trouble swallowin' the fact that Ms. Beulah was out in the woods at night. I mean, come on! She was ninety-somethin' years old! Ms. Beulah always was a tad...quirky. Their words, not mine. I think she was looney tunes. After the flood and her losin' everythin', then findin' out she was pregnant with Ms. Gertie—it done turned her brain to mush. I kept tellin' Jolene I thought we shoulda put Ms. Beulah in that home down in Greenville, you know, so she would have round the clock care. Jolene wouldn't hear of it though. And now look what's happened. Her body torn to bits by some damned critter, all because she forgot where she was and started wanderin' around in the dark. Nope. I think it's best to just let them continue to think she was sleepwalkin'. Got lost and had her a heart attack when she couldn't find her way home."

"Jared, you and I both know that little tale ain't gonna stick for long. When the death certificate arrives at your front door and doesn't match up your story, what then? I got a good crew of deputies, but people talk. If just one of them or the County Coroner or even Ralph, went home and told their wives what happened, the news will spread like wildfire. And that fire will hit your house before the death certificate does. Then all hell will break loose. Besides, I've got the rest of the county's safety to worry about. Whatever tore Ms. Beulah apart is still out there, and we've gotta find it before it kills again. People see us out traipsin' through the woods armed to the teeth, they'll put two and two together. Either that or they'll think Armageddon is acomin'. People will panic. And the last thing I need now is a bunch of armed rednecks combin' the woods, shootin' at every little sound. That happens enough durin' huntin' season."

Sheriff Gilmore made a noise that sounded like someone was choking him while he tried to laugh. I heard Daddy's deep and heavy sigh all the way from the other side of the porch. "I know, I know. I certainly don't want another family to go through this. I just...I just don't know how to tell them. I mean, how do I start the conversation? It's gonna break their hearts."

"Jared, give the gals some credit. They's tough stock, just like everyone else 'round here. After all, they's both mom's too. Think about little Sheryl and Barb in there. Ms. Gertie and Ms. Jolene's instincts to protect their youngin', and all the others in town, will kick in. Once the shock of the news wears off, they might surprise you. Maybe they'll grab their guns and help track the four-legged monster that killed their kin."

I couldn't sit and listen to any more. The hairs on my neck and arms stood straight up, and my stomach hurt. For a minute, I thought I might throw up on the couch. A wave of dizziness swept over me when the memory of the odor of the rusty blood slammed into me. Spit filled my mouth, and I shook with fury.

Without thinking about the noise it would make, I bolted from the living room and sped up the stairs. Thankfully, I made it to the toilet just in time.

I shook the thoughts of the last three days away. I didn't want to get in trouble for not paying attention or showing any disrespect. Nana's funeral service was underway, the church packed with mourners. The air conditioner hummed overhead, working furiously to keep the room at a tolerable temperature, a hard task for sure with all the warm bodies crammed inside its walls.

I snuck a peek behind me. It looked like the entire inhabitants of Locasia County had come to pay their respects to Nana. She may have had a reputation as a crazy loon, but people still loved her. Even the reclusive Witherspoon clan showed up, including my schoolmate, Dane V, with Ms. Emma, his momma, and his grandfather, Dane "Pops" Witherspoon III. My second-grade teacher, Lillian Shelby, sat at the organ, her pink summer frock already marred with sweat as she played. Pastor Wray stood near Nana's shiny silver casket, his face flushed red though he had yet to speak. The lid was closed, and a big, black and white picture of Nana, one I didn't recognize, sat on an easel next to it. When the last chord of "Amazing Grace" settled over the congregation, Pastor Wray cleared his throat, loosened the black tie around his neck, and began the service.

Like I always did during church, I tuned the pastor out and forced myself not to squirm in my seat. Sandwiched between my mom and dad in the first pew, I snuck a peek at Meemaw on the other side of my mom. She looked like a marble statue. With a quick glance around, I noticed Papa Joe and the rest of the crew from the diner filled up the spaces on the remainder of the bench. In honor of Nana's passing, Daddy had closed the restaurant for the rest of the week. Papa Joe smiled at me, but sadness shown behind his dark brown eyes. Daddy sat in silence, his eyes downcast as he stared at the closed hymnal in his lap and the card that read "Come! Celebrate the Life of Mrs. Beulah Roberts Kovlin."

I turned away, unwilling to look at the picture of her on the front cover or the one on the altar. I settled my eyes on Mom's quivering hand instead. It gripped Meemaw's as the pastor spoke about the promise of Heaven for Nana. I tuned back in and listened to him spout verses from the Bible meant to give comfort to those of us left behind, to ease our pain from losing her. They were just like the ones he said at Grandma Pat's service two years ago. He cautioned those of us listening to remember that departing this world was not the end, only the beginning. We were just travelers in a strange land and our ultimate destination was above.

Next, a parade of residents took the stage one by one and each offered their favorite recollection about Nana.

Some of the stories were funny, and uncomfortable laughter spread through the crowd. Seemed people were unsure whether it was proper to laugh at a funeral service or not. Other testimonies brought a round of tears and sniffles. I snuck a peek at Mom and Meemaw to see if they would get up to speak, but neither of them moved. Backs erect and chins set, they stared at the shiny casket and nothing else until the pallbearers hoisted it out to the waiting black hearse.

The sun was just beginning to set in the western sky. The heat of the day still held the area hostage. The shimmering waves of warmth hung heavy around me. The last visitors pulled out of our driveway, kicking up a light cloud of dust when they hit the main highway. I watched from the porch, swiping away at the mosquitoes buzzing around me. It was so hot, I wondered if I could get away with sneaking out to the pool in the back for a quick dip. It would have been easy since no one was paying any attention to me. But somehow, it seemed wrong. Today was not a day for fun.

The house was quiet, other than the low murmur of the radio by my side and the creak of the rocking chair I sat in. Only the four of us remained, surrounded by enough food to last a lifetime. Mrs. Ransford took Barb home with her after they paid their respects, along with a boxful of food Meemaw insisted they take. The large box full of southern delights didn't seem to make a dent in the mounds of food left. My stomach was packed, and I guessed everyone else's was too, considering how much food I watched people gobble down. In between the tears and hugs, they shoveled it in like they were starving.

Alone on the porch, I thought about Grandma Pat. She was my first go-round with death and all that followed it, so at least I had known what to expect. It had taken Daddy weeks to laugh and smile again, but eventually, he did. I knew Mom and Meemaw would too. Life moved on—returned to normal. I cried when Grandma Pat died. More from seeing Daddy upset than actually missing her presence in my life. Grandma Pat was a cold, hard woman whom I never felt comfortable around. I tried, but didn't recall a time when I snuggled up in her lap or enjoyed warm kisses and hugs. She had been nothing at all like Nana and Meemaw. Thinking about her funeral and how I bawled like a newborn kitten confused me because I had yet to shed a tear for Nana.

The lack of tears for Nana almost hurt as much as her passing. I loved her. Nana was a funny little thing, always flitting about from one project to the next. She wasn't able to sit still for more than ten minutes—just like me. Her mind revved up in constant motion—like her mouth. Her house smelled like talcum powder and warm apples fresh from the oven . Nana had a quick smile, hearty laugh, and a love for all things southern. Born in 1911, she loved to tell stories of her life growing up in Junction City, peppered with tall tales and crazy adventures.

Her favorite story, and one she told repeatedly, was about the great flood of 1927—her unbelievable tale about how she survived out in the woods, away from the raging waters that engulfed the region when the Mississippi River levee's failed and wiped out nearly all of Junction City. The story was legendary in our family—and the entire county. With a dramatic flair, she would recall how she survived. She'd been lured to the forest by screams she thought were from a woman in pain but turned out to be from a panther. Terrified, she started running and went the wrong direction, heading deeper and deeper into the woods. The sound of the big cat's heavy breathing and snarls behind her kept her feet pumping until she collapsed from exhaustion.

"I just knowed my life was over! I couldn't make my legs go no more. Thought my heart would burst from fear when the hairy beast jumped out from the bushes. Lawdy! I screamed and cried for help, tried to shoo it away, but it kept acomin'. I was clawin' my fingers in the dirt, tryin' to pull myself away. Didn't matter none. Thing was right on top of me 'fore I could blink. Mounds a black fur stickin' up every which way, and it stunk worse than an old dead skunk rottin' in the hot sunshine. It had these big yellow eyes and teeth as long as my fingers! I'm tellin' ya, it was *right here*."

Nana would stick her wrinkled hand inches from her nose for dramatic effect. She'd finish the story about how her shrill scream scared the creature away and she passed out from fright. When she awoke, she found herself high in a tree and surrounded by swirling, muddy water.

Mom and Daddy (and Meemaw, if around) would roll their eyes when Nana started the story, but I never did. I loved to listen to her sweet southern voice paint a vivid picture of her earlier life, even if it was a load of hog swallow like Daddy said.

My love for her was why I was so confused and had snuck outside to be alone. Why hadn't I cried yet? Not one tear had been shed, even when I watched the rest of my family cry. It didn't make any sense to me. True, I had only been seven when Grandma Pat died and it had been my first experience with death, but that shouldn't have mattered. I *adored* Nana, so why wouldn't the pain of missing her inside my soul come out?

What is wrong with me?

I pushed my feet against the smooth wood of the porch, and the chair began to rock in slow, flowing movements. I watched the last rays of the orange sun as they disappeared over the western sky. I was glad that Barb had gone home. I wasn't in the mood for talking, not even to my best friend. I hadn't said a word to anyone since Papa Joe asked me earlier how I was holding up and I muttered *fine.* Though he had been a guest in our house before, seeing Papa Joe all dressed up and the heavy sadness behind his eyes made my heart hurt even more. Papa Joe usually had a big smile on his face.

But not today. Instead, the old man's wrinkled face had been taut with emotion. Though unsure how old he really was, I suspected he was in his eighties. His dark skin, courtesy of his Choctaw heritage, looked thin and ashy from stress. His raven black hair only had a few hints of gray before, but I noticed quite a bit more at the funeral. Nana's death hit him hard, for the two of them were very close. Meemaw told Mom once, when she didn't think I was listening, that she found Papa Joe's weekly trek to Nana's after church on Sundays to be weird. Papa Joe made sure anything that needed fixing around the house got done. Helped out during the spring and summer months with Nana's humongous garden. Mom had brushed the comment off, telling Meemaw that Papa Joe was a sweet man who enjoyed helping Nana out. After all, Nana was the oldest citizen of Junction City and Papa Joe was the last remaining full-blooded Choctaw in the area, so it seemed natural the two were drawn together.

I stopped rocking when someone inside the house (Mom probably) started to straighten up the kitchen. The sound made me scrunch down further in the rocker, not wishing to be seen. I worried my thoughts would be written all over my face, followed by probing questions from whomever was knocking around inside. No, I didn't want to be seen until what I came out here to do was completed. I may have been young, but I understood what burned inside of me. I knew what emotion held the tears inside of me.

Guilt.

Guilt over what I'd done. Though it didn't make any sense—was beyond the realm of possibilities—Nana's death wasn't from some accidental run-in with local wildlife. She had run away from town into the deepest part of the forest, terrified of the thing chasing her. Maybe hoping she might lure it away from the rest of us. Almost like Nana sacrificed herself to save the town.

After Daddy told Mom and Meemaw the truth about what happened in the woods, my knot of guilt started to grow. It doubled in size when Sheriff Gilmore told Daddy earlier that the search party found evidence of something big in the area by Caney Creek. Claw marks on the tree and a few footprints deep in the bottoms of paws too big to be a cat's. The dogs followed the scent over to the next county, but lost it in the swampy mess. None of the tracks were fresh and no sign of the creature remained.

But the guilt swallowed me whole when I watched Sheriff Gilmore hand Daddy the necklace earlier.

The necklace Nana kept hidden in her jewelry box.

One she promised to give me when I was older and ready to hear the story behind it.

The one made from a soft, thin leather strap with a

crude charm carved out of wood in the shape of a cat's head dangling from the middle.

She called it her personal totem. A symbol of the guardian who kept her safe from harm, created for her by a Choctaw tribal elder years ago.

What she clutched to her chest the night in the woods.

I couldn't live with it. Couldn't stand the thought of what happened. I looked up and prayed in silence, hoping Nana heard me. *I'm sorry, Nana. I'm so sorry. Please forgive me. I didn't mean to hurt you.*

The sky grew darker. The brilliant silver stars glittered against the ebony backdrop. On my parents' porch in the dark, I shoved the awful visions of Nana's death out of my mind. I vowed to never to think about them or tell another soul. My body shook with force as I reached inside my mind. I gripped the edges of the rocker and hung on for dear life, mentally picturing the removal of the thoughts from my head. Like sweeping the dirt Daddy's boots left on the kitchen floor, I cleaned. I pictured myself burying them right alongside Nana's ruined corpse inside her casket at Ridgemond Cemetery, covered with six feet of heavy Mississippi clay.

Because they weren't odd dreams about the night she died.

They were memories.

My memories of the night I ripped into her soft flesh with my bared teeth, claws exposed and growl loud. As surely as I saw Tinker turn into an enormous white panther, I saw what happened to Nana with my own eyes. Because I was *there.*

Oh, God. What had I become? Why did I kill Nana?

Tinker's loud meow brought my mind's focus back to the front porch, out of the tortured halls of my mind. I swallowed hard and finished sweeping the recollections of that night away, then slammed the door shut inside my heart. The minute Tinker's soft coat rubbed against my bare legs, the memories became nothing more than fuzzy, unrecognizable images. Peace settled over me, like I just woke up from the best night's sleep I'd ever had.

Outta sight, outta mind.

A smile appeared on my face when Tinker jumped onto my lap. I stroked his smooth fur and let out a quiet laugh when he began to purr. He jutted his head into my chin and rubbed against it several times, then licked my cheek with his rough, pink tongue.

He curled up into a tight ball and gave one last little meow, closing his big green eyes. I was beyond thankful he was back since I hadn't seen him since the morning he ran from the house. Safe—that's how he made me feel. My protector was back. Everything would be okay now. Tinker would banish my dreams—and the monsters that resided in them.

To my surprise, I felt a hot tear slide down my face. It dripped off my chin and landed on Tinker's head. *No, not Tinker. Nahu'ala. Oh, why didn't you save Nana? Why didn't you stop me from...*I muttered under my breath, my voice but a faint squeak in the stillness of the night. The tears came faster, and soon, my shirt and Tinker's head were soaked. My eyelids seemed heavy, as well as my heart. Unable to keep them open any longer, I felt my body relax when they closed for the last time.

Over the singing of the katydids and the chirps of the night birds, I heard the same voice inside my head from three nights before. It was just as powerful this time, but quieter—softer.

I am here, Little One. Rest now. It was her time to go. I can-

not stop you from becoming. It is your destiny. Be still, and sleep.
You are not needed...yet. But soon, very soon, you will be. Hide
these thoughts deep within you. Do not speak of them again until
it is time. I am here to protect you. Sleep, and dream no more.

CHAPTER SIX - THE IN-BETWEEN YEARS

As my younger self predicted, the painful sting of Nana's death became a dull throb over time. Life went on as each of us learned to live in our new world without her. Mom and Dad worked hard every day to make their diner a success before Nana passed, but business boomed after Meemaw began to help out in the kitchen. Meemaw was an amazing cook, and people flocked to eat her signature fried chicken and cornbread. After losing her mother, Meemaw wanted to be as close as possible to her remaining family, so she and Papa Joe shared cooking duties in the kitchen.

She moved in with us permanently after she sold her

house and Nana's. Meemaw was a lot like her mother—funny, loud, full of pep and energy. Her natural warmth helped all of us work through the loss, and the daily connection with us helped her through her own. I loved that she was full of lots of warm hugs and kisses. The only real differences between the two of them were Meemaw was about three inches taller than Nana had been, and she didn't tell outrageous tales like Nana. And Meemaw's head wasn't full of solid white like Nana's, but a lot more filled her scalp after Nana's death. Meemaw refused to let old age settle in and made sure she went to see Norma Kendrick every four weeks. "Washin' the gray away," she called it. She wasn't quite ready to let the blonde hair she was accustomed to disappear.

We didn't talk about Nana's tragic death much, other than a comment or two about missing her at random moments. Mom and Meemaw remarked on more than one occasion that it helped being inside the walls of the house they both grew up in. Meemaw said once she was thankful Mom and Dad decided to buy the place and renovate it. For me, each night cuddled up with Tinker helped wipe away my crazy thoughts about my involvement in Nana's death. My worries completely faded three weeks after Nana's funeral, when Sheriff Gilmore stopped by and told Daddy they found the culprit—a male black bear. Ralph Wemscott reneged on his original statement about never setting foot back in the woods. He caught the scent trail again down by Caney Creek and spent two days tracking the thing before he shot it.

After the news spread through the town about Ralph's catch, things simmered down. Ralph didn't say a word to anyone. He just drove his muddy truck down Main Street with the corpse of the ugly black thing in the back, trussed up like a hog ready for slaughter. A collective sigh of relief wiped the fears of the townsfolk away, and Ralph had his fifteen minutes of fame. Mom and Dad fed him any meal he wished for an entire month for free. Mr. Hockington gave Ralph enough shotgun shells and bullets for his rifle to fill the cab of his truck full. News of his catch made it all the way to Greenville, and a taxidermist known for his work offered to prepare the creature as a trophy for Ralph's wall, free of charge.

People went back to their daily routines. Farmers tended to their flocks and their crops. School resumed, people shopped, hunting season came and went. Most of the town attended Friday night football games, then stopped in at the diner for a victory (or defeat) snack. Soon, thoughts of the morbid death of Junction City's oldest resident drifted away like the rice chaff from the fields on a hot summer breeze.

I clung to Meemaw like she was my personal life force. I had lots of friends but was only really close to Barb and Dane. I wasn't a loner, really, but preferred to concentrate on only a few relationships at a time. So I focused all my attention on Meemaw, Barb, and Dane.

Meemaw enjoyed running, like me. After she moved in, we began an after school ritual—jogging. The first day we ran together, she said if I wanted to be on the cheerleading squad, running would help keep me fit and limber, as well as increase my stamina. I knew that since I'd been running for about six months already, but I never said a word. Even though I had been young, I sensed Meemaw wanted to do something that reminded her of her youth. To feel alive and carefree, and maybe work off all the fried foods and desserts she loved to cook and eat.

First, it was just a mile, then two, then three, and

finally, five. She never slacked behind me. Meemaw matched my strong legs stride for stride with a smooth, even pace. Soon, we jogged all over town, and people would sit outside on their porches and watch us go by, tipping a glass of beer or tea at us as we passed. A few customers even started asking Meemaw how many miles we'd run each week when they came in to eat one of her stick-to-your-ribs-and-ass meals.

When I started seventh grade, Barb joined us. Initially, Barb told me she was sick of me being too tired at night to gab on the phone with her after I went out running with Meemaw. I told her she didn't need to worry none about that. Her momma owned one of the town's biggest mouths—a trap that never stayed shut, and one that surely would pass on down the line, at least the way Barb was heading. It was just a good natured poke we both laughed at, but secretly, I think Barb took my words to heart. When she began running with us, gossip never once left her lips.

Another thing Meemaw enjoyed was passing her skills on to me. After all, she'd say, that's what one generation is supposed to do for the next one—bestow knowledge to the younger family members. Train them in the ways of the world. She taught me how to cook, sew, make hand-churned butter, every available use for baking soda (who knew it was so versatile?) and how to clean and fry catfish. Told me I needed to know these things to prepare for when I was on my own, taking care of myself and my future family. I loved spending time with her. I was grateful for what she taught me, so I kept my sarcastic retorts about my thoughts on the out-of-date duties of a woman to myself.

I made the cheerleading squad after years of practice with Mom's friend and local gymnastics instructor, Kathy

Boddett. Mom and Kathy cheered together for the Junction City Panthers in high school. Mom married Daddy and stayed in town, but Kathy went on to cheer at MSU for two years. Kathy came back home, degreeless, when she blew her knee out. With Kathy's ability to tumble and flip gone, but not the desire, she decided to teach the next generation. She opened up a small gym three miles away from the Kilgore place, and soon, young mothers arrived in droves, daughters in tow.

Like me.

Apparently, I was a natural tumbler, at least according to Kathy. Took to it like a *duck on a June bug* she said to my mom one day after practice. I thought it funny since ducks didn't seem very athletic. "That girl's got some major skills, Jolene. She has strength and muscle coordination like a seasoned pro! Reflexes I ain't never seen in someone so young. And she ain't but just a child. Keep her comin' here and I guarantee you, she'll be on top of the pyramid in no time. She'll be the next town legend, surpassing even the two of us."

Mom had smiled and brushed the compliment off, but pride beamed behind her blue eyes. After we left the gym that day, we made a quick stop by the diner. Mom loaded me up with the biggest banana split I'd ever seen. While I attempted to make a dent in the sticky mess, Mom blabbed to anyone within earshot about her *star* daughter. After I made the squad my freshman year, *Newcomb's Diner* donated the most sponsor money. The day Mom and I went to Greenville to pick up my first uniform, the proud smile and shimmering tears of joy on her face were unmistakable.

Tinker became Tinker again. I never made the mistake of calling him Nahu'ala, not even when snuggled up alone under the covers together. He grew from a bedraggled, four pound stray to a large, healthy cat. He was an enigma, though: he only showed up at night. I never found where he hid out during the day, even when I enlisted the help of Barb. We scoured the neighborhood and not only could we not find him, but no one ever recalled seeing him wander through their yard. After months of searching, I gave up, content with the fact that my furry friend appeared at the back door each night.

After the summer of Nana's death, my dreams and visions vanished. As the years passed and I entered puberty, my childhood nightmares and fears were replaced by other things. When I got my first period and the hormones began to rage inside of me, my thoughts turned to boys. By the time I turned fourteen, Meemaw stopped her daily runs with me and Barb. She said it was because her knees hurt, but I knew better. Meemaw had grown tired of listening to us gab incessantly about guys. When I started making noises about how gorgeous Dane was and how I meant to marry him someday, Meemaw couldn't take anymore.

My calm, idyllic life changed during the summer I turned eighteen. Two weeks before I started my senior year, a violent storm slammed into the town. The EF-3 tornado damaged numerous homes and farmland when it blew through. The Kilgore farm and the town's biggest employer, Cohestra Industries, took the brunt of the storm. A few folks in town lost part of their roofs and debris littered the streets for a week.

Barb and I had been out running that morning, the sky a beautiful blue and not a cloud in it or a breeze to ruffle our hair. When we hit our second mile, right as we passed the entrance to the Cohestra plant, I sensed a shift in the air. Barb thought I'd lost my marbles when I told her we needed to head home because I sensed a storm coming.

"Storm? Sheryl, are you crazy? There ain't a cloud in the sky! Just another humid day full of sunshine and sweat! What's really goin' on? Oh, please don't tell me your knee is givin' you fits again? Cheerleadin' practice starts tonight!"

Barb whined but stopped running when she realized I wasn't following her. She had started to say more until she saw the look of fear on my face. "I'm not kiddin'. Look!" I yelled, pointing to our right. In the distance, a thick band of wall clouds rolled with anger. Even though they were far away, I sensed the shift in the electrical current around me. How, I had no idea, but some strange instinct screamed in my head we were in danger. "We need to get. Now."

"What the..." Barb sputtered. "Where did they come from? Those weren't there a split second ago! Do you really think it's headin' this way? The wind ain't blowin'..." Barb never finished her thought. Before she uttered another sound, a heavy gust of air slammed into us. It moved the ominous black clouds in our direction. Fast. The low rumble of thunder sealed any doubts either of us had. Barb and I exchanged glances and took off. We ran back toward my house. While running, I dug my cell phone out of my pocket and called Dad at the diner. Told him to keep everyone inside and that wicked weather was on its way. As soon as I hung up from warning him, the tornado sirens wailed. The piercing noise lit a fire underneath our feet, and Barb and I pounded the hot pavement even harder. Within ten minutes of crashing through the front door of my house and cowering in the basement, the storm was on top of us. Barb and I huddled together, holding hands and praying for the Lord above to keep us and the town safe from harm. We heard the sound of the funnel cloud as it approached. The freight-train-like noise was deafening.

Barb crushed her arms around me and yelled in my ear, "I love you, Sheryl. If this is it, I just wanted you to know that. Your friendship has been the best thing that's ever happened to me!"

I shouted over the storm, "I love you too, Barb. But don't talk like that! It will be over in a second! God is watchin' over us. You'll see."

Barb buried her face in my shoulder as the winds howled outside. The sounds of breaking glass, metal clanging, and the fury of the wind drowned out the sound of the warning system. Right as the noise reached its peak and the house shimmied and shook, it stopped. Barb and I scrambled to our feet and raced outside, our mouths agape as we stared at the mess in the street. Without saying a word, we moved in unison and hugged each other's necks. The love between us, and the thankfulness at being alive, transferred without uttering a single sound.

Though over in minutes, the damage it left behind was immense. No one died or sustained major injuries, which was a blessing, but Drexel Kilgore lost his entire rice crop, and the main building at Cohestra Industries was an unrecognizable pile of metal, wood, and glass. Everyone marveled at the destruction and the fact no one inside lost their lives. Dane's mother, Emma, ushered everyone out of the main building and over to the refinery area minutes before the twister descended. Accolades and murmurs of wonderment swept through town, almost as fast as the tornado. Ms. Emma's uncanny sense about the storm before the sirens started to wail saved many lives.

The majority of the citizens banded together to help clean up the mess. Newcomb's Diner supplied free food and drinks to the workers. Everyone pitched in, another perk of living in a small, close-knit community.

Cohestra Industries used the devastating event as a catalyst to not only rebuild, but expand. The company had been a part of Junction City since 1928. Every year, seventh graders learned about the plant in history class. After the flood waters recessed and people began moving back, Cohestra Industries started out as a grain and cotton refinery. Dane Witherspoon moved here from up north somewhere and saw the potential of the area and bought up numerous acres of the damp, empty land. Soon, people started to move in since the government offered chunks of land at rock-bottom prices. The loss of crop revenue and food produced from the area had hit the rest of the United States hard. Farmers from around the surrounding states flocked in by the dozens, eager to buy a piece of the fertile Delta soil. By the time Mr. Witherspoon died in the early 40's, his business was booming. Cohestra was the only mill within fifty miles, and after the new residents began farming, crop production soared. His son, Dane II, expanded the facilities in the 60's to include a small side business—bottled water production. *Spring of Youth* he named it.

From stories told by Nana, Meemaw, and Dane—and a tad from history class—I learned the water facility part of Cohestra's business didn't really take off until the mid-80's. Up until then, people in the Delta seemed to think it was insane to pay for water. If you wanted some, you grabbed a glass, filled it with ice, and loaded it full from your sink. If you wanted more, you repeated the process.

But after the sudden death of his father, Dane III (called "Pops" by everyone in the town—just not to his face) took over the helm of Cohestra in 1991, and he had big plans. He started a marketing campaign that touted the health benefits of drinking *Spring of Youth*. Glowing skin, youthful vigor, energy, and longevity were the selling points. The ads were sprinkled with a few pictures of some of the actors portraying the elderly residents of Locasia County.

"Get your bottle of pure, liquid youth serum today! The natural, spring-fed waters will rejuvenate your mind, body, and soul. There's a reason Locasia County residents live so long! It's all in the water—and we are sharing it with YOU!"

Local folks scoffed and kept to their tap water. Of course, they had the inside scoop that no one really lived any longer in Locasia County than any other part of the world. But the residents kept quiet and let the charade continue, just to save face. The target audience outside of Mississippi couldn't get enough of the stuff in their never-ending quest for youth. Soon, Cohestra's refinery business took a back seat to the bottled water side as it shot to the top of the money making section of the company.

As soon as Cohestra began rebuilding after the tornado, Pops Witherspoon decided to use the opportunity to expand the family's land ownership as well. He met with the other financial powerhouse family head in the county, his sworn enemy, Drexel Kilgore. Numerous local gossip tales about the reasons for the hatred between the two men had been whispered throughout the county for years. Some were utterly outrageous, born from the bored minds of the citizens. The one that stuck and made the most sense centered around botched, agreed-upon price for rice years ago. When Mr. Witherspoon wouldn't pay the verbal amount he offered at the beginning of the growing season, the argument caused the two men to almost come to blows outside the main building at Cohestra. Since that day many decades ago, the Kilgore and Witherspoon clans had given each other a wide berth.

One particular afternoon, however, was a different story. Pops Witherspoon offered to purchase Drexel's damaged fields, plus an additional hundred acres that connected the Kilgore spread past Caney Creek, deep into the forest and swamps beyond. I overheard the conversation between the two men. Mr. Witherspoon wanted the additional acres to build a new, bigger water plant closer to the source so Cohestra would be able to meet the demands of their water distributors. The discussion between the two old men had been loud and unpleasant. I heard every angry word from my position at the counter, along with all the other customers having lunch. For some strange reason, the meeting took place in the back corner table of our diner. Guess they both figured our little restaurant was neutral territory to conduct a meeting. Their voices went from hushed murmurs to loud words.

"I done told ya, Mr. Witherspoon, I ain't interested in

sellin' any of my land. Not to you or anybody else. Period."
Drexel huffed, clearly annoyed with the man sitting across
from him.

"I heard you the first time, Mr. Kilgore. But I don't
believe you grasped my more than generous offer. In case
you didn't, I will repeat it. Ten thousand dollars an acre.
And recall, I am not askin' to buy you out, mind you. Just
the damaged fields and the unused land by Caney Creek.
Leaves you plenty left to continue farmin', plus you won't
have to worry about cleanin' up the mess the twister left
behind."

"Y'all's really a vulture, ain't ya? Skulkin' 'round
waitin' for a member of the herd to just drop down to the
ground, too weak to stand back up and run. Then *swoop!*
You fly in and start peckin' at the carcass."

"Mr. Kilgore, ten thousand dollars an acre is beyond
generous! I assure you, peckin' at your carcass is not what
I'm tryin' to do. I'm tryin' to help you and your..."

Everyone in the diner jumped when Mr. Kilgore
slammed his fist on the thin Formica tabletop, cutting
Pop's words off with a loud *thump* and jangle of silverware
and glass. "I *ain't* like the others. Won't let the money you's
danglin' sway me none. Your words ain't worth a lick of
salt anyway! I won't let the money blind me from the truth
behind your words. And the truth is, y'all's either crazy as
Lucy-Goosey or sly like the schemin' fox 'cause the land
ain't worth a quarter of what you're offerin'. My money is
on sly fox. Y'all want somethin' out there in them woods
awful bad to make such a poor business choice. Don't
rightly know what it could be, but I'm here to tell ya, I
won't be a part of ya gettin' it. No siree. And don't ya ask
me...or my kin...again. I'm givin' ya fair warnin', Mr. Witherspoon—stay away from me and my farm."

Mr. Kilgore stood up in a huff, his face redder than a ripe tomato. He threw down a twenty on the counter, tipped his hat to me and my family, and left the diner without another word. Pops Witherspoon sat in the booth for a few more minutes and fiddled with his drink. He then rose and left without a backward glance. Stunned customers forgot all about their food and stared in shock. His face was unreadable when he passed by, but the heat of his anger was hot enough to brew coffee. As soon as the door closed, the murmurings of the crazy encounter started. Within the space of an hour, all of Locasia County heard about the meeting. The feud between the Witherspoon and Kilgore clans went from bad to worse.

I didn't realize until it was too late how bad things would get.

And it would make the damage from the tornado look like child's play.

Less than a week later, after the verbal sparring between the two powerful men in our diner, Pops Witherspoon died. When Kathy Hall, one of the two 911 operators in the county, came in for a jolt of caffeine after a long night shift, she told us all about it. Pop's housekeeper discovered his body on the back porch when she came to work less than two hours ago. A massive heart attack ended his reign as the head of the Witherspoon clan. I almost dropped the tray of biscuits. I was so glad Dane and his mom had gone down to Greenville last week. Dane's dad, the *fourth* Dane, had only been around Junction City long enough to knock up Emma, so it was just the three of them in that big old mansion. When Emma told him about her pregnancy, he hightailed it back east. He came back once to visit his son when Dane was nine.

Dane and Ms. Emma had been down in Greenville for the past week while Dane attended basketball camp. Lucky for them, they left the day the two elderly men almost came to blows in our diner. Hearing the news about his Pop's passing, I whispered a silent prayer of thanks. If Dane and his mom had been home, they would have discovered his body.

It was bad enough that Ms. Johnson found the old man. As Kathy related the 911 call, she said the poor elderly woman told her she was so upset, she'd nearly fainted. Ms. Johnson said it took her twenty minutes of running around inside the house to find the phone. After Kathy spread the bit of *really* juicy gossip, she left to go home. Well, she *said* she was going home. My guess was she planned on stopping by every house on the way to share what a difficult shift she'd just pulled.

My family didn't have time to even digest the news. And I didn't have time to snag my phone from my purse to call Dane before Ms. Johnson's beat-up Oldsmobile came to a screeching stop less than two feet from the front window of our restaurant. Mom, Meemaw, Papa Joe, and I were the only ones working at the diner. Shirley had the day off and Dad was in Greenville buying supplies. With the morning breakfast crowd gone and lunch a couple hours away, no customers were inside when Ms. Johnson burst through the front door. In her haste, she nearly jerked the door off its hinges with her beefy arms. The dainty jingle of the bell above the door sounded like a cowbell.

When she walked in, she looked like a zombie. Wisps

of her white hair had escaped the tight chignon on the back of her neck and stuck to her wet forehead. Her fair skin was white as snow, except for the two big blotches of red dotting her round cheeks. Her ample chest heaved as she struggled to catch her breath. Mom and Meemaw glanced at each other with knowing looks, worried, I'm sure, that the older woman was close to passing out. In a flash, they were by Ms. Johnson's side, and each one gently grasped an elbow and led the shaken woman to her favorite table. Papa Joe nudged my arm in the direction of the water pitcher. I nodded in response, grabbed a glass and walked over to the table. When I set it in front of Ms. Johnson, she picked it up with shaky hands and downed the first full glass in one, long gulp.

"Ms. Johnson, would you like somethin' to eat? I can whip up your usual in a snap."

"Thank ya kindly, Ms. Jolene, but I don't know if I'm *ever* gonna be able to eat again. I surely don't. After what I seen today, my appetite done skedaddled."

"Ah, now, sure you will. We...uh, just heard about what you walked in to this mornin'. I'm sorry about what you had to deal with, but death is just the beginnin' of eternal life. You know that, Lucinda. You just had you a shock, that's all. Who wouldn't be upset? I mean, you worked for Pops, I mean, Mr. Witherspoon, for how long?"

After she spoke, Meemaw lifted the empty glass up to me for a refill. While I poured, Ms. Johnson started fanning herself with a napkin from the table, and then began to wipe the wetness from her face and chest. The heavy humidity and rain had left her a dripping mess. I sensed her emotions. Terror streamed from her, just like the water. I slunk down in the seat behind her to listen. The compulsion to stay overwhelmed me, the booth like a magnet to my butt. Something seemed wrong—out of place. My own mouth was suddenly dry, and the outer skin on my ears burned.

"My nerves ain't shot from sadness of his passin', that's for sure. I've seen dead bodies 'fore, so it ain't that, either. I'm here to tell ya, he may be in eternity now, but he ain't flyin' in the Heavens with wings. No way Mr. Dane Witherspoon the *third* made it through the Pearly Gates. I worked for that old coot for over twenty-five years—more if you count the years I followed my mama's footsteps around the big old house when she worked for him. Three generations of my family took care of the Witherspoons. Ain't none of them been around when one passed. Lucky me, I drew that short straw."

"Sheryl, go fetch Ms. Lucinda a bottle of lemon-lime soda. It'll help settle her stomach so she can eat."

Ms. Johnson focused her attention on me for a second and then back to Mom and Meemaw. "No, I'm fine. Just need to breathe for a second. Get my wits back on track." She lowered her voice and motioned for all three of us to move in closer. "As I said, my nerves ain't on fire from findin' the old geezer stiff as a board. It's *how* I found him and what was left behind that's done freaked my ol' pea brain out. And I have somethin' to tell y'all. Somethin' I hid from the sheriff. Can you...will you lock the door? I don't want nobody to hear or see this."

The compulsion I felt seconds ago to stay and listen had been right on the money. Now, my stomach tightened and a dull headache danced around my temples. All three of us sat still, caught up in the fear in her voice. I heard light footsteps from behind me and realized Papa Joe had come out from the kitchen. He made his way to the front door. The *click* of the lock when he turned it seemed to calm Ms. Johnson's nerves somewhat. She leaned back and let her shoulders sag against the cool vinyl, watching with wary eyes until Papa Joe was safely out of earshot.

The black of her pupils blocked almost all of the blue of her eyes. She opened her purse, withdrew a small, amber colored bottle, twisted the top off, and tilted it back. She drained almost half of the liquid in one large gulp. Once finished, she smiled a feeble little grin, let out a huge burp, and began. "Sorry about that, ladies. But sometimes you gotta have a short snort to ease things up, you know? Not very ladylike, but..."

"None of us are judging you, Ms. Lucinda. Though after that big swig, I must insist you eat somethin' before you leave, okay? Maybe just a cup of bland oatmeal. Nothin' fancy."

"Ms. Gertie, you's about the sweetest woman in the county. Just like your ma, God rest her soul."

"You're too kind, Ms. Lucinda. Now, take a deep breath and tell us what's gnawin' at your insides."

"Okay. Well, like I said, death don't bother me so much. Seen several people pass over the years. Shed my tears at the loss of loved ones. But this time? Hmmm, it wasn't just a death. It was...murder."

Mom and Meemaw gasped in shock. The muscles in my neck tightened. Meemaw commented first. "Murder!? What makes you think he was murdered? Why, Kathy Hall told us he died of a heart attack. Shoot, the man was over eighty years old!"

"Ms. Gertie, I know how this town is—word spreads faster and farther than a fart on a windy day. Most of the words passed on stink just about as bad too. Listen, I'm tellin' you, old Pops was *murdered*."

"Does Sheriff Gilmore agree with your opinion?" Mom queried, her voice tight.

"Whether he does or not, Ms. Jolene, won't change my mind. But to answer your question...no. The sheriff and the coroner said the old man had himself a widow-maker attack. But the Governor of this great state himself could come and give a proclamation on the courthouse steps that the old man died of a heart attack, it won't matter to me. I'm tellin' you, the man's heart gave out because he was *scared* to death."

"Scared to death? What do you mean by that, Lucinda? I mean, really, how could you tell? And exactly how does bein' scared to death equal murder?"

"Gertie, you and I go way back, so I'll let your negative tone slide—this time. And I'll tell you how I know somethin' done frightened the life outta him. How many heart attack patients you ever heard about whose hair turned whiter than a goose feather when their heart failed?"

"Come again?" Meemaw blurted out.

"Girl, that pretty head of salt-and-pepper hair of his was *gone*. G-O-N-E gone. Looked like someone dipped his head in a can of white paint. Every single hair was not only white, but stickin' straight up from his head. Like he done stuck his finger in an outlet or turned his head upside down while blowin' it dry with a cupful of gel in it. I'm tellin' you, ain't never seen nothin' like it. Ever. Plus, his face was frozen in a silent scream."

"That is odd, but seriously, what in the world would have scared him? Witherspoon men are as hard as stone! Nothin' and nobody scares them. It's usually the other way around."

"Oh, I agree with ya, Ms. Gertie. No snake around these parts could hold a candle to old Pops. That is, until he had that run-in with Mr. Kilgore last week. When I came to work the next day, he seemed...different. And not just because Ms. Emma and lil' Dane was gone. Quiet, like someone popped his balloon and let all the hot air out. Deflated. After his run-in with Drexel, he stopped goin' to work and just followed me around while I cleaned. He checked the doors and windows about every twenty minutes. Made me give him my house key back...then went and changed the locks anyway. When his phone would ring, he wouldn't answer it. He'd just stare at the thing like it was on fire or somethin'. Oh, and bought himself the biggest, ugliest mongrel I've ever seen and kept it tight on a leash right beside him. And ol' Pops, he *hated* dogs. I mean, *hated* them. When a few strays dared nose around his property, he was right quick to grab his shotgun and dispatch them quickly. How does a man go from a tough snake to a cowerin' kitten in less than one week if he ain't terrified about somethin'?"

Mom furrowed her brow and looked out the window for a minute, then back at Ms. Johnson. "All that is mighty odd, I'll give you that. Wonder what sent him into such a tizzy?"

"Tizzy? Honey, he weren't in no 'tizzy.' He was lathered up like a rabid dog, foam danglin' from his jowls and all. When I left last night, he was mumblin' to that hairy fleabag. Kept tellin' him it had to *protect your master* and *warn me when he comes.* And I think, whatever ol' Pops was afraid was gonna pay him a visit, did last night. When I got there this mornin', the front door was wide open and the mangy mutt nowhere in sight. Knew somethin' was wrong right away. Sensed it, ya know? Then, like an old fool, I pushed my worry away, thinkin' I was just lettin' the heat get to me. I mean, Lawdy, this summer's been a doozy.

Don't reckon I recall a hotter one. So, I went to the kitchen and started to fix some coffee, hopin' maybe he'd just taken the dog for a walk and forgot to shut the door. Imagine my surprise when I opened the drapes overlookin' the back veranda. Ol' Pops looked like the Devil done waltzed in, snatched out his soul, and dragged it straight to Hell."

Ms. Johnson paused, took a deep breath and followed it with a long gulp of water. No one moved or spoke as we each thought about what Ms. Johnson told us. Finally, Mom gathered her thoughts together and asked, "You said you had somethin' to show us as well. What...what is it?"

The color that had seeped back into Ms. Johnson's face while she told her story, faded again. She wet her dry lips, then bit the bottom one. She tried to contain her tears and hold her trembling mouth still. She fumbled around with the napkin on the table until she unrolled it and released the silverware. With shaky fingers, she wiped at her damp brow and cleavage once again. She drew in a ragged breath and then cleared her throat. "After the sheriff finished questionin' me, I decided to go home and change into a drier dress before I came here to eat. I mean, I'd been sweatin' like a city whore in a country church the whole time. But the second I stepped inside my front door, I knew someone had been in my house. Grabbed my shotgun from the closet and warned the bastard to show his face 'fore I found him and blew it off. Right when I reached the phone to call the sheriff, I noticed bloody paw prints on the floor. I sort of laughed at myself for gettin' so wound up, 'cause after seein' the prints, I figured a critter snuck in and hurt itself tryin' to get out. Happened to me before with a raccoon and another time with a skunk, remember that Ms. Gertie?"

Meemaw nodded her agreement in silence, motioning with her hands for Ms. Johnson to continue her story.

"So, I put the phone down and followed the trail. The prints stopped at my bedroom door. I pushed it open and saw the mutt on my bed. At first, I was angry the hairy thing was not only in my house, but on my bed. Thought maybe it followed my scent trail or somethin'. Figured whatever got to ol' Dane scared the critter and it ran to my house. But then, I saw all the blood. Gobs and gobs of the red stuff was all over the walls and my comforter. Room was covered in it. When I looked back on the bed, I noticed the beast was dead. Ripped apart and its guts nowhere in sight. Lawdy, I ain't never gonna get all of the mess clean. Never. Or sleep on the mattress again. It's ruined."

"Oh, my word! How awful," Mom whispered to no one in particular.

"Honey, you ain't heard the awful part yet. That story was just the appetizer. This here is the main course. This was a hangin' outta its mouth."

None of us took a breath when Ms. Johnson reached into the pocket of her dress, extracted something, and then opened her hand for us to see. She held out a piece of paper marked with faint scribbles. Ms. Johnson's arm shook as she moved her hand closer to Meemaw. Instinctively, Mom put her arm out in front of her own mother and pushed her back against the seat.

She senses something is wrong, too.

"Lucinda... why did you bring it to us and not give it to the sheriff?"

"If you read the note, you'll understand why."

"What does it say, Lucinda?" Meemaw asked.

"I done already read it once and ain't repeatin' it. Read it yourself."

"Oh, for Heaven sakes! You're actin' like it was written by Satan himself, Lucinda," Meemaw snapped. She reached over and snatched the paper from Ms. Johnson's hand. She spread the crumpled mess on out on the Formica. "What in the world could be so...?"

Meemaw's voice dried up, her bravado long gone. I thought her eyes were going to bug out of her head they grew so wide. Mom leaned over and read it too, her lips moving in silence as she squinted at the small print. Both of their faces blanched, and Mom's hand rose up and covered her mouth. My own fear had skyrocketed and not just from Ms. Johnson's eerie story. Though I didn't want to know what it said, I was unable to stop myself from asking. "What? What does it say?"

Again, the diner was silent. Even the air conditioner stopped running, like it waited for the note to be read aloud. I glanced over my shoulder to see if Papa Joe was still in the kitchen but didn't see him. I hoped he was out back, smoking, leaving us alone to calm down Ms. Johnson. I wouldn't have admitted it to anyone out loud, but I was scared and hoped he hadn't left for the day. I glanced up at the old clock on the wall. Was Daddy on his way back yet? A brief flash of anger hit me because none of the important men in our lives were here when it seemed we needed them.

Irritated now, I reached over the seat and grabbed the paper from Meemaw's unsteady hand. When I did, a familiar aroma hit me and made my head spin with old, childhood memories. I remembered the scent—apples and talcum powder.

Nana.

I choked down my fear, forcing myself to read the words. Though already dry and dark brown, I smelled the rusty odor of the blood used to create them. I tamped my rising terror back down and read:

Dane was weak, so I took care of him. Now he's gone, and my time has come—and I am strong. Stronger than all of them put together. I've been waiting for a very long time to reclaim what's rightfully mine. Give this note to SIN. You know her as Sheryl Ilene Newcomb. Watch her face when she reads it. I know what she did. She knows what she did—and who she really is. Let her know I am coming for her. Tell no one except the Kovlin women. Their reign is about to end. Tell the Kovlin clan I'm coming. Going to collect what should have been my inheritance—my birthright. Tell any others and you're a dead woman, Lucinda. The death of this mutt will pale in comparison to yours. And I'll know—because I'll be watching. I have your scent. You'll never see or hear me coming.

"And, there was this," Ms. Johnson murmured. Her faint voice was followed by a small *thwack* as she tossed another item from her pocket onto the tabletop, this time in a hurry like it was on fire. My fingers shook as I lifted the object up to get a better look at it under the light. My heart thundered in my chest. The sickening taste of bitter bile rose up from my stomach. A shudder of cold panic slammed through me as I stared down at the item in my hand.

It was a necklace. One made from thin leather and a crude rendition of a cat's head carved in wood, woven into the center.

"Just like Nana's," Meemaw whispered in disbelief.

Kovlin reign? What did that mean? Oh, God, the writer of the note knows what I did to Nana. How? Did someone see me that night? Who is coming and what birthright? What the hell is going on?

As the four of us sat hunched together like a bunch of frightened chickens waiting out a thunderstorm, Papa Joe walked in from the kitchen. With slow, sure steps he crossed the small space with silent footfalls. Something about him seemed different. His body posture seemed odd—made him look taller and stronger than usual. His gait was smooth, fluid. Confident. The entire dining area seemed to darken and the temperature soared as he moved closer to the booth. Warm heated radiated from him. I cut my eyes to the front window, thinking the earlier rain-storm was about to turn into a downpour and the dark storm clouds were the reason for the change in light. To my surprise, it was sunny outside, yet the yellow rays didn't seem to be able to penetrate inside the restaurant. When I turned my attention back to Papa Joe, I had to blink twice to ensure I wasn't dreaming. His big, limpid brown eyes had morphed into a golden sable color. They pulsed with energy as his deep, throaty voice cast a cloak of soothing balm over us all when he spoke. His focus was pinpointed on Ms. Johnson. "No need to worry, ladies. The note is but a prank, written by bored teenagers. Ones who are jealous of Sheryl for one silly reason or another."

"A prank? But...but what about the dead dog at my house? And this weird necklace?" Ms. Johnson balked.

"There was no dog, Ms. Johnson. You saw nothing. Heard nothing. Read nothing. Found nothing. You are dreaming. A very vivid dream, brought on by the shock of finding Mr. Witherspoon's body this morning. You are going to go home, pack up, and prepare for an extended vacation with your family once you take a long, refreshing nap on your couch. You deserve some time away after all the years you gave to the Witherspoon family."

Ms. Johnson started to protest, but Papa Joe's words seemed to mesmerize her. The thrumming cadence of his voice and the intensity of his gaze befuddled the stressed-out mind of the poor woman. When he put his hand on her shoulder, her eyes clouded over like she was in a trance, her head nodding in agreement. Without another word, she stood up and followed Papa Joe to the front door. She never took her eyes off the glass door while he unlocked it, and then she walked out of the diner. The tingle of the bell above the door was soft and light as she exited. Her footfalls silent as she shuffled out to her car.

Three sets of worried eyes focused on Papa Joe, our mouths agape and hearts still pounding. My mind raced with a gazillion questions. Ms. Johnson acted like a puppet on a string, controlled by the smooth lies Papa Joe had uttered. Did he use some sort of mind trick on her? What would happen when she returned home and found the dog? Would she see it? Was that even possible? No, no way. Fairy tale and fantasy—unless—Papa Joe hypnotized Ms. Johnson. I stole a quick glance over my shoulder and the sun was still bright, yet the inside of the diner held the same dreary darkness. The heat radiating from Papa Joe was intense, though his eyes had returned to normal.

My mouth was dry and my head spun. I wondered if he was using some sort of ancient Native American hocus pocus on all of us. For a split second, I stole a peek at Mom and Meemaw's faces. Although they didn't look like a deer caught in the headlights like poor Ms. Johnson had, they didn't look *right*, either. Something behind their eyes—something I couldn't quite pinpoint but still sensed. I looked over at Papa Joe who had a smile on his face, but the emotion didn't slide up to his luminous eyes. "Come, Kovlin women, we have much to do. We must prepare food for the grievin' family."

None of us said a word or even looked at each other as we rose in unison from the cramped booth. My guess was Mom and Meemaw had the same gut wrenching sensation swimming around in their insides as I did. Because somehow, some way, my heart and mind sensed nothing would ever be the same for any of us again.

Ever.

CHAPTER SEVEN

PART TWO – THE CHANGE

The bumpy ride across town ended the second I turned my truck onto the long, paved driveway that led up to the Witherspoon place. Each side of the wide lane was blanketed with massive magnolia and weeping willow trees, strategically interspersed to create a shaded, living canopy. When breezy, the limbs of the weeping willow danced with grace and beauty across the pavement. But not today. The trees stood still like statues under the blistering heat of the Mississippi sun.

Between the heat and the weight of the heavy trucks carrying farming goods hither and yon, Locasia County's roads were full of a ton of potholes. When dodging them, it made any driver look like they were drunker than Cooter Brown on a Saturday night. My ability to drive wasn't helped any by the lack of sleep and all the crazy thoughts careening around in my noggin. I laughed out loud at the analogy, one of my mom's favorite sayings.

Jesus, I really was tired if I was quoting my mother's silly expressions in my head.

It had only been a few months since Dane's grandfather had the driveway redone, and it was like driving on a sheet of glass. Of course, compared to the jarring ride on the way there, even a drive on pea gravel would have been an improvement. Once parked, I paused for a moment and gathered myself together while I checked to make sure the food crammed in the backseat survived the ride intact. Satisfied the contents were safe, I snuck a peek at my reflection in the rearview mirror and scowled. My blue eyes were surrounded by a sea of red, and the dark circles underneath them made me look like I should don a jersey and hit the football field. Actually, I looked like I just left a party at Stony Bamford's house after a long night of passing blunts around. I scrounged in my purse and found a ponytail holder, gathered up my unruly hair and twisted it into a messy bun, and then slathered some pink gloss across my lips.

I grabbed my purse and forced my shoulders to relax before stepping out into the sweltering heat. My insides felt like watery Jell-O. Once I climbed up the massive brick stairs that led to the wide wraparound porch, I wiped my sweaty hand on my shorts before I rang the doorbell. I noticed a slight tremor in my hands and willed myself to concentrate on happy thoughts. I thought about fluffy bunnies, rainbows, unicorns, adorable cat videos on YouTube—anything to steer clear of the smoldering panic in my gut. Thankfully, within five seconds, the door opened.

"Hey, babe! Missed you!"

Dane stood aside after opening the large front door of the house, a forced grin spread across his tired face. I wanted to jump into his arms and plant a kiss on him but held myself back. With my luck, his mom would be right behind him and use her cocoa-colored eyes to cut me to shreds. The woman seemed to hate every hair on my head.

A prick of anger danced up my back. She hadn't done a very good job of hiding the fact that she did not approve of her son dating a "whiter than rice" girl. I overheard her snarky comment one night on the phone months ago when Dane and I had been jabbering until way past midnight. He apologized a hundred times for his mother's prejudices, and I laughed it off, but it still hurt. It was a wonder he turned out sane at all between his grandfather's stone-aged teachings and his mother's racial issues. I mean, come on! She was as dark as two day old coffee, and Dane's family was part Native American—or had she forgotten that little tidbit of information? Maybe it slipped her mind when young Dane IV slipped her something. I said a silent prayer of thanks for my parents. They may have been southern to the core, but they lacked the particularly nasty southern trait of racism, and thankfully, they passed that along to me. "Glad you're back home. I'm just sorry your trip was cut short because of what happened. Hate it about Pops. At least you got to attend most of the camp though. So, how was it?"

Dane ushered me inside and pushed the door shut with a loud *bang*. He leaned down and nuzzled his face in my hair. It wasn't too much of a stretch for his six foot four frame, since I stood right at five feet ten. Our bodies fit together like we had been made for each other. His warm breath and strong arms set me on fire when he pulled me in closer for a full bear hug. The tension in my muscles, present since the visit from Ms. Johnson the day before and lack of sleep for over twenty-four hours, disappeared with one crushing embrace. "Oh, just a bunch of long-legged giraffes like me, learnin' how to tighten up our ball-handlin' skills. And *all* of me missed you too. Texts and phone calls weren't enough," he said, his husky voice muffled as his lips brushed over my hair. He moved his hips into mine and my heart skipped a few beats. Passion warmed my lower body when the bulge pressed against my hips and his strong pectoral muscles mashed my breasts. "Mmmm. You smell good. You baked some peach pie today, didn't you?"

He nipped at the nape of my neck in a playful bite, and then pulled his head back, his dark eyes dancing with desire. I swatted his tight rear through the thin shorts he had on with a loud *smack*. His familiar scent hit me and left me a bit unsteady on my feet. He smelled delicious as well. His personal aroma was an intoxicating mixture of fresh cut wood, citrus, and a hint of musk. His hair was still damp from an earlier shower, and I caught a whiff of the shampoo and body wash I bought him for his birthday, Scented Rain. Combined together, I had to stifle my urge to push him back on the couch and jump him right in the living room. Didn't matter to me whether his mom was home or not—and he knew it too. His liquid-brown eyes, full of wanting—needing—stared into mine, the smattering of light-green flecks glittered with passion. His full lips curved up in the kind of grin that would make him millions if he decided to give up playing hoops and become a model. Jesus—it was getting really hot in here. I wondered if he was trying to sidestep discussing his grandfather's death by making my brain turn to mush.

I decided to tread back to safer territory before my raging hormones took over. "Of course I did. It's your favorite, and I made it all by myself. And there's a ton of food in the backseat of the truck. You and Ms. Emma will have enough meals to last through the winter. The whole family's been cookin' nonstop since we learned about Pops' heart attack. We spent the entire day and night at the diner."

His sexy smile disappeared in a flash. He released his tight grip on my waist and pulled away, motioning with his head for me to follow. My steps matched his as we walked, and my peripheral vision caught all his movements. He ran his long fingers through his thick, black hair and sighed as he moved across the polished hardwood to the main living area. The bronze skin on his wide forehead furrowed with worry, and he closed his eyes. He pinched the bridge of his nose with his thumb and index finger, a habit he involuntarily did when he was stressed.

Even though they lived in the same house, Dane wasn't close to his grandfather—but death was death. Dealing with it, no matter your personal feelings toward the deceased, was never easy. And the passing of his pops wasn't going to be an easy task to recover from for Dane and his mom. I shot a quick glance at the ornate, over-the-top decorations of the living room and wondered if they would stay or move out. If his grandfather was as mean as local legend made him out to be, the old bastard probably left them high and dry.

A twinge of guilt hit me at the lie I'd just spoken to him. I pushed the emotion aside and kept my face warm and neutral. After all, his grandfather *did* die of a heart attack. At least according to his obituary and the two page spread about his life and contributions to Locasia County in *The Daily Grinder* this morning. Only the four of us in the booth yesterday knew the rest of the bloody story—though that little morbid detail was about as clear as Mississippi mud in my mind.

So far, Ms. Johnson had followed the cryptic note's instructions to keep her mouth shut. In fact, while Mom, Meemaw, and I finished wrapping up the food earlier, Ms. Johnson stopped by the diner. In a rush and her face still as pale as a newly opened bud on a cotton plant, she spoke in hushed tones. Told us goodbye and asked us to keep an eye on her house until she returned from an *extended* vacation to visit her family up North. The three of us refused to exchange glances with each other, worried our facial expressions would give our true thoughts away. It was obvious to all of us that Papa Joe's mental suggestions from the day before were still working on Ms. Johnson. I had to bite my lip to keep from asking her about the dog.

Though none of us said a word, we all knew it was a load of swill. First of all, Lucinda Johnson didn't have any other relatives alive, at least none we knew about. And we lived in a small town, which meant everyone's business was, well, everyone's business. Ms. Johnson never married, never bore any children. She was the only child of Rayburn and Nanette Johnson, both of whom had been only children themselves. And if Lucinda Johnson had any distant cousins or other relatives alive, she had never spoken about or visited them before. Where she was really going we had no idea, but it seemed the instructions to leave for a while from Papa Joe had worked.

Her big eyes kept looking at the door as she spoke, like she was watching for a ghost or Satan himself to come through it and snatch her soul. The woman seemed scared out of granny panties and, if I gambled, I'd place my bet on her not returning to Junction City.

Ever.

I let out my breath in a small huff, chased the memories from earlier away, and shoved my concerns about Dane's living arrangements aside. I would deal with the matter of all that mess later. Right now, my baby needed me. I watched him plop his tall, lanky frame down on the plush couch behind him. I followed and sank down on the over-stuffed cushion next to him.

"Thumbs up for home-cooked food. Thank goodness. Momma and I are both dangerous in the kitchen. Last time Momma made meatloaf, I think I was about six. She nearly caught the damned oven on fire. Pops ripped her a new one, tellin' her to let Ms. Johnson fix our food since that's what he paid her for. That he didn't move us in here to burn the place down. And me? Shoot, I ain't no help. I can boil water for tea and that's about it. If I had to cook for myself, I'd starve. It's the woman's job to cook. Well, it's *supposed* to be. With Ms. Johnson gone, Momma better learn how to—and quick. Or hire another housekeeper. After all, I'm a growin' boy who needs to eat. A lot. Some of my activities burn up a lot of energy."

He looked over and winked a luminous brown eye at me, assuring me he was joking. Last year, when we first started dating, I exploded and gave him an earful about my feelings on the subject of feminine duties when he brought them up. His grandfather's mindset seemed trapped in the 1700's. His Pops had some pretty archaic ideas about the role and place of women. No wonder his wife died at such a young age after giving birth to their son. Ol' Pops liked them one of three ways: barefoot and pregnant, cooking and cleaning, or naked under the covers. Oh, and he took the same approach to *children should be seen and not heard* to womenfolk as well. The old bastard tried his best to instill the asinine ideas in his grandson's head.

I made sure to retrain my new boyfriend's brain with a thorough dressing down. Told him if he didn't yank his mind out the caveman era and into the present, we would be over before we really began. Guess my loud tirade was quite convincing. The first time he told me he loved me a few months later, he said my fiery spirit and passion were two of the reasons he fell for me.

And, of course, my own tight ass and firm boobs. Traces of the Neanderthal remained no matter how hard I tried to erase them. Oh well, at least he wasn't prejudiced.

I ignored his attempt to needle me and decided to cut him some slack, considering why he was home and in a semi-foul mood. Thinking about those issues would put me in a rotten mood as well, and I didn't need any more on my overloaded plate. So much was rumbling around in my head, it felt like a tote sack full of rocks was loose up there. I reached over and tugged at his hand to get up. "Help me unload my car before all our hard work spoils. I got to get back to the diner and help prepare before the dinner crowd arrives."

Without a word, but with a feeble smile, he obliged and we traipsed out to my car to bring in the meals. We exchanged the cool air of the inside of the house for the wall of heat outside, and it was like we stepped into a steam room. This summer had been hotter than any I recalled in all my eighteen years. Everyone around town whined and moaned about the overbearing heat. It was so bad that Barb and I changed our running schedules from early morning to late at night.

It took less than three minutes to gather everything up and get back inside, but it didn't matter. We were both sweating bullets by the time we set the boxes on the kitchen counter. As we unloaded and started stashing the prepared meals in the fridge, I asked, "How's your mom holdin' up? Is she out settin' up the funeral arrangements?"

"Fine, like me. You know, there wasn't a whole lotta warm, fuzzy feelin's around this place. Wow, that came out rude. Don't get me wrong—I'm sorry Pops passed on and glad I wasn't here when it happened—but neither of us feel the need to, oh, what's the word?"

"Mourn?" I offered.

Dane snapped his fingers. "Yeah, that's it. Can't really mourn for losin' somethin' you never had, right? I mean, yeah, I saw Pops every day, but seein' someone all the time don't mean you're close to them."

I looked away and grabbed another packet of food. A lump formed in my throat for the sadness of it all. How people lived under the same roof, no matter how the circumstances of their living arrangements came to be, and not become close to each other was beyond me. I decided to shift subjects. "Couldn't convince Ms. Johnson to stay, huh?"

"Oh, don't think Momma didn't try. She practically was on her knees beggin'. Course, that little visual didn't do much good since she was on the *phone* with Ms. Johnson. She even offered her a raise, but it didn't work. Conversation didn't last too long, and Momma said it was weird."

"Weird?"

"You know Ms. Johnson. Never a dull moment around her with her gums flappin' and hands always busy either cleanin' or cookin' or workin' out in the garden. If she weren't tryin' to talk your ear off, she was hummin' one song or another. She was happy, you know?"

I handed him the last container of chicken and dumplings, and he focused his attention on squeezing it into the packed freezer. Yeah, I knew. But I also was aware of the new Ms. Johnson—and he wasn't. A woman so frightened, she seemed to have aged twenty years in less than twenty-four hours. "So, I guess Ms. Emma didn't sense any happiness, huh?"

"Nope," he said, grunting in frustration as he tried to close the freezer door.

"Understandable, considerin' she worked here for longer than you've been alive. I'm sure walkin' in and, uh, findin' her employer gone was hard. Eww, I would have freaked."

"Oh, please. She may have been a naturally happy person, but she and Pops weren't friends or anythin'. I mean, guess I might freak a bit if I found him...like that. But he's my kin—even though we weren't close or nothin'. Momma said Ms. Johnson was actin' like Pops was her kin too. Said she got all sad and quiet, like she was mournin' him or somethin'. Yet, she told Momma she wouldn't be able to make his service. And when Momma asked if she'd like to come over to visit us, she didn't answer. Totally ignored her like she didn't hear the question Momma posed to her. I mean, I don't understand. She's known me ever since I was in diapers, and I always thought we were, you know, close. I kinda always looked at her as a second mom of sorts. And she can't find the time to even stop by and pay her respects? Like I said...weird."

I paused a moment and considered whether I should tell him what was really going on, but the words were locked inside my throat. After Ms. Johnson dropped the bomb in our laps yesterday at the diner, Mom, Meemaw, and I closed up the diner and huddled in the kitchen. To say we were scared would be an understatement. Mom and Meemaw tried their best to hide their fears from me, but I saw right through their act. We were all shaking in our boots, so to speak. The events of the previous twenty-four hours popped into my mind.

CHAPTER EIGHT

Whatever funky juju Papa Joe used on us earlier had apparently worn off. Mom and I were both so wound up, we starting yelling at each other. We sounded like two ramped-up feral cats screeching and hollering at each other over the rights to a dead mouse carcass. I told Mom to stop treating me like I was a child and just spit out what she was thinking, no matter how odd or stupid it sounded. After all, the note specifically mentioned my name. Mom told me to mind my own business and let the "adults" handle whatever was going on. I countered that it was my name used so it certainly was my business to mind and that I *was* an adult as well. She spit back not to sass her, so I answered by flinging a cup full of corn meal across the kitchen in her general direction. Papa Joe stopped the frantic argument, and possible food fight, with a squirt of cold water in both of our faces from the kitchen sprayer.

After Papa Joe calmed us all down a bit, we cleaned

up the mess we'd made and ended up talking for hours about the strange events. When we got to the part about the morbid note and the fact that Ms. Johnson delivered an exact replica of Nana's totem necklace, all of us felt the chill in the air. When Daddy called hours later and told Mom he was staying overnight in Greenville because of car trouble, Mom had a hard time holding in her sigh of relief. Though she didn't say it out loud, I knew she didn't want to alarm Daddy with any details until we understood exactly what we were dealing with.

Mom wanted to call Sheriff Gilmore. She thought we might be in danger and wanted the threat investigated. Thought an inquiry should be made as well about the death of old man Witherspoon. Maybe get the coroner to check for unusual things that weren't part of a normal autopsy. But Papa Joe reminded her that Mr. Witherspoon was mostly Native American, so no autopsy would be performed unless the signs of death pointed to homicide, which of course, they did not. Mom countered with Ms. Johnson's vivid description of the terror frozen on the old man's face, along with a brand new head full of powdery white hair. Papa Joe asked her what part of that pointed to homicide, to which Momma didn't have an answer. He planted a seed of doubt in the minds of Mom and Meemaw when he mentioned Ms. Johnson might be lying. After all, none of us had seen the dog either at her house or at Dane's. And it was common knowledge that Pops Witherspoon despised canines. Maybe the entire show she put on was just a well-acted farce, concocted to elicit sympathy, Papa Joe reasoned. Meemaw tried to defend her lifelong friend, saying it wasn't true. But Papa Joe reminded her that during the time Ms. Emma moved into the Witherspoon estate, Ms. Johnson had been one of the worst gossips in town. He offered that maybe this was Ms. Johnson's way of getting back at them and used my interracial relationship with Dane V as a catalyst. After all, though rarely talked about, the stigma and deep seated traditions of the past were still alive in the small minds of some of the townsfolk.

I watched Mom and Meemaw chew those little nuggets around and spotted the moment their attitude changed from raw terror to partial acceptance. My hands shook and my body trembled because I was waiting for the question about Nana's necklace to come up, but it never did. Nor did the question of "what she did" come up. It took every ounce of mental strength I had not to blurt out my guilt. I almost did when the pain, which I had buried deep, ripped out of the hiding spot in my heart and bolted to the frontlines of my head. Right in the middle of making the crust for Dane's peach pie, I almost blurted out, "I killed Nana" until a warm hand touched my shoulder. I looked up into the sable-brown orbs of Papa Joe staring at me. The intense heat and warmth from his hand calmed me. Though his lips never moved, I distinctly heard him say, *No, not now Little One.*

Oh, God—maybe I was losing my mind. Was Nana's insanity hereditary and passed along the bloodlines to me?

As though he heard my panicked thoughts, Papa Joe shook his head no, his brown eyes unreadable. A surge of heat swept through me, and it felt like my blood was flowing lava in my veins.

Hush, Little One. All is well. Do not fear.

Papa Joe's words of comfort rang through my mind. I watched in silent awe as he easily steered the conversation to lighter topics and suggested we get a move on with cooking for the remaining Witherspoons. Mom and

Meemaw were entwined in the world of food preparation, as was I, and we settled our frayed nerves by cooking. It seemed trite since I would never admit to anyone that the simple act of creating sustenance with my bare hands calmed me in a profound way. The satisfaction of preparing the food was made even stronger, considering I was cooking for my boyfriend. But it worked. It gave the three of us something to occupy our worried minds for a while as Papa Joe regaled us with strange stories about legends from his tribe, passed down to him from his elders. As we bustled about the kitchen, the mundane task and Papa Joe's engrossing tales of Choctaw history provided us all a sense of comfort. We listened, and for a while, the cryptic note and the gruesome discovery in Ms. Johnson's house faded from our thoughts like it never happened.

For a while.

Once we finished cooking the mountain-high pile of food for the remaining Witherspoons around three thirty in the morning, we began to clean the kitchen and prepare for the early morning breakfast crowd. All of us were punch drunk from being up all night, and when Shirley Ramsey arrived for her morning shift, Mom insisted Meemaw go home and get some rest.

Considering my relationship with Dane, I was given the task of playing delivery girl. Though standard southern tradition when paying respects for the loss of a loved one was for the entire family to stop by to pass along their condolences, everyone knew I wasn't about to let that happen. Not before I saw him first. He had been gone for over a week and my family was intuitive enough to know the two love birds needed a few moments of private time together.

No, I couldn't tell Dane about all that. Wouldn't. My

brain still hadn't processed it yet, so trying to explain to someone else would be impossible. Besides, he had enough going on in his life.

CHAPTER NINE

Telling him the part about Ms. Johnson's visit to the diner earlier seemed harmless. I decided he should hear it from me rather than the local gossip queens. "Ms. Johnson stopped by the diner earlier. Told us she was takin' a vacation to visit family up North. Didn't say when she'd be back, though. Asked us to keep an eye on her place while she's gone."

Dane snorted. "Family? That don't make no sense. She doesn't have any. And she ain't never taken a vacation before, not since I've lived here. She couldn't wait to leave until after Pop's service? It's only two days away! Huh, if he didn't die of a heart attack, I'd smell a rat."

"Oh, please, Dane. Ms. Johnson loves you two! Did you ever think that attendin' a funeral might be hard on her? People her age don't like to be reminded about their own mortality, at least that's what Meemaw said this morning. They also don't like change. And Meemaw should know because they're the same age. Some folks just don't deal well with passin' on or all the emotions death brings to the surface. Ms. Johnson was always a happy woman, just like you said. Maybe she doesn't like the idea of cryin' in front of others. Who knows? But I don't think you should take her absence or decision to retire as a personal slap against you or your mom. I know she cares for you all. I saw the way she doted on you. She treated you like you're the next Indian Chief round these parts or somethin'."

Dane didn't say a word. He looked out the kitchen window toward the veranda, his eyes focused on something and nothing at the same time. I followed his gaze, sensed his sadness and worry through the thin material on his back. Out of the corner of my eye, I saw his throat muscles working. His Adam's apple jostled a bit while he tried to hold back his real emotions. I didn't want to let on that I felt his pain, so I concentrated on the beautiful view.

Waves of heat from the intense morning rays of sunshine shimmered across the expansive backyard. The bright blue of the water in the kidney-shaped pool sparkled with a rainbow of colors as the beams bounced across it. Even though the French doors were closed tight, the sweet scent of the jasmine and gardenia bushes Ms. Johnson planted out back tickled my nose.

The Witherspoon spread was a stunner for sure. A typical southern manse surrounded by weeping willows, magnolia trees, and too many rose bushes to count. During the spring, the place was a sea of pink and white from all the red bud, tulip, and pear trees. Eight spacious bedrooms and ten enormous bathrooms were inside the two story estate. The rest of the fifteen thousand plus footage was made up with a formal dining room, sitting room, library, three living areas, and a kitchen the size of the entire first floor of my house. How Ms. Johnson kept the place so immaculate all by herself was beyond me. I thought I was on top of things when I cleaned up my room and put my clean clothes in the drawers and closet. No wonder the woman never married or had children. When would she have had time for them?

The beauty of the space disappeared when my eyes settled on the veranda. Grape and wisteria vines wound all through the latticed railings and consumed the graceful white portico with fragrant greenery. The lavish bamboo and wicker patio furniture sat in silence. I wondered which one had been Pop's final resting place. A few lovely hanging baskets full of colorful flowers gave the area a warm, cozy feel. But even with all the lush surroundings, everything seemed wrong. Out of place. And I knew it wasn't because my boyfriend's grandfather died out there.

That was just the tip of the iceberg.

Dane took in a slow, deep breath, so I squeezed his hand with a little more force and focused my attention back on his face. God, he was a beautiful sight to look upon. His mixed heritage created a spectacular human being. Tall with sinewy muscles, he had the height of a basketball player, but the build of a running back. Trevor Ropert, Junction City's high school football coach, had hounded Dane without mercy to play, but Dane brushed his pathetic pleas aside. A basketball player through and through, no doubt. His heart and skills meshed with the joy of handling the ball up and down the court. Dane had no interest in slamming his body into another's and running over them like they were a bug under his shoe. It just wasn't in his nature to be violent. Oh, yeah, my baby was a lover, not a fighter, which is exactly why I fell for him.

His skin was the color of warm cocoa, his lips full, and

his eyes a deep, chocolate brown interspersed with thin flecks of gold and green. His broad forehead, nose, and high cheek bones revealed his Native American heritage. But the most eye-catching thing about him was his hair. It looked like polished black leather and fell in soft, ebony curls around his face and past his shoulder blades. Most of the time, he wore it in a ponytail or hid the flowing mane under a baseball hat. But on the occasions he wore it down and loose, it was breathtaking. It was the perfect combination of thick, wavy hair with luscious curls that every girl in the county lusted after, including me—and I had curly hair. I recalled Barb crying in second grade when Dane came to school with a short haircut, thanks to a bout with a wad of chewing gum lodged in his hair. Barb had been devastated when she realized she would no longer get to fiddle with Dane's hair at recess any longer.

Dane's jaw was clenched. The cords in his neck strained against his skin. I figured he was thinking about his situation and the unknown future, so I tried to inject a bit of humor before I left.

Always leave 'em smilin' is what Nana used to say.

"No vacation in over twenty years? Yikes, I guess it was about high time Ms. Johnson took one, don't you think? And if she hasn't had one all these years, she's due for at least a six-month stint on a warm beach somewhere. You know, surrounded by folks who'll take care of her for a change. Once she gets her fill of bein' pampered and waited on hand and foot, she might just come back. We gals can only stand bein' fawned over for so long before we have to take the reins back, ya know."

"Okay, I get that. But why didn't she just tell Mom that? I mean, she coulda' asked for the time off. Mom woulda given her all the time she wanted. Oh, who am

I kiddin'?" he muttered. He grabbed my hand and pulled me close. "We don't even know if we're gonna be livin' here for much longer. Everythin' is all up in the air. Havin' a housekeeper only works if you have a house for her to keep. That's why Momma ain't here. She's down at Cohestra, meetin' with the higher ups and Pop's attorney. She was in a mood when she left too. I think she's afraid of more than losin' a place to live and her job at the plant, now that Pop's gone."

His words made the hair on the back of my neck stand up at full attention. His voice was throaty, full of heavy emotion. I tried to shake the worry off, attributing it to my lack of sleep, the foreboding, blood-written note from yesterday and the unreal explanation offered by Papa Joe. "What else would she be afraid of?"

Dane buried his face in my hair again, his hug stronger than the one before. Through our clothes, I felt the muscles of his body tense. The edginess and angst poured out of him, and it seemed he was trying to extricate it by diving into my hair. He took a heavy sniff, then pulled back, the heat of his worry filling up the space between us. "Oh, guess afraid wasn't the right word. More like pissed as Hell. Yeah, pissed as Hell. That fits better."

"Pissed? Why?"

"Well, because my sperm donor is on his way here. Matter of fact, he's probably at the plant already," he muttered, glancing down at his watch. "Them two in the same room will make the tornado look like a slight wind blew a few pieces of paper from the garbage. I can only hope he's here for the funeral and then leaves right after. If he's comin' for an extended stay or, God forbid, to try and take over the plant...oh, I don't even want to go there. If he and

Mom have to work together, you and I are skippin' our senior year and movin' to Memphis early."

It took me a few seconds to figure out how to respond. Not that I hadn't considered the fact that Dane IV would come to town for his father's funeral. I had. But I really didn't think he would...and surely not this soon. I wondered who called him and told him the news about his father's sudden death. My guess was someone from Cohestra. He was probably on the ownership papers somewhere and needed to be informed. I doubted it had been Dane or his mom. To my knowledge, there had been no contact between any of them since his last trip to Junction City. And that was nearly ten years ago. Dane IV didn't call, didn't pay child support, never sent any birthday, Christmas, or Easter cards or presents, not even once. Nothing. He never acknowledged Dane was his, but it didn't matter. He tried to run from his duties, but he could go to the moon and it would still be obvious to anyone looking that Dane V was his offspring.

The hatred between Ms. Emma and Dane's father was a legend of its own in Locasia County. A sweet, high school romance, made more enticing since it was forbidden by both sides of the respective families. It soured like curdled milk when the stick turned blue. A very public screaming match between Ms. Emma's father, Lionel Carter, and Pops Witherspoon occurred on the front steps of the courthouse when Mr. Carter was leading his wife and pregnant daughter in to file paternity papers. Dane IV had already hightailed it out of town, leaving Ms. Emma in quite the pickle. According to my mom, who happened to be coming out of the beauty shop across the street, the volatile situation was diffused when Sheriff Gilmore showed up and led the feuding families over to his office to chat.

Two days later, Lionel and Cherise Carter died in a car accident on their way back from Greenville. Ms. Emma didn't go with them since her morning sickness was in overdrive. Probably the first time in history someone had been thankful they were puking their insides out. Local rumors (not from my mother this time) said the trip was made to hire a high-priced attorney to take on the Witherspoon clan but ended in a twisted pile of metal on the road after a head-on collision with a tractor trailer full of rice. The death of her parents left Ms. Emma alone and pregnant at the age of seventeen. A young, African American woman still in high school, impregnated by a half-Indian, the only son of the wealthiest family in the Delta. Meemaw told me tongues wagged for *years*.

Before the red clay had time to settle over her parents' graves, Ms. Emma was offered a job at Cohestra and a new place to live—the Witherspoon mansion. After the death of his beloved Belinda, Pops lived alone with his only son up until the seed was planted in the fertile soil of Emma Carter. Pops Witherspoon never remarried or even dated again. He devoted all of his time and passion to his business. When I first started going out with Dane, Meemaw told me all about the situation. Said the stories about Pops were mostly garbage and he was a decent, honorable man—just a bit crankier than the average person. She said Mr. Witherspoon not only bucked tradition but thumbed his nose at it by taking in the girl who carried his grandson in her belly. A *black* girl no less—in a town, county, and state not known for its tolerance.

Mom said there had been some talk around town in the beginning. Well, actually, *lots* of ugly gossip. Some said

Emma's bun in the oven was really planted there from Pop's loins, and that was the reason his son had skipped town. Said Dane IV was ashamed by the deplorable actions of his own father, who had been knocking boots with his young girlfriend behind his back. Others shrugged that scenario off. They thought Pops put on a well-acted façade of caring about the wellbeing of his future grandchild only because he wanted himself a black house maid. A young, pretty thing indebted to him for taking her in and more than willing to thank him in any which way the old fart requested. Mom said that particular tale died a quick death since Ms. Johnson was already employed as the housekeeper/maid at the Witherspoon estate just as her mother and grandmother had been.

Most rumors had been squashed when Dane V was born and his birth certificate named Dane Witherspoon IV as "father" and Dane's last name was listed as "Witherspoon" rather than "Carter" like his mother. That one little act silenced the gossip about the identity of the father since everyone said there was no way in Satan's burning Hell that Pops Witherspoon would have agreed to such a thing if it weren't true.

Once Emma Carter started to work at Cohestra Industries and people began to see the two of them interact on a daily basis, two things became crystal clear: One, the strong-willed individuals were nowhere near kind and considerate of one another, and two, there was no way Emma Carter would *ever* be controlled by someone else.

The shock of the situation waned with each passing year. Like the bright, new paint on a wall, the vibrancy of the rumors faded with time. New chunks of scandal replaced the withered pieces that remained of the Witherspoon shocker, and soon, chins wagged and tongues blabbed about the other latest goings-on in Locasia County.

I pulled my thoughts together and tried to give Dane my best smile. "Oh, stop. I'm sure they're goin' over all the normal stuff people do when someone like your pops passes on. And I'm sure your mom will keep her claws sheathed while your dad is around—for your sake."

"Sperm donor. He doesn't deserve the title of father, dad, or friend."

"Oh, sorry. *Sperm donor.* I think you need to chill. You're workin' yourself all into a bother and you don't have a reason to quite yet. Your pops took care of you both all these years—no reason to think that won't continue now that he's gone."

Dane's lips contorted as he chewed on the bottom one before he responded. His muscles relaxed a hair, and I saw some of the worry leave his face. "You're right. You're right. Can't help myself, though. I'm a natural-born worrier. That's what Ms. Johnson always said."

I ran my hand across the warmth of his back, and then moved quickly to his rear. I smacked his tight rump once more. "You worry because you have a good heart and have this strange need to take care of everybody. Another reason I love you. Listen, I've got to get back to the diner. Mom's probably cussin' a blue streak right about now. I know you've got a lot goin' on, but if you want company later on after I get off from work and finish cheerleadin' practice, come on over, okay? I should be home by eight, and then we can go for a run. I'll ask Barb to bow out tonight, so it'll just be the two of us, okay?"

"You realize you said *get off* and *come* in the same sentence, right? Is that an offer?"

The heat from before roared back, the longing between

the two of us strong enough to turn icicles into daggers of fire. I scooted away and out from under his embrace and made sure to over exaggerate the roll of my hips as I walked toward the front door. I did love my petty torments.

And don't' forget to leave 'em wantin' more. Nana's other favorite saying.

"Always big boy. Always. Two sweaty bodies rollin' around underneath the stars after a hot run to get the juices flowin'. Mmm, can't wait. But I won't be able to do a *thing* if you don't let me leave. I'll text you later."

He smiled and I returned it. The depth and love behind his brown eyes pulled my soul to his like a magnet. No silly banter, no smarmy comments, no teenage stupidity from raging hormones—just plain love. If my face reflected even half of the emotion his did, there was no doubt he knew exactly how much I loved him. I surely had no doubts about his love for me. It shone like the North Star on a cloudless night. Our lifelong friendship had molded and shaped our hearts for each other, and the cosmic melding was complete.

With everything going on around us—all the craziness of the last two days—I should have left. Continued to the door and headed straight to work. But I didn't. The look on Dane's face, the electricity between the two of us, the craving to feel his skin against mine—all consumed me. Without thinking, I let my desires overrun my senses, and in a flash, was in his arms.

I kissed him with hot fervor. My lips ground into his; my arms fully wrapped around his body. I clung to him, sought out every inch, like it was our first time exploring each other. He responded with as much heat and longing, his long fingers intertwined in my hair. He pulled me closer, hungrily devouring my mouth in his. Clothes seemed to magically disappear as we tumbled to the floor. Growls of pleasure filled the air from both of us as we rocked in heated harmony, our bodies covered in sweat. Neither of us spoke as our bodies instinctively sought out our mutual pleasure spots. We both yelled out in unison, our voices full and deep from ecstasy. Spent, we collapsed in a heap on the cool hardwood, our naked chests heaving.

"Wow. I've heard that death makes the livin' want to feel alive. And sex is the best way to do that. Guess it's true."

I bit his chin and jumped up and began a mad dash to retrieve my clothes. With my luck, his mom would walk through the door any second. The heat of embarrassment flushed my already hot cheeks. I threw his clothes at him, then slipped my own on. "I'm not even gonna dignify that with a response. I...I got to go. I'm late already. So, tonight we just run, okay?"

"Hey babe—one more thing before you go—and I promise it's not about *that*. Wait a sec, okay? Let me go get it."

I paused, my finger on the door latch. "Sure thing. Make it snappy, though. Got hungry people in this town to feed besides you."

I heard the thumps of his heavy footsteps as he raced to the kitchen, slammed a cabinet door, and then thundered back to the front door. "I have no clue where this came from, or why it's even here, but ain't no use in wastin' it. Thought you might take it to Barb...or someone else with a dog."

I stared at the bag of dog kibble in his hand and swallowed hard. The brief interlude of happiness disappeared as I looked at the food meant for the dog that had been gutted in Ms. Johnson's bedroom. "I...oh sure. Barb will appreciate it. That hairy mutt of hers eats like a horse. I'll drop it off to her on the way back to the diner."

Dane handed it over to me and a shadow of confusion passed over his face. "Weirdest thing. Found it this morning when I was searchin' for a garbage bag. I mean, what the hell was Ms. Johnson doin' buyin' dog food? Thought when I found it that maybe she left it here by accident after doin' our shoppin'. But I don't recall her sayin' she had a dog. Do you?"

"You know, don't think so, but then again, I don't pay much attention to anythin' anymore, what with our senior year comin' up and all. And cheerleadin' practice, workin' at the diner, makin' your eyes roll back in your head..."

"No tellin'. Who knows? Maybe Ms. Johnson was gettin' older than we thought. Got confused while shoppin'. That must be it! And maybe that's why she's actin' so strange now. What's that disease called....Althieters?"

My laugh was dry and came out more like a cackle. "Alzheimer's disease."

"Yeah, that's it. Alzheimer's disease. Betcha that's what it is, 'cause there ain't never been a dog in this house. Pops *hated* dogs. Hmm, now that he's gone, maybe I could get one?"

Afraid to say much else, I blew him a kiss and forced myself not to run to my car. "Gotta go, babe. See you later. Love you," I blurted as I opened the door and kicked up my pace to my car. The blood was pounding so loud in my head that his "I love you too" sounded like he was miles away rather than a few feet from me in the doorway. Even though it was near one hundred degrees from the radiant sun, the chill of fear turned my body ice cold.

Fuck me runnin'—this isn't good. Not good at all. Daddy's

favorite saying, one he mumbled many times over the years, never seemed more appropriate than right at this moment.

CHAPTER TEN

I kept my phony smile plastered on my face until I reached the end of Dane's driveway. Once I pulled out on the main road, it disappeared. The last forty-plus minutes had been spent shoving down my real emotions while I cuddled and coddled my love. Now, they'd busted out of my mental prison and run amok inside the cab of my truck.

What the hell was wrong with me? I was certainly not a prude, but I *never* acted so...sleazy. It was like I couldn't control myself. I just acted like a dog in heat, mounting Dane like an animal. The hunger, the need, the desire for him had destroyed all rational thought and made no sense to me now. My cheeks burned from embarrassment. It wasn't like that was the first time we'd been together, but it certainly was the first time it had been so completely lustful. Our relationship, even our sexual one, was full of tenderness and love. Dane had the heart of an angel. He was patient, sweet, funny, and full of quick comebacks. Always the first one to step in and stop a potential argument if he was near enough to hear one begin. He was a big ol' teddy bear and hated confrontation of any sort. He was also a lover of the outdoors, like I was, and stayed clear of anything that had to do with what the local rednecks called *hunting season*. He thought it was a farce, the way the men and boys cloaked themselves in the scent of their prey, camouflaging themselves while armed to the teeth with powerful weaponry, waiting to shoot. Made him sick to his stomach. I knew my original gut instincts about him were right on target. Dane was part Native-American and didn't have an issue with eating what he killed; however, he found no challenge, no sense of fairness or test of skills, in the way the heavily armed fools chose to hunt. Those qualities, and more, drew me to him in the first place, and allowed me to overlook his few negative ones.

I was in love with all of what made up Dane, not just enamored with his physique. The moment our lips touched the first time, it was like the entire journey of my life shifted. I knew he would be my companion on the trek, which is why what just happened on the floor of his living room made no sense at all. There had been, at least on my end, nothing but raw carnality to the act. It was intoxicating and repulsive at the same time.

I wouldn't even look at the sack of Pure-Grade Bits! on the floorboard. Looking at them made the last thirty-plus hours come alive again. Through sleep deprivation and fear, it seemed I had almost believed the sack of crap Papa Joe fed us last night and early this morning. No, that wasn't fair—we *wanted* to believe him. We craved the simplistic answer of the note's origin just as much as Ms. Johnson had. His voice was as smooth as sweet molasses and full of just as much sugar, and the stories acted like a soothing salve on us all.

But then he started talking *inside* my head. Could he do the same with Mom and Meemaw? Others? Or was I just a sliver away from plunging into insanity to even believe such a thing? Had I just been fooling myself all these years, thinking I had gotten away with killing Nana?

Oh, Jesus, what is wrong with me? Please, please help me, Lord. I don't know what to do or say. Or think. If I'm going crazy or this is some form of divine punishment, please make it fast.

I slammed my fists on the old steering wheel so hard, the entire truck shook from the impact. No, I am not going to let stupid, silly childhood fears invade my life again. I was eighteen years old for goodness sake, not some naïve nine-year-old child, easily swayed by my emotions. What...did I really think I had turned into some werewolf or furry monster and snuck over to Nana's, chased her down through the woods in the dead of night, and then ripped her to shreds? How insane was that idea? Improbable. People didn't turn into other beings except for in movies and books. And my little nightmare about the Shadow-Man, and Tinker turning into an enormous panther-like cat, was just like Mom said—a dream. One brought on from listening to Nana's crazy stories. Besides, I loved Nana. I would never hurt her. Period. She died from her wounds after being attacked by a bear. Ol' Ralph even caught and killed the nasty beast.

But that rationale didn't explain my vision. I was *there*. Felt it in my heart and soul. Was it possible my mental ties were so strong to Nana's I had actually seen what happened through her eyes? Had she somehow reached out with her mind, maybe because she was so frightened, and sent her last moments on Earth into my brain?

Another improbable scenario but one that made a bit more sense to me was telekinetic in origin. Even though

I didn't believe in psychic ability, it was surely a better explanation than thinking I had morphed into some blood-thirsty creature and killed my sweet great-grand-mother. Plus, if I had turned into some monster, why hadn't I turned again? What could Nana have ever done to make me want to kill her?

No. No way. It was just some weird fluke, a freak of nature. And the dream about Tinker was simply a nightmare brought on from the overactive imagination of a child. Maybe my nine-year-old self was still freaked out from the nightmare about the Shadow-Man. Made my brainwaves more open to suggestion and Nana's life force—energy or whatever it was—transferred itself across the expanse of the town and into my malleable mind.

"Yeah, keep tellin' yourself that, Sheryl. Still doesn't explain how Papa Joe spoke inside your head, now does it?" I said out loud inside the cab of the truck. The sound of a car horn screeched in my ears, and it jerked me back to reality. Great, how long had I been sitting at the four-way stop, lost in these crazy thoughts?

I gave the pedal some gas and continued to drive. Lost in my own mind, not paying any attention to the road, I nearly jumped out of my skin when my cell phone rang. As I turned right onto Highway 73, I broke one of Daddy's cardinal rules and answered it when I saw the call was from Barb. I needed the distraction from my disturbing thoughts.

"Hey sweetie. I just left the diner. Your mom said you went to visit Dane. How's he doin'?"

"Hey, Barb. Yeah, just left his place. He's okay...just a bit unnerved. Who wouldn't be though, right?"

"Girl, I wouldn't be able to set foot in my house again if

one of my family members died in it. That's too creepy for me. I'd insist we move. Or I'd move in with you until after graduation."

"It's not like it's a crime scene or somethin', Barb. The man had a heart attack. He was over ninety years old. That's what happens when you get older—you die."

"I don't care how it happened. He *died*. Took his last breath there in the place. Yikes. And if he wasn't ready to go, his soul might hang around and haunt the place. Wouldn't surprise me one bit. I mean, the place is beautiful, but it's also old and full of a lot of other sad events, I reckon."

"Barb, lay off the horror movies, will you?"

Barb laughed, her voice light and airy across the airwaves. "It's all your fault I watch them to begin with, you know. Now, enough talk about the dead. Are you still pickin' me up for practice at six?"

"Well, duh. You're the one who told me your car won't be fixed until next week, remember?"

"Gee, you're wound tight today, aren't you? And here I thought a visit with your honey would make it all better. Guess you didn't have time to get any, huh?"

"Barb!"

"Oh, I'm just yankin' your chain. So, six, right? And what about our run after? We still on for that?"

"I'm not sure. I asked Dane if he wanted to run and really didn't get an answer. If he decides to take me up on the offer, do you mind?"

"Bowin' out? Of course not. Wouldn't want to get in the way of you two love birds. Remember, you've told me before about your wild sessions. I might get hurt."

"You are too much, you know that?" I said, laughing as I pulled into my driveway.

"Would you please try to convince Roger Hinkley of that? Can't get that boy to look twice my way. He needs someone to tell him how wonderful I am and that he should ask me out. Oh, and you could mention the fact I've been takin' gymnastics forever and how bendable I am."

"I will do no such thing! You want him...you go after him. Any prize worth havin' is best won by usin' your own skills, not relyin' on someone else to pick up your slack. Listen, I've gotta run. If I don't get back to the diner, Mom will skin me alive."

"Hmph! Some best friend you are. I'll remember this the next time you ask me for a favor."

I shut the engine off and started to step out of the truck when I spied the full bag of dog food on the floorboard. My stomach did a little flip flop, and I couldn't open the truck door fast enough. "Barb...call the dude. This isn't the Civil War era, you know. Women are allowed to take control of their lives—encouraged to do so, actually. If you want Roger, go get him."

"Oh, if I only had a tenth of your confidence. I'm not brash like you. I'm a reserved southern lady—at least that's what my mother wants to believe."

"Reserved? You? Wow, you've got your mom snowed. Remember, I've seen you in action at some of Stony Bamford's parties. Ain't nobody in this county who can shake what her momma gave her better than you can! Listen, you just work on your *va-va-voom* when you're sober, okay? You are gorgeous, funny, and have a wicked sense of humor. Any guy would be lucky to call you his girlfriend. *You* need to believe that and quit whinin' about what you *wish* you had and go get what you want. It's as simple as that. You can still be a lady while snatchin' your bit of happiness. Nothin' wrong with that. Unless, of course, you pull a Tami Rogers. Now *that* I have issues with."

Barb sighed. "Ugh. Don't mention that tramp's name. She makes me sick to my stomach. Bad enough we have to see her at practice every day, not to mention school. Skank. Oh, and recall, out of the two of us, I'm still pure. I may like to slug a few beers back and let my booty rock, but that's it. So, back on topic. Your solution is easier said than done."

"Hey, my number is at one and will *stay* at one. You're pea green with envy because I've found my soulmate. Now, all you need to do is remember practice makes perfect, sweetie. Work on your confidence and make that call to Roger. Listen, I'll see you at six, okay? Really, I've got to go. Catch you later."

I clicked my phone shut before Barb had a chance to speak. As much as I loved her, I didn't have time to cajole her into asking Roger Hinkley on a date. The girl had been pining for him for years. And in less than one week, we would start our senior year which meant she better hurry up before graduation took them both away from Junction City.

Before I climbed the stairs to the front door, I stopped and sent a quick text to Mom.

Food delivered @ home to get gym bag then on my way

The second I closed the front door, my phone beeped a response.

No need. Meemaw came back. Slow as Xmas here. Get some rest before practice. XO C U 2nite

I stood in the hallway and considered typing a response back, telling her to send Meemaw home and let me come finish the shift. She had to be exhausted. An irritating thought poked around inside my head, so instead I asked:

Where is Dad?

The house was quiet, only the slight hum of the air conditioner and fridge in the air. While I waited for Mom's reply to my text, I glanced around the small living room. Nothing seemed out of place. It looked exactly like it did when we all left for work yesterday—lived in but homey. A cushion from the couch was on the floor, tossed haphazardly next to my worn out running shoes. The pile of newspapers was off kilter where Daddy had stacked them next to the fireplace after he read each one. Mom's favorite coffee cup sat, half full, on the end table next to her recliner. Meemaw's bag of knitting materials, with pink, green, and yellow yarn spilling out, rested next to her spot at the end of the couch.

Everything *looked* the same, but I couldn't shake the sensation something was missing. Not right. Out of place. I backed out of the living room and into the kitchen, the sound of my flip-flops the only noise other than my breathing. In four strides, I was inside the doorway. My eyes scanned the area for anything amiss, only to be greeted by the same thing as in the living room—nothing. Even the bowl I had toasted bran flakes in almost two days ago sat in the exact place I left it—on the table.

Oh, good grief. This is ridiculous. Just go take a nap. Your brain needs a break.

I shook the silly fears away and headed to the stairs. When my phone beeped, I almost dropped it.

Dad is here. Cooking. Gave Papa Joe afternoon off. Stop by b4 practice. Luv u.

Okay, so I had the house to myself for a while. I considered calling Dane, but squashed the idea the second it appeared. All my ideas, even the thought of a shower, dis-appeared the second my feet landed on the top stair. My body froze as the stench assaulted me like a physical entity. The familiar aroma permeated every inch of me, wind-ing through my body like snake venom. The hair on the back of my neck and arms stood straight up. It felt like my skin was on fire. The only other time I smelled it before, I thought it was fear. Somehow, I knew that was wrong.

It was the scent of death. A disgusting combination of mud, musk, decay, and something else I couldn't quite place, yet I recognized.

Without conscious control, my body crouched and I hugged the wall. I made my way down the hall, following the stench. Though repulsed, I couldn't fight the urge to discover the origins of the odor. As I neared Meemaw's room, it grew stronger. My eyes cut both directions to ensure I was alone, and then they swept the small area of Meemaw's bedroom. Nothing. Not a thing out of place or missing, just like the rest of the house.

But something, or someone, had been inside the house. Every nerve in my quaking body screamed the undeniable truth.

The scent trail was easy to follow, almost like it was a living, visible entity. It led straight to Meemaw's dresser and ended at her jewelry box. Adrenaline raced through my veins, and my legs quivered in response. I knew, before I even reached the dainty box, what I was looking for would be gone.

It's been in my house! In Meemaw's room. Snooping, explor-ing, and it left its rank stench embedded inside the confines of our home.

I pushed away the disgust from the scent and picked up the box. On the underneath side was a hidden catch where Meemaw hid her real jewelry. Her diamond engagement ring from Papaw...the red ruby necklace she only wore during the holidays...and her most prized possession.

Nana's totem necklace.

With a quick flick of my fingernail, I sprung the clasp and pulled out the hidden slip.

Please, please let it be there.

The pieces all fell into my sweating palm, accompanied by a small piece of paper crumpled amidst the gems. All except the one I was looking for. I had to force myself not to fling the contents across the room in anger. Instead, I set the box back on the dresser and walked over to her bed. My legs shook while I sat perched on the edge of Meemaw's bed. I dumped the contents in my hand onto the stark white comforter and gave a final scan.

No necklace.

The crumpled note begged to be opened. When I picked it up, the scent of death made me gag. I grit my teeth and forced my rising anger down as I unraveled the paper.

Where you are, I've stood before. Where I am, you soon shall be. Nothing can protect you now.

I tried to control myself. I tried to squash the fury that burned inside of me as it raced through my bloodstream. Tried to ignore the compulsion to run and find whoever it was playing games with me and my family. Tried to tamp down the rage at the knowledge the *thing* had been inside my house. But the impulse to seek and destroy was too strong, my wants and needs ravaged by the red hot fury that turned my blood into flowing lava. Without thinking, I leapt from the bed and raced down the stairs, taking them two at a time. I veered to the right, tore through the kitchen, and yanked open the back door, my flip flops long gone.

I ran faster than I ever had before. A small part of me whispered to turn back, to get my keys and phone, to at least let someone know where I was going. I stomped the pathetic idea into mush with each *thump* of my feet on the grass. When I got to the six foot privacy fence that separated our yard from the McNeils', I didn't stop to open the gate. I simply jumped it as if it was only an inch off the ground.

What the hell?

No. No thinking. Only instincts guided me now—instincts to follow the scent of death inside my house. Strength pulsed through every muscle. Each step was sure and smooth. Heat tore through my body, but my breath came even and steady. My eyes sharpened, and I saw every movement around me with uncanny accuracy. I could hear every blade of grass bend under my bare feet, the shudder of car engines in the distance, a dog barking miles away. The dull thuds of hammers as they connected with their targets I knew came from the construction site at Cohestra.

Thoughts of those important to me vanished as the poison of rage devoured my soul. The deeper my respirations, the stronger the scent and constriction of my mind until nothing remained but pure, all-consuming wrath.

Find it. Kill it. Shred it into bloody pieces.

The scent controlled me now. I knew it wasn't Nana—whatever or whomever it was just used her to get to me. Well, it wanted SIN? It was going to get me. Every single part of me—claws, fangs, and all. The carnal desires to kill and maim overrode everything else, and my body sprinted through the quiet, hot streets of Junction City and out to Caney Creek.

I was on the hunt.

For blood.

CHAPTER ELEVEN

In less than ten minutes at a full-out run, I was deep in the woods. Sweat poured off of me as I navigated my body through the dense forest. Each gulp of the humidity-soaked air made me feel like I was swallowing a mouthful of water. The smell waned but was still strong enough to follow. My ears were overloaded with the competing sounds around me. The shrill cadence of the insects, the throaty croaks of the frogs, the incessant chirps of the birds in the trees, and the sound of my feet as I ran seemed amplified with each breath. My legs thundered across the ground. Power surged through the muscles with each extension.

As I came to an opening in front of me where the sun's rays peeked through the heavy canopy of shade trees, my muscles tensed as I jumped. The force propelled me nearly twenty feet, and I landed with a soft *thump* in the open glen. I stopped and crouched low, feeling exposed in the open area. Without moving my head, my eyes scanned the surroundings. My heart dropped into my stomach when I recognized the location. I stood in almost in the exact same spot where Nana's mutilated corpse had been left to die. I sniffed the air and choked back a sob when the aroma of apples and talcum powder slammed into my nostrils.

No! It's not possible. It's been too many years. Oh, God, my mind is playing tricks on me. What is going on? Why am I here?

My body began to shake from anger and exhaustion when I realized the scent trail I had been following was gone. I stood up and took a deep, long breath through my nose. Nothing. I spun around in a full circle, trying to catch the trail again, but it was useless. Other than the normal odors of the forest and the heartbreaking remnants of my nana, I lost the rank stench I had been after.

"Damn!" I screamed, my yell heard by no one but the inhabitants of the wooded area. Breathing heavily and heart beating so fast I was afraid it would pop out of my chest any second, I collapsed in a spent pile onto the damp ground. Though I wasn't a crier, tears of grief, anger, pain, and sorrow erupted out of my eyes, soaking my shirt in seconds. The rush of blood thrummed inside my head, and a wave of dizziness threw my sense of balance out of whack.

What was wrong with me? Why had I run nearly six miles into the middle of nowhere, following some scent like a rabid dog? Why did the trail stop here, right by the place Nana took her last breath? Was I being punished for what I had done to her and suppressed in the back corners of my mind for so long? Was this what insanity felt like? Hearing things, seeing things, *smelling* things that didn't exist?

"Dear God, help me!" I sobbed out loud into the muddy ground.

Come home.

I shook my head to rid myself of the intruding voice inside my mind. Wet dirt molded to my damp cheeks and edged its way inside my mouth. I spit out the mess and crushed my hands to my ears in desperation, hoping my palms would block the familiar voice. No—I wasn't crazy! Something killed the dog—something stole Nana's totem necklace and left the note as a warning. Someone—*something*—had been inside my house. Left me a note. Those things were *real*. I saw them.

Come home, Little One. All will be explained at home.

Under the intense rays of the late afternoon sun, my body contorted into the fetal position, I crushed my hands harder against my ears. "Go *away!*" I screamed.

The ground beneath me began to vibrate. I felt the rumblings in my legs, chest, and thighs. It rippled and grew until I had to let go of my ears and bury my fingers into the soft mud for support. As the quake intensified, I noticed the forest was deathly quiet. When I lifted my head up and looked around, I swear I saw the trees sway, their bright green leaves shimmering in harmony with the movement of the ground.

An earthquake with no sounds? Not possible. Did my break from sanity make me imagine it? Oh, God, I was going crazy.

The tremors stopped as quickly as they started. I gathered my bearings back and began to rise, then froze in place as a wave of sheer terror tore through me. Cold chills spread across my back and chest. A low growl rose in timbre and turned into a deafening roar. The sound seemed to be coming from nowhere and everywhere at the same time.

I command you! Come home.

The voice I recognized, though I had not heard it in almost ten years. It was Nahu'ala. It dominated me—a primal urge to listen and obey overshadowed my fear. The impulse to submit took control over my body and I began to run, exiting the sunny glen. Inborn instincts—just like the ones earlier to seek out and find the owner of the evil odor from inside my house—propelled me forward. Toward home. To submit to the voice without question. To obey.

Though I fought the calling with all my might, it was no use. My body was on some sort of cosmic autopilot, controlled by who or what, I had no idea. All I knew for sure was that the pull was too strong to ignore.

Within minutes, my legs pumping at full speed, I emerged from the woods and on to the main highway. I was backtracking the way I came before. The scent I had been chasing earlier grew. The stench made my eyes water. The craving to follow it fought for control over the compulsion to submit to the voice of Nahu'ala to return home. My lungs screamed for air, my legs burned, and my heart thundered against the walls of my chest. My breath came in great gasps, and my arms shook as the blood raced through my veins. It felt like my brain was on fire as it tried to grapple with the dueling instructions.

Then, I hit a wall. At least it seemed like I did. The scent of the thing slammed into me like it was alive. The reeking aroma surrounded me as though I had fallen in a garbage dump. The urge to kill trumped the command to go home. My body veered to the right, zigzagging through the parked cars and construction trucks. In mere seconds, I came to a halt, my quaking body in the parking lot of Cohestra, and my eyes trained on the vehicle closest to me.

The sleek, black sedan glistened underneath the late afternoon sun. With the way it smelled, it should have been covered in rotting flesh. I knew, without a shadow of a doubt in my heart, that the owner of the car had been inside my house. I shot my eyes over to the license plate and noticed the tags were from Illinois. Figures—it was damned Yankee stink. The raging inferno of anger and confusion in my head dimmed a bit because I knew my enemy was *real*—a living human being. Not some four-legged monster that smelled like the carcasses of a hundred dead skunks. A sense of relief hit me, for this was solid proof I wasn't crazy or imagining things. Figments of the imagination weren't able to drive a vehicle, nor could some made-up monster. This was a real foe to confront and ask why the hell he or she was playing such a morbid game with me and my family.

And then, after asking, my plan was to tear them into unrecognizable pieces. I would leave nothing but a pile of blood and flesh behind.

I pulled my eyes away from the car and started to walk toward the smoked glass doors of the smaller, outer building that hadn't been destroyed by the tornado. The scent trail was so strong it seemed to illuminate in front of me—like a glowing wave to follow. Before I made it to the curb, the voice inside my head exploded. It was so loud it was painful. My head felt like it would burst, and I fell to my knees on the hard blacktop, my hands clamped around my ears.

Go. Home. Now!

The roar that followed the order made my entire body quake in fear and pain. This time, I realized the earth wasn't shaking. It felt like a noose was around my neck, yanking me from behind. My chest tightened, and I couldn't pull any air into my lungs. Intense, searing heat burned inside my head and for a split second, I wondered if I was having a stroke or aneurysm. I cowered on the ground with my palms pressed firmly against my head, and mewed like a small kitten.

"Okay, okay. I'll go."

"Sheryl, you okay, honey? What in the world are you doing here? Oh, Lord, you're filthy! Are you hurt?"

The voice above me seemed familiar. The smooth tone felt like a cold compress on my burning head. The minute it spoke, the booming growl inside my head stopped and the tension around my chest disappeared. I dropped my hands from my ears and went to all fours, gasping in a lungful of the blessed air.

"Sheryl, can you hear me? Oh, Lord, do I need to call an ambulance?"

Get up. Let her take you home. Now.

Like an obedient child, I complied. Every muscle in my body screamed as I pushed myself up off the hot pavement and stood up. I pushed a wisp of my hair from my face and was surprised when my hand came back covered in red clay. Then, I remembered I had been wallowing in the mud minutes before. No wonder the look of worry on Ms. Emma's face was of sheer panic.

"I...I'm fine. Sorry. Just pushed myself too hard on my run today. I...um, tripped and fell down by the creek. Lost my footin' in the mud."

"Child, you realize it's over one-hundred degrees outside right now, dontcha? Only crazy people, or ones who want to die from a heat stroke, run in this heat. You...are neither. And out in the woods? Alone? That's just plain dangerous. And you know better than to run during the day! Here, let's get you inside and cool you off. And some water. It's worryin' me, you ain't sweatin' like you should be."

Do not go inside. Leave! Now! The voice of Nahu'ala was adamant.

"I know. Don't know what I was thinkin'. Guess I wasn't. You know, teenagers have that problem sometimes," I said, producing a smile that I hoped conveyed I was sorry. "I'm fine, really. Just needed to catch my breath."

"No, you need water. Right now. Come on, let me take you inside..."

I backed away from Dane's mom and moved toward the parking lot. "Ms. Emma, I really would like to go home. Do you mind droppin' me off at my house before you go home? You were leavin', right?"

I saw a wary look cross Ms. Emma's dark eyes as she scanned mine. Her parental instincts seemed to be on high alert, for I could tell she knew I was hiding something from her. I remained calm and forced my eyes to reflect nothing but a blank stare. After a few seconds, she shook her head and grabbed my elbow with her soft, warm fingers. "Yes, I was. Come on, I'll take you home. But only if you promise me two things."

"Okay. Shoot."

"One, you don't *ever* run when it's this hot outside again and in those woods," she said tersely, which I followed by a nod of agreement. "And two, stay away from here. It's dangerous with all the construction."

"Yes, ma'am."

Once we crossed the parking lot over to Ms. Emma's sports utility vehicle, the tension between the two of us from moments before melted. I tried to control my body, but it still shook as Ms. Emma put an old practice shirt of Dane's down on the seat so I could sit inside without ruining the leather. My legs felt like jelly. Though my breathing was still rapid, the thundering in my chest was gone. I climbed inside and shut the door, hoping it would put a barrier between me and the odor, but it didn't. It was just as strong as before, like I had rolled around in it. Ms. Emma didn't seem to sense it because she gave no sign she did. When I reached up to push my damp hair out of my face, my hand reeked of it. Thankfully, the overwhelming urge to run inside the building and shred the owner of the stink had lessened.

Of course that was only because another stronger force controlled me. Though another word had not been said inside my head the last few minutes, I still felt the presence of Nahu'ala. It was like I could feel the big cat watching me from *inside* my own mind.

Ms. Emma backed out of the parking lot and onto the main highway. I could tell she was looking at me from her peripheral vision, so I decided to try and act normal. "I'm sorry to hear about Mr. Witherspoon. My family had me bring over some food to the house for you and Dane earlier. Hope you like what we fixed. If not, you're gonna have a lot of garbage bags full of food to throw out. We kinda went overboard."

The smile on her full lips only reached her cheeks. "That's mighty sweet of you all. I will make sure to thank your family. Dane and I are kind of in a tough spot at the moment."

"He told me earlier that Ms. Johnson left. I'm sorry to hear about that too."

"Well, today is the day for that word for sure. Heard it a thousand times if I heard it once."

"I'm sure you did. Everyone at Cohestra must be in shock."

"That's puttin' it mildly. Between the tornado and Mr. Dane's passin', most are terrified the plant will close down and they're gonna lose their jobs. Thankfully, fears were soothed today by promises from *upper* management that wouldn't happen."

I heard the irritation in her voice and suspected it was because of Dane IV's presence at the meeting. While Ms. Emma drove, I noticed her jaw was clenched and the veins in her neck engorged with blood. I also caught a whiff of the scent of her anger mixed in with her sweat. She was still reeling after her encounter with her ex. I wondered what the conversation inside the four walls had been like earlier. Judging by her demeanor, not pleasant at all.

Do not ask about that.

I jumped when Nahu'ala's voice growled inside my mind. Ms. Emma noticed and questioned, "What's wrong, sweetie?"

"I, oh, nothin'. Muscle contraction. My thighs are super mad at me for pushin' them so hard today. I just need a big glass of water, a banana, and a shot of orange juice to put things right."

"And a good smack upside the head for scarin' the daylights outta me. I mean, I walk out of my office and find my son's girlfriend on the sidewalk, shakin' like a leaf, covered in wet mud and lookin' so pale she musta seen a ghost or somethin. My first thought was you were dyin', and I can't handle any more death right now."

I tried to stifle my laugh and it came out sounding like a frog's croak. "I'm sorry I upset you, Ms. Emma. Guess my body took over when it had enough and decided to go somewhere familiar. It won't happen again."

Ms. Emma turned onto my street, her face a bit more relaxed than before. She smiled and this time, it reached her luminous eyes. She maneuvered the SUV into my driveway and parked, then surprised me when she reached out and grabbed my hand. "I'm sorry I'm actin' so uptight. The last thirty-six hours have been a lot to handle. One minute I'm watchin' my superstar son practice his slam dunks and the next, our lives are flipped upside down. Just from one phone call."

"Please, you don't have anything to apologize for. With everythin' going on, you took time out of your day and brought me home. That was very kind of you—so thank you."

"I can't have the woman my son loves dyin' from a heat stroke or heart attack—at least not on my watch."

I swallowed hard and licked my dry lips. I must be going insane because Ms. Emma actually sounded like she cared about me. Her eyes were moist and open, and no hidden agenda or malice swam behind them. It was the first time she had ever looked at me with an emotion other than irritation or anger.

"Oh child, don't look at me like that! It's just, well, with everythin' that's happened, it made me take a hard look at myself, you know? Focus on my loved ones...the things in life important to me. And the most important thing in my world is Dane and his happiness. Though I've had trouble admittin' it before, you make him happy—it's as simple as that. Which means *you* jumped from minor annoyance to part of the family, at least in my book."

"I...uh...well, thank you," I stuttered, completely taken aback by her candor and intensity.

"Honey, sometimes it takes death to make you realize you're alive. Now, scoot and go get yourself cooled off and rehydrated. I'll see you later I'm sure. And don't worry, I won't be tellin' my Dane about this. He worries enough about you already."

She let go of my hand and shooed me out of the truck. I flashed a smile at her and stepped out, and then waved as she left. In a daze, I just stood in the driveway and tried to remain upright as all the dizzying thoughts of the last few hours jockeyed for attention in my mind. I nearly jumped out of my skin when a cold hand touched my shoulder. "Dad! You scared the crap out of me!"

"Well hello to you too, honey. Sorry, didn't mean to startle you, but I must say, you had us all worried too. Where have you been, and how in the world did you get so muddy? Oh Jesus, sweetie, are ya okay? Injured? And...was that Ms. Emma?"

"Oh, Dad, I'm sorry. I...I went out for a run and forgot my phone," I said, looping my arm around him, herding him toward the front door. I couldn't control the urge inside of my mind to hurry up and get inside, even though the aroma of the intruder hung heavy in the air. "And yes, that was Ms. Emma. I fell durin' my run after gettin' too hot. She was just leavin' the plant as I was walkin' by, and she was kind enough to give me a ride home. Other than bein' filthy and a bit sore, I'm fine."

Dad gave me a good once-over. When he noticed I was barefooted, he raised one eyebrow and gave me the look. The look that said he called bullshit. "Uh huh. Your disappearance wouldn't have somethin' to do with that boyfriend of yours, would it? Looks to me like you've been breathin' heavy and rollin' around on the ground."

"Dad, really? Come on—his *mother* just dropped me off! Seriously, I went out for a run and got overheated and fell. That's it."

"So what, your shoes get stuck in the mud or somethin'?"

I hoped my lie sounded plausible and my face wouldn't betray my real emotions. "Uh, no. I took them off before I got in Ms. Emma's truck, since they were so muddy. I'll have Dane bring them by later."

He stopped me before I walked in through the front door, his face a mixture of irritation and humor. "Your mom has been worried sick about where you went. I had to convince her not to call Sheriff Gilmore to send a search party out lookin' for you. We may live in a small town, but that don't mean bad things don't happen on occasion. I realize you needed to spend some alone time with Dane, but next time, bring your phone. Okay? I don't enjoy havin' your mom get all riled up thinkin' somethin' bad happened to her one and only child."

Something happened to her, that's for sure. What, exactly, she has no idea. Mister, your daughter's lost all her marbles.

I shook my twisted thought away and put on my best smile. "I'll go call her right now and take the butt chewin' I have comin'. Then, I'm takin' a hot bath, callin' Barb to bow out of practice, grabbin' some grub, and going to bed. I'm beyond exhausted."

Daddy didn't have time to respond. I smacked a quick kiss on his cheek and went inside, taking the stairs two at a time. The need to be alone hung over me like a heavy cloak, smothering out everything else—even the sickening stench of the monster who'd invaded our home. Within minutes, I got reamed out by my mother. Then I listened to Barb whine and moan about not being able to practice our opening routine, complain about having to run alone tonight, and pester me to find out why I was so tired. I endured it all without saying much to either of them, then turned my phone to silent, filled the tub with scented bubbles and hot water, and settled my sore body down in the frothy suds.

I thought the minute I was alone and a tad more relaxed that my mind would begin rehashing the crazy events of the last thirty-six plus hours, but it didn't. Instead, my brain was a blank canvas. It was almost as though all the interior lights in my soul shut off and I was alone in the dark. The tension in my muscles eased as the warm, fragrant water soaked into my skin. The aroma of sweet pea and jasmine floated around me, embedding the fragrant scents into every pore. With my eyes closed and mind adrift in the soothing, tranquil waters of the bath, a sense of weightlessness embraced me. Peace surrounded me, wrapping my body, mind, and soul in a cocoon of warmth.

The time is now, Little One. Time to relive the past, so you will understand your future.

The voice of Nahu'ala beckoned to me. The deep, low rumbles drew me to it just as it had before.

Only this time, I didn't feel any pressure to obey. I followed on my own.

CHAPTER
TWELVE

I stood on a high mountain peak, overlooking unfamiliar terrain. The brilliant blue of the afternoon sky was dotted with plumes of wispy white clouds, dancing in the light breeze. The air was crisp as it blew through my hair. My bare feet stood in heavy snow, yet I didn't feel cold. My eyes scanned the scenic beauty around me with wonderment and awe. From the majestic, snow-covered trees as far as I could see and down to the inverted valley below, it was breathtaking. A wide river cut through the earth, winding its way like a slithering snake between the towering mountains. Even from my perch hundreds of feet above it, I heard the raging rapids and saw the frothy caps of white as the rushing water cascaded over the enormous boulders underneath it.

The smells that assaulted my nose were unknown to my mind, but my soul seemed to recognize them somehow. The hearty fragrance of ancient redwoods; the sweet scent of fir trees; the musky aroma of moose, reindeer, and bear—all melded together with other, familiar scents. Warm tears began to trickle down my cheeks at the untouched beauty I was surrounded by, just as an eagle glided on silent wings in front of me.

Though impossible, I knew I'd been here before. The pull was strong...insistent.

Home.

Through my blurry vision from my tears of joy, I saw tendrils of smoke from small camp fires rise up from the forest floor. Voices floated across the distance and up to where I stood, almost like they hitched a ride on the smoky vapors. The language was beautiful, the lyrical singsong quality full of appreciation and respect for the land they stood upon and lived off of. They praised the Great Spirit for another day of life. They spoke to each other with respect and dignity, acknowledging their devotion and joy to one another. Their voices seemed to be in harmony with the natural bounty around them. I closed my eyes and let the sweet vibrations of their words wash over me.

When I opened them again, I was shocked to discover I no longer stood on the peak. I was in the valley, standing next to one of the small, open pits of fire. The smell of smoke was stronger, mixed with a variety of herbs and local fauna. I looked over at the closest person to me—a young woman about my age with long, ebony hair, woven into an intricate braid. It cascaded down her back and ended just above the rise of her backside and swayed gently as she tended the fire. She hummed as she worked, stirring the embers once, and then moved back to a small mat. It looked like it was some type of animal hide—maybe bison or deer. She began to shred into smaller pieces some type of green plant.

Her face was smooth, the lines of maturity not visible yet. Though I had never seen her before, she looked oddly familiar. As she worked, her humming grew louder, her countenance a sea of serenity. The creamy mocha of her skin and her enormous brown eyes almost glistened as the afternoon sun caressed her with its warmth. She was the most beautiful creature I had ever seen. So young, so naïve and innocent. Entranced, I watched her perform her tasks with grace and ease. I found myself drawn to her and moved closer.

"Hello."

Silence.

She didn't move or give any indication she heard me. I squatted down next to her and tried again, this time a bit louder. "Hello. My name is Sheryl. Can you...can you hear me?"

Nothing.

I started to reach out my hand and touch her shoulder, but was interrupted by the sounds of laughter. I turned and watched two young boys running in our direction. The sense of familiarity hit me again, but only with the one boy closest to me. His features blurred under the dirt, sweat, and disheveled hair, but something about his eyes I recognized though couldn't quite place. They stopped less than two feet from us and dropped to the ground, their squeals and giggles bouncing around me as they wrestled on the ground.

"Looks like they're enjoying themselves."

Again, nothing.

I took a deep breath and wondered why she didn't respond. For a second, I considered if the young woman was deaf or something. But even that wouldn't explain why she hadn't seen me or noticed when I sat down next to her. Maybe she was blind as well? I reached out and put my hand on her shoulder but felt nothing. My hand slipped through the air and landed on the ground.

Little One, you cannot touch memories. You can only see them.

Shocked, I spun my head around at the sound of Nahu'ala's voice. Though I'd heard it in my head, it also seemed to be coming from behind me. When I saw the body attached to the voice, I gasped.

Oh, Little One. Do not fear. I am here to guide you. Not to harm you. Come, I have much to show you—and time is of the essence.

The enormous mouth never moved, yet I heard the words as though they were spoken out loud. The pair of luminous gold eyes the size of lemons held my gaze, the black pupils a mere speck in the afternoon sun. The thick, arctic white coat shimmered under the rays of the sunshine, like it had a million diamonds embedded inside of it. The paws were bigger than my head, and the claws that poked out from under the tufts of white fur were at least three inches long. The muscular body had to be at least eight feet.

Wow, some bath I'm having. Bath salts are drugs, just like what I've seen on the news. I've got to wake up.

The gigantic cat chuffed, and I felt the vibrations ripple through the ground underneath me. If I didn't know better, I would have sworn it raised its thick, black-tinged lips into a smile before the voice boomed inside my mind again.

Sheryl, rise and follow me. You aren't asleep, merely in another plane of existence. Come.

My body betrayed me and stood up. Just like earlier, when the voice of Nahu'ala unleashed commands inside my mind, I was overcome with the urge to obey. My legs shook with trepidation once erect because I noticed the beast in front of me had legs longer than my own, its head towered above mine by at least two feet.

I took a quick glance behind me to the young girl and boys. Inside their own world, they seemed completely oblivious to my presence and the gargantuan predator less than three feet from them. I turned back around and bumped right into the hard snout of the great cat. My entire body locked in frozen terror, waiting for it to gobble me up as a small, afternoon snack. The citrine-colored eyes bored into my own. I gulped and waited for the death bite. To my shock, the eyes blinked once, and with a twist of its head, I felt the rough fur against my face as it gave me a loving head butt and began to purr.

Just like Tinker.

The warm head and gruff coat connected with my skin, and all the fear inside of me vanished. It felt like an enormous weight had been lifted from my chest. The worry about the intruder in my house, the terror the mysterious notes caused, the fear for my family, poof—gone. Calmness, tranquility, and an almost electrical surge of power flowed between woman and beast. Without thinking, my hand reached up and stroked the heavy coat, immediately disappearing under the mounds of fur.

The purring was so loud it sounded like a diesel truck carrying a heavy load of grain down the highway. I smiled and melted into the euphoric emotions speeding through my mind. I closed my eyes and rode the waves of bliss. The sensation of pure, unending love washed over me and removed all traces of anything else. Never, in my entire life, had I felt so safe, loved, or at peace.

Or strong.

My eyes opened at the nudging of Nahu'ala's head. I followed his gaze over to the trio in front of us, the boys now calm and sitting on each side of the young woman. Their hands mimicked her movements as they learned while watching her work. The one who looked familiar turned his head in our direction, his dark, chocolate eyes staring right at us. Full clarity slammed into my ribcage and almost knocked me down. Tears formed behind my eyes.

"Oh...my...god. Is that...?"

Yes, Little One. Me, as a child, along with my mother, Talulah, and my brother, Hattak'katos. The day you are witnessing was the last one we spent here, in this place, before we travelled to our new home. You call it Mississippi—we call it Nanih Waiya. It means our place of creation.

I clamped my gaping jaw shut and blinked a few times. Chill bumps covered every inch of my skin when he said the name Hattak'katos. Old childhood fears of the night of the awful dream from so long ago came bursting forth. My head swam from the input overload.

No way—it can't be!

My fingers grasped a handful of the fur and hung on, afraid if I let go, my mind would slip into insanity. My throat let out a small gurgle when I no longer felt the coarse coat in between my fingers. I spun around and jumped backwards in fright.

All will be revealed now, Little One. Your time has come to take your place among us. The journey will be long and full of great joy. But as with all life, great joy comes by way of great sadness. Light balanced by darkness. Life balanced by death. I have much to teach you. Come.

Flabbergasted, my tongue didn't want to work. I watched Papa Joe's hand extend toward mine, his fingers bent and creased with age. The smile was the same as always, full of warmth and mischief, but there was something else. A combination of strength, power, and an all-knowing look.

My mind burned with questions as I took his waiting hand in my own. The minute our skin touched, the connection before with Nahu'ala was re-established. My pounding heart slowed and again, as it had done before, the worry and fear slipped away.

CHAPTER
THIRTEEN

We were no longer in the snow-capped mountain range. The scenery changed in the blink of an eye, and I recognized our surroundings. Though I couldn't place exactly where in Mississippi we were, I recognized the terrain.

Papa Joe and I stood in a small clearing at the edge of the mighty Mississippi River. The muddy, murky water swirled and rushed by, ignoring our strange intrusion on its banks. The first thing I noticed was a quiet stillness. Other than the sounds of the water and the wildlife, I heard nothing else. No cars, no machinery, no voices, no sounds of humanity.

So many questions hammered inside my head. Instead of trying to corral them and pick out the right one to ask, I blurted out a whole string of them.

"Papa Joe...what is going on? You said back there, wherever *there* was, your brother was Hattak'katos. So, you're Nahu'ala? The big cat from my dreams? Is this a dream? Oh, boy, I'm really confused. Maybe I did suffer a heat stroke earlier."

"Little One. I believe your Holy book says, 'oh ye of little faith.' I also believe it mentions, in the book of Ephesians, that our fight is against spirits and principalities—things man cannot see with his eyes. Only with his soul."

"Yeah, that's right. It does. But none of what you just said even came close to answerin' my original questions."

"If you truly wish to learn and understand, you must master one task at a time."

I was beginning to get frustrated with his doublespeak. "What does that mean?"

Papa Joe pulled his gaze away from the dirty water and found my eyes. His stare was neither judgmental nor frustrated—simply curious. "Sometimes, I forget the generation in which you were born. The ways of the past have been lost. It means, Little One, to ask simple questions first. Once you comprehend the answer, move on to the harder ones. Build a strong base of knowledge before you attempt to climb to the next level. Without it, your shaky base will eventually fail you and you will remain hopelessly in the dark, the next rung never climbed."

I let his words sink in for a second. Not that I didn't understand what he was getting at, but I needed the extra time to cool my racing nerves down. Though I loved Papa Joe, and had ever since I could remember, things seemed different now. Our connection was mystical—transcendent—and nothing I had ever experienced before. But how could that be? Of course, that was probably because I was high as a freaking kite on the stupid bath salts my body was soaking in at home.

"Sheryl, this is not a dream. Our conversation is as real as the bathroom full of the scent of sweet pea and jasmine where your physical body is currently at. Again—we are connecting on another plane—not the one you are used to."

"I...okay, instead of fightin' this, I'm just gonna roll with it. So, I'm not dreamin'. We're really talkin'. On the shores of the Mississippi River in the middle of the summer and not one mosquito has bitten me, and I'm not drippin' in sweat. While my body soaks in the bathtub at home. Right, so far?"

"Correct."

"And you, the man I have known ever since I was a little kid and who has been a part of my family since my nana was young—you are also Nahu'ala? The big cat from my dreams who transformed from the stray, Tinker, to save me from umm, oh, what did I call him?"

"The Shadow-Man."

I snapped my fingers. "Yes, the Shadow-Man." I stopped, unable to control the sarcasm dripping from my mouth. Even though Papa Joe wasn't really here and was just part of my screwed up dream, I didn't need to be disrespectful to him. "And your brother, Hattak'katos, is the Shadow-Man, the one you protected me from that night, right?"

"Yes, that's right."

"Papa Joe, excuse me for my rudeness. Guess even my sharp tongue has a hard time being tamed when I'm asleep. But please, tell me, am I supposed to believe you are some kind of shape-shifting were...were...cat? One who's been hangin' around in my dreams since I was a little girl?"

"Skin-walker."

"What?"

"The correct term is a skin-walker. Not shape-shifter...or werewolf or werecat. Those are names made up by imaginative minds. And again, you are not asleep or dreaming."

I chewed on that for a minute. Skin-walker. The second the word left his lips, the hair on the back of my neck stood straight up. Though my mind told me I had to be dreaming because people weren't able to turn into animals, my heart told me different. The polar opposite opinions running around inside of me made me dizzy. "So...you can change into the form of a white panther or ordinary housecat?"

"Yes."

"And you haven't attacked me or anythin', so what, all these years, you've just been hangin' around me, guardin' my dreams from your brother Hattak'katos?"

"Yes. Among other things. That is only part of my connection with you."

I dug deep into my childhood memories of the dream and the circumstances surrounding it. It was buried deep, full of painful images and feelings about the death of my nana. All the sensations, the guilt, wrapped around my heart in a vise, thinking I had somehow killed her, flooded back. Without prompting, my mind went back to the moment I ran through the forest and found Nana. Watched and listened to her bitter defiance at the beast in front of her during her last moments alive. The stoic words she spoke, but the absolute terror behind her eyes when she saw me. The excitement I felt at ripping flesh, my own insatiable need to kill smothering everything else.

Tears formed, and I let them come. Gut wrenching sobs burst out of me and my knees gave out. I collapsed into a sobbing heap and wept.

"Little One, cry no more for her. Ms. Beulah didn't die from your hands. Hattak'katos is responsible for her death. What you saw was just a vision of my reaction. I arrived too late to save her."

His words didn't make any sense. "What? I don't...I don't understand. You don't understand. I...I was there. I know what I did."

Papa Joe leaned down and cupped my wet face with his warm fingers. "It is you, Little One, who does not understand. Dry your tears now, and listen. Not with your ears, but with your heart."

The second our skin touched, the connection was back. An electrical surge of warmth spread throughout my body and somehow, even though it made no sense and couldn't be real, I didn't believe Papa Joe was lying to me. For a second, doubt crawled through my mind. Did I just want to believe so I could finally remove the gnawing inside my gut that I was the one who killed Nana?

"Put your doubts to rest, Little One, and listen."

Papa Joe eased down and sat next to me in the soft grass. Instinctively, I snuggled closer to him, my head resting on his shoulder. With one arm around my body in a protective grasp, the other moved out across the water, and he began to speak.

"Water is the substance of life. It is necessary for the survival of all living creatures. Food is important as well, but hunger can be satiated by other things. The need for water cannot. To live, to grow, to be strong, water is the key to life. From the beginning, man and all other living entities have been ingrained with this knowledge. This is why all societies, from human to animals to plants, congregate around a water source.

"This mighty river before you is the lifeblood of North America. The longest and largest of its kind here, it is the source of legend and the birthplace of many a thriving city. It has given life but also taken it over the years it has flowed. Man, in his ultimate prideful stupidity, has tried to tame it, but this kind of power cannot be contained.

"There are several legends of how we came to be here many, many moons ago. Some believe the original clan migrated to this continent after the destruction of King Solomon's Temple in 722 BCE, not long after it was conquered by the Assyrians. Still, others believe the entire Native American population in North and South America are direct descendants of one of the twelve tribes of Israel. Those who adhere to that storyline believe they were brought to the North American region by God himself because they were the only tribe left who truly kept the connection with *Yahweh*. No matter which story a person believes, the conclusion is always the same: every person is part of the Creation. There is a bit of truth in each legend, but the real reason we are here, and why, is a secret known only to the guardians.

"What is known and agreed upon is that the tribes from the Pacific migrated here, following two brothers who were the tribal leaders—Chata and Chicksah. This was back in the time way before any settlers from other countries arrived and America wasn't even a place anyone had ever heard of or knew existed. The land was wild and free; the animals roamed in peace. When the lands of the Northwest ceased to care for them, Chata and Chicksah were given a vision to move. They had all the remaining members of the tribe collect the bones of their ancestors and place them in buffalo sacks to carry with them to their new home. Chata and Chicksah carried a large staff and led the group away from all they'd ever known. The first night, after they made camp, Chata and Chicksah placed the staff in the ground and told the tribe members that whatever direction the staff pointed the next morning, it would be the path they followed. This would be repeated each night for several years as the clan migrated east, until the staff remained upright. Once it did, Chata and Chicksah said that place would be their new home.

"When they came to this mighty river, crossing it took a toll on the group, and many did not survive. The ones who did crossed the remaining miles in sorrow and heartache. The loss of their loved ones, alive and dead, nearly broke their spirit and will to live. Chata and Chicksah even began to argue. A few days later, when they all awoke, they were surprised to see the staff remained upright. Of course, this was the sign all of them had waited for. It meant they were home. The people danced and sang and prepared a feast. But Chata and Chicksah did not join in the excitement. They sensed the land would not hold all of them. So they decided to build a burial mound and place the bones of their ancestors inside and then split up. Chicksah took half of the people with him and went north, eventually finding a place to settle. The group became known as the Nation of the Chickasaw.

"Chata remained in the Mississippi Delta, and his clan became known as the Nation of the Choctaw. The burial mound still remains, and it is called *Nanih Waiya*. It is where we buried our ancestors. Though ownership of the land, if there could ever really be such a thing, has changed hands many times over the centuries, *Nanih Waiya* is considered the place of our creation."

I wanted to ask Papa Joe so many questions but was lulled into a state of bliss by his words. As he spoke, I saw the images of his story dance above the swirling water, like watching the story unfold on a large movie screen. It was very strange, for his speech had never affected me this way before in all the years I'd known him. When it dawned on me *why* it did, my mouth went dry.

It was because he spoke in his native tongue. Though I had heard him drop a few words now and again over the years while he worked at the diner, I didn't speak or understand Choctaw. Now, I did. It was yet another reason to relax and enjoy the strange dream because I certainly wasn't experiencing reality.

"There are other theories, other legends, passed down from different tribes. None of them really know the entire truth, only bits and pieces of it. Over time, things get lost when passed down from one generation to the next. The truth fades with each death of those who actually experienced particular events. Each generation has taken their story and added their own interpretation to it. Then, they pass the newer, updated version down to the next crop of young ones. This is the way of humans. We take something once pristine and beautiful and ruin it with our own ideas of what it should be—especially if the truth doesn't fit into our way of viewing the world. We mold it to fit our needs and wants. Each time a tainted version is passed down, the beauty fades and all that is left is ugliness.

"What I am about to tell you, Little One, is the truth. I can claim it as such because I experienced it with my own eyes. I will tell you what I know, and when I am finished,

I will answer all the questions I know you will have. I am prepared, for there will be many."

I didn't answer Papa Joe. I simply nodded my head in agreement.

"The woman and two young boys you saw earlier, as I said, were me, my brother, and my mother. We were part of the clan in the Pacific Northwest, the clan called to move from a vision experienced in unison by Chata and Chicksah. Only my father, Chata, was given the true understanding of the journey—and why we were being called.

"Talulah, our mother, was the mate of Chata. Hattak'katos and I were his children. When our tribe began to migrate, of course we followed. Hattak'katos and I proudly carried two buffalo sacks each day, full of the bones of both sets of our grandparents. We were young, eager, and wide-eyed, ready to venture to a place where the cold didn't rip into your heart and the sun was warm on the skin and the air wet and fragrant. At least, that was what we were told by our father. Our mother carried on the tradition as we walked each day through the rugged terrain. To keep us occupied and close to her side, she told us all sorts of stories about what our new life would be like once we arrived.

"Like all children and brothers, we tired easily and fought. Sibling rivalry knows no ethnic, religious, or racial bounds. It simply is. I knew, from a very early age, that Hattak'katos wished to be tribal leader once our father passed. Though I knew I should care about such things, I did not. I had no issues with him taking the position because, to be honest, I didn't want the responsibility of our entire tribe on my shoulders. Being out in nature, alone, living off the land, was more my style. The problem was, I was the older one, and the title rested with me.

"Our daily journeys turned into weeks, the weeks into months and then years. Hattak'katos and I grew up and apart, and his bitterness toward me took root in his heart. He was my blood and flesh, and I would have given him anything to make him happy. I loved him deeply. But he wanted something I was unable to give, and his heart turned dark. I didn't realize how deep his anger and how dark his evil was until we reached this place."

Papa Joe motioned again toward the river in front of us.

"The night we camped on this side of the river, resting before the crossing the next day, everyone seemed at odds. Some were afraid to cross the river, as you can imagine, and the others scoffed at them, calling them weak. Tensions rose and the arguments soon turned into brawls. It took several tries, but finally, Chata and Chicksah calmed everyone down. Everyone, that is, except my brother. He was livid, stomping around and challenging anyone who showed any fear of the water. He called them out for their cowardice, saying they should end their pathetic lives so their weaknesses wouldn't be passed along to their children.

"He finally quieted down after Chata admonished him with harsh words in front of us all. Hattak'katos did not back down from anyone except our father. Ever. At the time, I thought it was because he respected him as our elder and leader. Of course now, I know different.

"That night, everything changed—at least for me. You see, my totem came to me, and I believe Hattak'katos's did as well. Well, I didn't then, but I do now. Do you know what a totem is?"

Unwilling to break his magical story, I shook my head no.

"Most Native American tribes believe in a totem. It's

an animal guardian. Your own personal guiding force, if you will. When it comes to you, whatever animal it is, it tends to happen during great times of stress or when the person is near death. That, it seems, is when the heart and soul are most open to the connection and our true self emerges. It is always some type of animal and the type of creature to come to you is directly tied to the inner soul of the recipient. Each one represents different things to different tribes, depending upon their own oral legends. For example, the panther is considered a supernatural deity from the Underworld by most of the Southeastern tribes, like the Choctaw. Because certain tribes believed in an Underworld that houses creatures in constant battle for control of the Upperworld, the panther totem was often called the 'water panther.' Legend has it, when the battles raged between the two worlds, the water panther had the ability to control certain natural elements. Earthquakes, thunderstorms, rain—they all were thought to be controlled by the water panthers.

"The panther was feared because it is considered a monster that destroys its enemies in violent ways using nature against its own creation. It was often associated with war as well. Many a young warrior or shaman hoped to claim the panther as their totem, for it meant they would be feared by others when wars broke out...or have the ability to control the elements.

"But there are those, myself included, who viewed the panther totem as a protective guardian. To see one meant you would be blessed with courage, power, and valor. My mother told me stories of our ancestors who had panthers as their totems and how those people were intuitive and very spiritual. Oftentimes, those who had a panther totem became healers or holy men because they had been blessed with a deep understanding of spiritual things.

"As with everything, there is a side of light and a side of darkness. When a totem comes to an individual, the result is dependent upon the heart of the witness. If the heart is pure, then the totem will help guide the soul down one path. But if the heart is dark, well, the path followed is never light. Tradition has it that if a member of the tribe with a dark heart had a black panther as their totem, they would be able to embrace the dark moon and the powers of the night. They would be a great warrior, feared by all, but guided by the forces of evil.

"The night we bedded down along the shoreline, each one of us was exhausted and doing the best to grapple with our own fears about trekking across the river the next morning. It didn't take long for sleep to descend on most of them, but I was having trouble. Something kept my eyes open and my focus on the water's edge. I felt this pull—this urge—to get up and go check on Hattak'katos. He usually slept near our small family, but he hadn't returned from his walk earlier to cool his temper. I tried to ignore it, to pretend I didn't feel the worry tug at my heart, but it was no use.

"I made sure not to make a sound as I wound my way through the sleeping bodies around me and toward the shoreline. I didn't want anyone to wake up and question me about being up...or what I was doing and why. Mostly, I didn't want my brother to get trouble if it was discovered he was gone. As I neared the last cropping of protective trees, a twig snapped behind me. Before I spun around, something slammed into the back of my skull and knocked me to the ground. I remember feeling a tremendous amount of pain, but I tried to stand back up anyway. I thought we might be under attack from another tribe—wondered if maybe we had encroached on their territory. My mouth opened to give a shout of warning, but before my vocal chords could move, the second blow hit—right in the middle of my back. The force was so hard all the air left my lungs.

"Things started to blur after that. My body wouldn't move, like it was frozen. I heard the sounds of strange screams and tried one more time to move. All I managed to do was raise my head a fraction from the ground. I swore, before everything went black, I saw an enormous white panther charging toward me, and I asked the Spirits to let it take me and spare the rest of the tribe. Then, everything went dark.

"I came to a long time later. So long, in fact, it was late afternoon. I was miles and miles away from where I had been, but I didn't realize it at the time. When I woke up, I was face down in the mud and every inch of me hurt. I was covered in bruises and my head throbbed. I finally got my bearings and managed to sit up. When I looked around, for a minute, I thought I was dreaming. I was in the most beautiful place I had ever seen. Describing it is impossible. Words cannot aptly capture the beauty. It is something that must be seen with the eyes, and even then, the mind can barely comprehend. But what happened next is something I believe *you* will understand."

A cold chill traced a path down my spine. "What...what do you mean?"

"I met my totem, face to face. Sensed his presence before I heard a sound. I looked behind me and there he stood. My heart fluttered with a brief sense of fear, but it passed as quickly as it appeared. I felt the ground move as the enormous cat moved closer; the gold eyes never left my own. Just as I have spoken in your mind, he reached out to mine."

Aghast, I stuttered, "What did he say?"

A deep, warm smile appeared on Papa Joe's face as he closed his eyes, reliving the memory. "He said, *Do not fear, Little One. You have been chosen. Your heart has been judged and found to be pure. It is time for the torch to pass from me to you. You are blood of my blood, four generations down from me. Should you choose to accept this path, your old life will pass away. The new one will begin, and you and your descendants will be blessed with this duty, just as I was—the burden to stand guard of this ancient place and the secret it holds. The journey will be rewarding in some ways, harsh in others. You must leave behind all you know and step forth into this new existence without fear or hesitation. And, you must swear your allegiance and be willing to sacrifice your life to protect it until the time comes for you to pass the duty to another."*

Confused, I asked, "I don't understand, Papa Joe. How does this tie to me? Why are you showin' me all this?"

"The lineage gifted with this duty spans back to the beginning of man's time here on earth. Only one heir every four-hundred years is shown the location of the sacred place, passed along from the previous guardian. Though a few decedents of the original tribe are gifted with the ability to skin-walk, only one of them will become the guardian. I became guardian, and then was shown the sacred place. Hattak'katos also possess the ability to skin-walk, but his totem was the black panther. The Great Spirit saw inside my heart and knew I would take on the responsibility for the good of mankind because what rests hidden deep inside the Delta is of great importance, and should it fall into the hands of humans, life as the world knows it would be forever altered."

"That didn't answer my question. Why me?"

"Little One, some things cannot be explained with words. They must been seen with the heart. Here, let me show you. Once you see, you will understand."

He moved and stood up. I didn't have a chance to respond or even blink before he changed. In a split second, the elderly body of the man morphed into a gigantic white panther. He was bigger than the buffalo I remembered seeing as a child at the Memphis Zoo. He made no sound, no pain-filled yelps or shrieks of agony. His clothes didn't rip to shreds and fall to the ground, they were simply gone. The change happened in the space of one full breath. The great animal I knew as Nahu'ala stood less than two feet from me, his eyes unblinking and his huge mouth slightly open, exposing his long fangs and pink tongue. With a gentle bob of his head, he motioned for me to stand. On shaking limbs, I did so and reached out to touch his face. When I did and the connection happened, my mind was overtaken and everything became clear. I was stunned into silence as the images swept over me. My mind, body, and soul flushed with wonderment and awe at the unbelievable scenes.

Without him explaining, I knew I was looking at the entrance to the location where humanity began in naïve innocence and ended in shame-filled banishment. I watched, mesmerized, as two glowing angels sealed up the entrance and took their positions as guards while a man and woman fled in guilt. It was as though a portal through time opened, then closed, as a ring of fire made the entrance disappear. But it left one thing. The scene shifted, and alone in an open glen stood a single tree, its branches spread far and wide and the roots gnarled and twisted, firmly implanted in the ground. The leaves were a shade of green I had never seen before and so vivid, it looked like they were pulsating in time with my heartbeat. Vibrant, azure water lapped in gentle waves less than ten feet from the trunk, shimmering with the movement. The foliage surrounding the area was lush, the fruits, berries, and flowers bigger and brighter than what they should be. The water stretched for miles, and then eventually met with the Mississippi River. As the bright blue liquid mixed with the murky brown of the Mississippi, the sparkling slivers of blue were swallowed by the swirling light chocolate.

In a whoosh and blur of colors, time sped forward. The outer layers of scenery shifted and changed, but the lone tree never altered its majestic stance. Not one leaf fell, nor did they change color as years of seasons raced by. The frantic pace of the images slowed when a tall man appeared by the trunk of the tree. His body was lean and sinewy, his skin a deep, copper brown. Thick, raven-colored hair cascaded down his strong back. He spoke in his native tongue while kneeling in worship at the foot of the tree, his long fingers caressing the exposed roots. The atmosphere around him brightened, and my body jerked in shock when he transformed into a white panther. He bowed his mammoth head toward the tree in humble obedience. He turned and released a deep, throaty growl and then burst from his position and disappeared into the woods.

Time sped up again. It was like watching through a camera lens as it pulled back for a wider shot. On the perimeter, miles away, I saw Papa Joe's tribe as they navigated the area after crossing the Mississippi. Soon, the area pulsed with the Choctaw Nation, campfires releasing tendrils of smoke in the air. The sounds of laughter and joy danced in my ears as the teeming throng lived in harmony with each other and the land. Immense joy filled my soul as I watched, tears welling up in my throat. I sensed their pure hearts and their loyalty to each other and nature as they raised their voices in song, praising the Great Spirit for providing for every need.

Warmth spread through my body as the connection grew, and I basked in the harmonious encounter. I had been granted the amazing opportunity to watch history as it unfolded. Something inside my heart, body, and soul changed. But the blissful state of tranquility evaporated the second the images migrated. The encroachment of others with light skin and weapons appeared as the screams of agony and pain slammed into my ears. Thick, white smoke appeared as the entire village was destroyed, and when it cleared, I let out a gasp of sorrow. Soldiers mounted on horses surrounded what was left of the once proud people, herding them from all they'd ever known. Children and women wept near the bodies of their loved ones whose mangled corpses littered the bloodstained ground.

My heart broke and my own tears flowed down my face at the utter devastation. The collective sorrow—from not only the broken people in front of me but from Papa Joe's torment as well—hung over me like a heavy cloak. No history book or movie portrayal could ever even begin to come close to capturing what was happening in front of my own eyes.

Then, I heard it. Heard *him*. The triumphant growl reverberated throughout the empty valley before his body appeared from the shadow line of the trees. Anger burned away my tears of sorrow as I watched his ebony, fur-covered torso stomp through the crimson dirt. His claws sank deep into the damp earth while he lifted his head and sniffed the moist air. His eyes held the glint of satisfaction as he watched the last soul disappear over the horizon, the trail littered with their tears and blood. Without another sound, he turned and slunk back to the woods, free to search for the Tree of Living Water.

Do you see, Little One? Do you understand now?

Yes, Nahu'ala. Oh, God, yes.

Then, he showed me my destiny, and I sobbed.

CHAPTER FOURTEEN

"Honey, you okay in there?"

The sound of my dad's voice pulled me out of my dream. Or vision. Or mind break—whatever it was. My body shook, and I was freezing cold. I looked down and noticed the water had no bubbles left, and it was colder than the water in Caney Creek during the winter. I blinked a few times to focus my eyes, wondering how long I had been in the bathtub. Obviously, it had been long enough for the water to cool and my Dad to worry. "Yes, Dad. Just...paintin' my toenails. Girly stuff, you know."

I stood and the cold water dripped from my wrinkled skin. I stepped out of the tub and grabbed a towel and began to dry off. I was so cold my teeth chattered.

"Okay, darlin'. Listen, dinner is almost ready. Would you come down and set the table please?"

"Sure. Be down in a minute."

Dinner?

I glanced out the window above the tub and was shocked to see the sun had set outside. Well, at least I had an answer as to how long I'd been soaking. At least an hour. Great, no wonder my skin looked like an old woman's. I bent down and pulled the stopper from the tub and watched the water swirl around as it drained. I considered myself lucky I hadn't drowned.

Once dressed in fresh clothes, I looked in the mirror. The girl who stared back at me looked the same on the outside, but the inside? A completely different story. After what I'd just experienced, I knew I would never be the same. There wasn't a shred of doubt churning inside of me any longer. None of us would ever be the same. I thought back to the day Nana died and the frightened younger version of myself as I stood in the hallway. Thoughts of all the shame, guilt, and pain I felt all the years since, thinking, somehow, I had either killed her or been responsible for her death. The tormented anguish I buried inside, unwilling to examine it with mature eyes.

Until, that is, today.

Now that I knew the truth, as off-the-wall and utterly preposterous as it was, for the first time in my life, I felt true peace. Not happiness—but peace. I was not responsible for Nana's death, and knowing that fact took the heavy weight of sorrow off my chest. Once Papa Joe showed me—in the vision, or dream, or altered state—whatever it was, what really happened and why, I changed. Everything changed. I knew what I was, and that knowledge answered some of my questions but left so many others open. The last thing Papa Joe/Nahu'ala said to me before I woke up resounded in my head:

You must cut your ties to your mate. Do not see him again. He poses you great danger.

Of course, I had bowed up and demanded he tell me why. I was greeted with silence for a brief second before I woke up in the tub to the sound of my dad's voice. Fully awake, warm, and all my wits back about me, anger rumbled through me.

Papa Joe—can you hear me? I whispered in my mind. For a second, I wondered if he would hear me. I never tried to reach out to him and had no clue if I was capable of such a thing. I jumped when his answer rang through my head.

Yes, Little One.

Please, come here tonight after my parents go to sleep. I have much more to ask.

No, you have much more to learn. And I am already here—as I have always been.

He was here?

I turned and yanked the bathroom door open, racing down the stairs. When I made the turn into the kitchen, I almost knocked Meemaw over. But somehow, my body arched in a strange way and, with grace and ease, I missed bowling her over on her rump.

"Well, someone sure is hungry."

"Sorry, Meemaw. And yes, starved. Your chicken smells great, as usual."

I moved past her with minimal effort and came to a full stop when I saw Papa Joe sitting at the table. A flash of curiosity at who was left running the diner crossed my mind, but I dismissed it. At this point, it didn't matter. Seeing Papa Joe *outside* of my vivid dreams made him look older and much more tired. I noticed a few more strands of gray intermingled in his ebony hair, and his face seemed drawn... tight. His posture was all wrong—like his body was limp because his bones had turned to mush inside of him. He looked like a deflated balloon and near physical exhaustion. Of course, now that I knew exactly *how* old he really was, I cut him some slack. After living over four hundred years, he looked damned good. But still, he looked off, out of sorts. I cocked my head to the side and gave him a look of concern. Did his mind-meld trick with me somehow drain him of his energy?

We...we must hurry. There isn't much time.

I swallowed hard and gave a slight nod of agreement. On autopilot, I smacked a quick kiss to each of my family members and began to set the table. A lump in my throat appeared when I set down the last dinner plate. The delicate scrolls of the blue and silver pattern on the worn china reminded me of the past. Memories of the time in my life when blissful innocence ruled my world hit me. Hard. A life full of playing, laughing, loving, and being loved was what I knew. I listened with a heavy heart while friendly banter and chit-chat filled our small kitchen. The sound of the clock on the wall seemed louder than normal as each second ticked by. The chirps from the katydids were so loud outside it sounded like a horde of them had invaded the house. I almost laughed when I caught myself looking at Tinker's bowl of uneaten nuggets on the floor, like I expected him to be there chomping away. It dawned on me that he was eating here in human form—and at the table and not the floor. The weird *Twilight Zone* factor made me shudder.

Yeah, like that was the only weird thing that happened in the last few days...

The aroma of fried chicken, mashed potatoes, green beans, and—was that chocolate cake?—hung heavy in the room. The lump formed in my throat earlier grew in size with the knowledge this very moment would be the last time things were normal for me, my family, and the entire town.

A few minutes later, the sumptuous meal covered every open spot on our small dining table. We all held hands with our heads bowed as Dad said grace. Once finished, the food was passed around and plates loaded with enough calories for each of us to pack on twenty pounds. After a few bites were swallowed by everyone, Papa Joe spoke. "Thank you for invitin' an old man for supper. It's nice to have others cook sometimes. Feels kind of odd, though, closin' the diner down early."

"Ahh, come now, Papa Joe. You know this time of year it's just too hot for folks to venture outside to go eat. They'd rather keep cool inside their homes and take their meals sittin' next to the air conditioner. It's perfectly acceptable to close by seven. And you're part of the family. And you're welcome here anytime," Mom said, reaching over and patting his gnarled hand. I saw the look behind her eyes and smile. Something else lurked there. The look it took me a few seconds to place. It was apprehension. It dawned on me she brought Papa Joe here to tell Dad about Ms. Johnson and the note.

Boy, she was going to get way more than she ever thought. She thinks she's only opening a can of worms. Turns out, it will be an entire case.

"Sheryl, how are Dane and his mother doin'? Did they like the food?"

My eyes shot over to Dad. He wasn't looking at me, thankfully, as he worked on mixing his food all up on his plate. His hair, once thick and honey-colored, had thinned and was more of a milky white than honey. I saw light pink patches of skin under the glare of the overhead bulb. I couldn't stop staring at it, for I had never noticed it before.

It was like, for the first time, I realized he had aged. The wrinkles around his eyes, mouth, and neck—when did they arrive? It sent pangs of regret through my chest like a burning arrow. I'd been so busy in my own life, so caught up in growing up and escaping this place, I failed to notice the people closest to me were slowly dying.

I forced my eyes to look away from Dad's aging features and back to his plate. Anything to keep myself from choking up. I almost laughed out loud at the mess he'd made of his food. You couldn't tell one entrée from the next. He liked it that way. All the flavors and textures intertwined. It made me feel queasy when I watched him mash everything together. Then I remembered I was supposed to respond to his question. "Um...yeah, best as can be expected. Don't know about the food—Dane didn't eat any when I was there, and Ms. Emma was at work." I paused and slid my glance over to Papa Joe and then to Meemaw and Mom. The imperceptible nod of each of their heads went unnoticed by Dad, so I continued. "But I know they are grateful for it since Ms. Johnson quit them."

Dad stopped tearing his chicken apart and looked up. "She did? When? Why?"

Mom cleared her throat. "She decided to quit after findin' Mr. Witherspoon. It was quite...rough on her."

"Well, that's understandable. Seein' death up close and personal ain't never easy on anyone. But she quit? That's kind of odd, dontcha think? A vacation, sure—I can see that. But quit? What's she gonna do now? I mean, she's been with them for, well, ever since I heard tell. Didn't her momma work for the family as well?"

"Yes, she did. I believe Ms. Johnson was the third or fourth generation to work for the Witherspoons. Isn't that what she said, Mom?"

Meemaw piped in. "I believe she said she was the third generation when she came in this mornin' to say good-bye."

Dad stopped chewing and wiped the grease from the corners of his mouth. "What do you mean, 'to say good-bye?' She's gone? Like, moved away? Ain't she gonna wait to go after attendin' the funeral?"

Mom folded her napkin in her lap and reached for her tea. I noticed her hand shook as her fingers latched around the glass. "She...went to visit family up North. And no, she isn't plannin' on payin' her respects at Mr. Witherspoon's service."

"Well, I'll be. Never woulda figured Ms. Johnson as that kind of person. She seemed so, you know, old school southern. Gotta say, I'm surprised."

The ticking of the clock grew louder with each passing second. Mom and Meemaw exchanged worried glances with Papa Joe and then me. For a split second, I thought Mom was going to change the subject, but then I saw her jaw set. She took a large swallow of her tea before she continued. "Now Jared, don't go judgin' Ms. Johnson too harshly until you know all the facts."

"I'm not judgin'."

"Good. Because...well, there is a reason she up and skedaddled outta town, and it ain't got nothin' to do with losin' her manners."

The tone in Mom's voice made Dad set his fork down and look up from his plate into her eyes. "Oh? Somethin' besides just visitin' long lost kin?"

Silence. The greasy chicken sat on my stomach like a lump. Finally, Meemaw reached into her purse and rum-maged around, producing the wadded note Ms. Johnson left us. A flutter of anger danced across my chest as she opened it. A light tremor of worry made her hand shake as she slid it over in front of Dad. "I believe, Jared, you need to read this."

"What the...?" Dad mumbled. He wiped his hands on his napkin before picking up the note. None of us moved while we watched his eyes scan the crinkled paper. I held my breath at the stench that wafted from it. It was so strong, I could almost see the scent molecules rising from it. I swallowed hard and clenched my teeth to keep from yanking the paper from his hands and shredding it into a pile of unrecognizable strips. Dad's expression changed from shock to curiosity and then over to horror and anger. He dropped the flimsy paper like it just bit him. "Where did you get this?"

Mom pushed her chair away from the table and stood up. Visibly shaking now, she held out her slender hand and motioned for Dad to stand up. "Jared, I believe it's time we have a family meetin'."

On cue, the rest of us stood up and followed my bewildered dad into the living room. Family meetings were only called under the direst of circumstances and had only happened three times prior. The first was Nana's death. The second, when Meemaw decided to move in. The third happened when I began dating Dane. Now, the fourth would be the last one I ever participated in. Mom and Meemaw thought they were going to drop a bombshell in Dad's lap, which in truth, they were.

They just didn't know exactly how big the explosion would be. Had they really known, they would have never lit the fuse.

So much for my senior year...

Almost an hour later and countless footsteps across the hardwood floors by Dad, we all waited for his response. As was his way, Dad never spoke during the time each of us took turns and talked. He listened intently and let the entire tale about the strange death of Mr. Witherspoon soak into his mind. I sensed he was rolling it around his head as he tried to sort through it all. Once he ingested all of it, his pacing picked up speed—keeping in time, I assumed, with the spinning wheels in his mind. He stopped moving and I saw the change in him. His back stiffened, and he squared his shoulders, cracked his neck and fingers, and took in a deep breath. "Sheryl?"

"Yes, Dad?"

He turned his big eyes over to me, his focus sharp and steady. The way he looked at me, his piercing gaze full of accusations, almost physically hurt me. "What's goin' on here?"

Mom jumped up from her spot on the couch. "Jared! How in the world would she know? She's just a child, for goodness sake! Don't you go takin' that tone with..."

Dad cut her off, his eyes never leaving my own. "Jolene. Sit down."

Mom's face blanched, and Meemaw let out a small gasp as her hand flew up to her mouth. Never, not once, had Dad *ever* spoken like that to my mother—or anyone for that matter. Dad wasn't cut from that type of cloth. He liked to smile, to tease, to make others laugh. He hated confrontation and did everything in his power to avoid it. "Sheryl. Talk."

"Jared, why in the world do you think...?"

"Ms. Gertie...you read the note. You know exactly why I'm askin' her."

The tension in the room was so heavy, it felt like someone just tossed a wet blanket on us. I knew if I didn't speak, things would deteriorate, fast. "Dad, before I answer, I need to ask Mom and Meemaw somethin', okay?" No response. Just an icy stare. I waited to see if Papa Joe was going to admonish me to be still but heard nothing. Turning to Mom and Meemaw, I asked, "Where is Nana's totem necklace?"

"Sheryl Ilene! Are you accusin'...?"

"No, no, of course not. Please, everyone...calm down. I can't stand all this anger and distrust swirlin' around. Let's not forget we're all family. Please...I need to know if either of you moved Nana's necklace from the jewelry box."

"Well, of course not. Why would we? It's hidden safely away upstairs...wait, do you think the one Ms. Johnson had is ours? Is that it? You think someone broke in here and stole it?"

Why did I even bother to ask? I already knew the answer.

"We don't think someone stole it. We know they did." Three sets of eyes converged on Papa Joe. I stared at my hands, trying to gather the courage to continue.

"How do you know that, Papa Joe? Sheryl, what is goin' on?" Dad asked.

I sighed and stood up. It was like moving through mud or quicksand. I didn't want to do this. I didn't want to come clean and tell them the truth. Didn't want to break their hearts and destroy their idyllic worlds, but I had no choice. I reached into my back pocket and produced the note I found in Meemaw's jewelry box and set it on the coffee table. All three of them moved closer to read it, yet none of them reached out to touch it. Instincts seemed to warn them of the danger the note contained.

I moved over next to Papa Joe and let the tips of my fingers graze his shoulder. I needed the connection with him to get through this. The need to pull from the depths of his strength, to explain the unexplainable and downright unbelievable to my family, raced through me. My heart skipped a beat when I felt the intense heat burning through him. He was fading, fast. He said my transformation needed to happen soon because the danger was high. My heart broke when I realized what he really meant by the statement. For me to transform, he would have to pass the gift, which meant his physical body would die.

That is the way, Little One. Do not fear or be sad. I will always be with you. Now, you must hurry.

"Mom. Dad. Meemaw. I want you to open your hearts and listen with it. Not your minds, okay?" Three curt nods were my answer. "Remember all those crazy stories Nana used to tell us? The ones about the big cat that saved her from the flood and how she would see the white beast in the forest sometimes late at night? The one she said gave her the totem necklace and watched over her?"

Tears sprang from Mom and Meemaw's eyes. Mom looked   horrified,   but   Meemaw looked—what?—accepting? On the same page with me almost. No, the look was one of understanding.

She knew!

I struggled to retain my own composure and let the words flow out in a sensible fashion. "The one she called Nahu'ala? And my dream years ago? About the Shadow-Man and how Tinker turned into a big, white panther and saved me? And the next day I called him Nahu'ala?"

Mom and Meemaw gasped when I said the name. Dad

didn't react as strongly, but I noticed the fire behind his eyes dimmed a little. He sensed something was wrong. Really wrong. None of them said a word, so I continued. "Well, there is a reason for all of that. A crazy, out of this world, aliens-have-just-landed-on-the-planet and the zombie plague just started type reason. In other words, somethin' it will take your eyes to see for your brains to understand. So, Papa Joe is goin' to demonstrate what I'm talkin' about, and then we'll do our best to explain the rest. What I don't know or can't answer, Papa Joe will help you understand. Ready?"

"Ready for...what, Sheryl?" Meemaw whispered, her voice dry and husky. Mom reached over and clasped her right hand in Meemaw's and then her left with Dad's. I saw the confusion behind Dad's face but swore I saw a hint of recognition behind Mom and Meemaw's.

Do they both know?

I backed away a few steps from Papa Joe and whispered, "Tinker...here kitty kitty."

In a flash and without a sound, Papa Joe's body disappeared and my furry bed companion, Tinker, sat in the chair. His fluffy tail curved daintily around his feet, his green eyes unblinking. My eyes moved over to my family as I watched their reactions from across the room. Part of me feared one, or all of them, might faint from the shock. After all, watching someone change into an animal was not an everyday occurrence.

Freakin' ever.

The color disappeared from all of their faces. Each one looked like they'd just been drained of blood by ol' Dracula himself. Mom and Meemaw were both visibly shaking, and Dad looked like he was about to toss his dinner all over the couch. Dad's wispy hair looked like it turned whiter about as fast as Papa Joe turned into Tinker. Jaws hung open and eyes bulged out of their sockets. A collective quiet overtook the living room—even the clock wasn't ticking anymore—as the enormity of what just happened inside the four walls of our home crashed down on top of them.

Tinker/Nahu'ala broke the silence with a dainty, Meow.

The minute the silence was broken, it seemed to bring the three of them back to life. Dad shot up out of his chair and in a flash was in front of Mom and Meemaw. He took a protective stance about two feet from them like he was guarding them from what he probably assumed was a demonically possessed cat. Mom reached out and grabbed his hand, and Meemaw closed her eyes and swallowed hard, her throat muscles undulating.

"Sheryl, get...get away from it."

"Dad, it's okay. Really," I said. I leaned down and scooped up what used to be Papa Joe and cuddled the cat to my chest. "It's not what you think, believe me."

"You tryin' to convince me this thing ain't straight from the bowels of Hades? Unless dinner was made with peyote and we's just havin' an awful hallucination, that there beast is evil."

"Please, sit down and listen. I have much to tell you and not very much time to do so."

"I ain't gonna do no such thing until *that* thing goes away," Dad grumbled.

"Jared, sit. It's okay," Meemaw whispered. "Can't you feel the power? The love? There is no evil here—only love."

Dad shifted his eyes over to Meemaw and gave her a stern look. The kind of look made to question a person's sanity. Through her shimmering tears, Mom smiled weakly up at him. "She's right, Jared. Can't you feel it? The energy? Look, even the hairs on my arms are standin' up!"

Dad's mouth dropped open. "Have y'all lost your minds?"

In three quick strides, I was by Dad's side. Out of the three of them, he was having the most trouble. I touched his shoulder and said, "Daddy...please. It's okay. Let me explain."

With reluctance behind his wide eyes, he eased down on the couch between Mom and Meemaw, his gaze never leaving the furry body in my arms. I backed up and sat on the chair closest to me, and Tinker jumped down and back over to the chair where he'd changed. The second his furry feet touched the cushion, Papa Joe was back, his body erect in the chair. Out of the corner of my eye, I saw Dad jerk, but Mom and Meemaw never moved or said a word.

I smiled at Papa Joe before training my eyes back on my bewildered family. With a deep breath, I began the tale.

CHAPTER FIFTEEN

"The night I dreamt about the Shadow-Man seems to be the startin' point for me, so I'll lead off with it. You see, he is real and not someone I made up. His name is Hattak'katos, which roughly translated, means *man and cat*. He is the brother of Nahu'ala. He came here that night to kill me while I slept. Thankfully, my guardian protected me," I smiled, motioning with my hand over to Papa Joe. "He was here, in the form of the cat you know as Tinker. But when he changed to his true form, I discovered Tinker wasn't his real name. When I fell back asleep, he stood guard over me. When Hattak'katos appeared again, that is when Papa Joe's true form took over, and I woke up and saw him. I heard the conversation between the two great powers in my mind. Hattak'katos wanted me, but Nahu'ala informed him I was already taken."

"Taken? Sheryl, what in the world...?"

"Dad, please, let me finish? Everythin' will click when I do, okay?"

"I remember Nana sayin' that name. Nahu'ala. Sometimes, late at night, she would mumble it in her sleep. One night, when I was around ten, I asked her about it. That's when she showed me the totem necklace. Told me her guardian gave it to her. Said his name was Nahu'ala but I was to never mention it or speak it out loud. Ever. She was adamant about it. The look on her face was so sad when she spoke his name. And then, when you came along," Meemaw said, turning to Mom, "the same thing happened—remember?"

Mom nodded, her eyes lost in the memory. The look on Dad's face was laughable as his eyes bounced between his wife and mother-in-law like a ping pong ball. "Yeah, and I was around the same age. I'd spent the night with Nana...heard her whisper the name in her sleep...asked her about it the next mornin'. She did the same thing with me. Showed me the necklace, told me about her protector, and then said to never mention the name. Of course, I didn't listen to the last part—I told you. And, if I recall correctly, you flipped your lid."

"I did," Meemaw said, her voice quiet and heavy. "Because after the first time I asked about Nahu'ala, I began havin' nightmares about a huge, black panther chasin' Mom down in the woods. I...I heard her screams of terror as she ran. Watched her shimmy up a tree as the water rose behind her. The dream terrified me—and I didn't want the same thing to happen to you. I...I sensed the...oh, I don't know what to call it. The energy, the force? Whatever you call it, the dreams were forebodin'."

I watched a lone tear trickle down Mom's face, her eyes closed as she listened to Meemaw. Worry creased her forehead as she nodded in silent agreement. I wondered if she was reliving the day I called Tinker Nahu'ala and her reaction to it.

"But it did. I started havin' the same dreams. Watched my petrified Nana run through the forest. Heard the monster behind her. Listened to her scream. I had the dreams up until...oh, God...until I had Sheryl." Mom's eyes popped open, and both she and Meemaw stared at me.

"Mine stopped the day I gave birth to you, Jolene," Meemaw croaked.

I let their words settle over the room before I said anything else. Poor Dad looked like he was watching a spaceship full of little green men land in our backyard.

"And the cat! Oh, gosh, Mom. Remember the stray I named Fluffy? The white one with the green eyes that showed up on our doorstep—oh, Jesus! Right after my first dream!" Mom gushed. She grabbed Meemaw's hand and hung on for dear life. "Remember, Mom?"

Meemaw nodded her head, her tears flowing faster now. "Yes, yes I do. And I had one, too. Named him Ralphie. He appeared the first night after I overheard Nana cryin' in her sleep."

Both of them turned their attention over to Papa Joe. His lips parted in a genuine, heartfelt smile so full of love, it would have melted an iceberg. Waves of love rolled off of him and coated the entire room with an invisible embrace of warmth. "Yes, Little Ones. I've watched over your family for many generations and have been known by many names. Ralphie. Fluffy. Tinker. It is part of my duty, guarding the next in line—and my kin."

"Wait...are y'all under the same delusion here? Because it sure sounds to me like y'all are. Seems to me y'all are tryin' to convince yourselves that Papa Joe is some kind of...I don't know what to call it. A werecat? And one who is older than dirt?"

Mom shushed Dad with a wave of her hand. He was the one who looked appalled now. "What are you sayin', Papa Joe? Kin? Many generations? I don't..."

I stood up and went over and knelt down in front of my mom and Meemaw. Tears of my own clouded my vision as I looked at their confused faces. For a split second, they looked like little girls rather than grown women. The buried memories of the interactions with their guardians and visions of their possible futures barreled back from the depths they each hid them in. With wide-eyed wonderment, both of them stared at me, waiting to hear the answers to their numerous questions. Telling them this part was what I feared the most. I knew it would be the hardest for them to hear—especially Meemaw. "Remember how Nana told us how she survived the 1927 flood? How she was out down by Caney Creek, pickin' collard greens? How the scream of a woman in pain lured her further out into the woods until she got lost? Then a black panther chased her up into a tree?"

No answer. Just two sets of impatient, glossy eyes stared at me. Neither woman blinked.

"And recall she said the big cat ran away before the flood waters came? Well, that isn't entirely the truth. The cat ran away, but way before the waters rose. Hattak'katos left because he didn't want to face his brother, Nahu'ala, or drown in the flood he, for lack of a better word, conjured up."

"I...I don't understand..." Meemaw muttered.

I swallowed hard and kept my voice steady. "Nana was out in the woods gatherin' collard greens, like she said. She liked to be outside, communin' with nature—a habit she never gave up, as you both well know. And she *did* follow a scream she thought was of a woman in distress. But...it wasn't. It was a ploy by Hattak'katos to draw her deeper into the woods and pull Nahu'ala out—away from the spot he guards."

"What? Why? And what do you mean '*flood he conjured*'?" Mom whispered.

"Hattak'katos was unable to find the location of the sacred place his brother, Nahu'ala, is charged with watchin'. He tried for centuries to find the spot. It has been his drivin' force ever since he turned and embraced his abilities. It is what he lives for. Over the centuries and after many defeats, his obsession made him go mad. He went so far as to enlist the help of the government. Of course, he didn't exactly tell them the entire truth—only enough to catch their interest. The rest they did on their own."

"Wait...*our* government is involved?" Dad asked, shocked.

"Yes. Hattak'katos, in his human form, was instrumental in craftin' the Indian Removal Act of 1830. Recall from history the first Native Americans forced to move were the Choctaw—from right here in Delta country in 1831. The history books I read in school taught that it was because of the government's interest in ethnic cleansin'. That President Andrew Jackson was just continuin' the work of cultural transformation started by George Washington and Henry Knox. And maybe, for them, it was. But that wasn't the reason Hattak'katos was involved. He wanted to rid the Delta of his brother—and any possible descendants—for free reign to pursue the location of the sacred place."

"How do you know all that, Sheryl? I mean, he let all those people—his own people?—die the horrible way they did, yanked from their homes, just to find some supposed sacred tract of land? That's a mighty big claim there, Sheryl. A mighty big claim. Again, I ask, how do you know?"

"Heartbreakin', isn't it, Daddy? One of the worst acts of hatred ever committed, and it was orchestrated by one of their own. I know because I saw it with my own eyes, in a vision that I'll explain later. But it doesn't end there. That tactic didn't work, so Hattak'katos opted for a different approach. In a fit of anger, he decided to destroy the entire area by unleashin' the flood. Since he couldn't find the location, he decided to destroy it. Plus, he knew his brother was in love with Nana and hoped he would leave his post to save her. Hattak'katos planned on wipin' everythin' away all at once. He would destroy his brother and his descendants in the flood. That was his plan. With his obstacles gone, he would have free reign over the territory he has always wanted. The opportunity to look for the sacred place without interference or fear his brother would find him."

"Boy, howdy. I think I'm gonna need a drink," Dad said as he moved over to the small decanter on the bookshelf near him. In one swift movement, he snatched a glass, filled it to the rim with tequila, and chugged it back. On any other day, Mom would have given him a thorough dressing down for drinking, but today, she didn't even flinch. She and Meemaw were frozen in their spots on the couch, trying to grasp it all. I waited until Dad sat back down to continue.

"It almost worked, too. Nana *did* scurry up a tree when the waters began to rise, but she slipped and fell back into the water. She...she drowned before Nahu'ala got to her. Once he did, he was devastated. He was too late. He broke the one and only rule he had been given and took her to the place he guarded. The place no one but the guardian knows how to get to. The place of healin' and mercy—a sacred place where the Tree of Living Water sits—the flowin' water created by God's hands in the Garden. He took Nana to the spot Hattak'katos longs to find, and she was brought back to life. But after everythin' she'd suffered, her memories of that time sort of got jumbled around inside her."

"Mom *died?*" Meemaw said, the shock and disbelief seeping out of her. "How...how can that be?"

"Yes—technically. It was only for a few minutes between the time she was found and taken to the sacred place. But Nahu'ala's love and prayers for her swayed the Lord. He allowed her to come back by drinkin' from the waters by the Tree. But the gift of renewed life came with a very high price, which is what leads us to where we are now. Hattak'katos is after the location—as he has always been. He wants to control the power of the water. Removin' his ancestors from the Delta didn't work. Causin' the flood that wiped out a huge section of the Delta didn't work. His tactic this time started when he tried to make Nana tell him where it was the night he stalked and killed her. That didn't work either and is why he came after me—and why she died. You see, it was impossible for Nahu'ala to protect us both at the same time. Though it broke his heart, he had to let the love of his life go to watch over me. After he saved me that night, he realized too late why Hattak'katos left without puttin' up much of a fight. By the time he arrived in the glen, it was too late. Nana was already gone."

"Oh, dear Lord," Mom gasped, her face a sickly shade of white. "So Papa Joe's real name is Nahu'ala, and his brother's is Hattak'katos—and they both have the ability to...to..."

"Skin-walk. Yes, they both have the ability to change forms, and they have been here for over four-hundred years. One guards. One hunts."

"Skin-walk? Like shape-shiftin', right?" Mom ventured.

"Yes. But there is more, Mom. What I've just relayed is the easy part. The difficult, flip side comes next."

I watched the wheels spin behind both of their brilliant blue eyes as they tried to digest my words. All the color had drained from their faces, and they looked like two ghosts sitting in front of me. I glanced over at Dad and flashed a feeble smile, but he didn't return it. My attention returned to Meemaw when she gasped, "My birthday...Mom said I came late. That she musta gotten pregnant the last week Pop-pop was alive, before the flood. But, that's not true, is it?" The knot of tears in my throat kept me from answering. I responded with a slow shake of my head. "Bernard Kovlin isn't my father, which means..."

Papa Joe rose from his spot on the chair and moved across the floor with fluid grace. He squatted down next to me and reached his gnarled, wrinkled fingers out and took Meemaw's hands in his. He didn't say a word. He didn't have to—his face said it all.

"You?" Meemaw croaked.

"Yes, my daughter. Me."

Mom began to softly cry. Dad's lips were drawn so tight, it looked like someone had stitched them together. Meemaw and Papa Joe were lost in a world they seemed to be the only people in at the moment. Even though Papa Joe had been a part of her life since her birth, the sudden shift in his role must have made her head swim. I understood her pain and confusion, for I experienced a fraction of it when I found out that Papa Joe was much more than a close family friend. He was family. But it hurt my heart to see her so upset. We all were having great difficulty absorbing the fact that he was my great-grandfather, Mom's grandfather, and Meemaw's father.

In a word, it was damn near incomprehensible. Then again, maybe this part would be easier to accept after seeing him turn into a furry house cat in front of their eyes. Good thing we started them off with just that. Had Papa Joe turned into Nahu'ala...I shuddered to think about what would have happened. Dad would probably have drunk the entire bottle of tequila and Mom or Meemaw would have had a stroke.

"Gertrude...my Gertrude. I haven't missed a day of your life since you were born. Nor yours, granddaughter and great-granddaughter," he said, looking over at Mom and then to me. "The three of you are my greatest joy, along with Beulah. But I hope you understand, at least a little, why the secrecy has been in place all these years."

Even though the secret had been kept for over four generations, it didn't seem to matter anymore. Papa Joe was different—otherworldly. Peace, joy, and love surrounded him. Like an invisible blanket, it stretched out from his body and enveloped us all in a cocoon of love and strength as he spoke softly about the woman he loved from afar all his life.

And how he'd watched his family from a distance with a heart full of pride and sadness for over seventy years.

It was close to midnight when Papa Joe and I finished our stories. The tears that flowed down all three faces during the last few hours dried up. My guess was no one had any liquid left in them to spill. The questions posed by Dad, Mom, and Meemaw had all been answered, heard with their disbelieving ears and destroyed minds. Shell-shocked from our words, the three of them sat in silence as they each tried to make sense of it all.

Watching my loved ones experience such a wide variety of painful emotions tore at my heart. Their lives, once full of the normal worries about money, food, shelter, raising a family, operating a business, spending time with family and friends—it all crashed down around them. Everything they knew to be true, things ingrained in them since childhood, slipped out of them with each tear shed.

I had the distinct advantage in dealing with all this new information because I had experienced it through my connection with Papa Joe. Though I still was somewhat unnerved—no, a *lot* of unnerved—by my new reality, I had the privilege to see it all. To grasp the enormity of the mind-blowing alternate universe I would be living in. Mom and Meemaw at least had some idea, some connection, because they both had experienced similar interactions with their father and grandfather over the years. His blood flowed through their veins. But Dad was hopelessly lost and had asked the majority of the questions earlier.

After Papa Joe finished explaining how he and Nana fell in love and kept their secret—how through visions he showed me the true history of things—I dropped the bomb. When I told them how all of this tied back to me, and what was to come, none of them seemed capable of forming a question to ask or respond with any discernable emotion. They sat like three solid pieces of marble, unable to grasp the entire situation.

The house was quiet now, but I was beyond nervous. I felt jittery and anxious, like I had consumed two entire pots of straight espresso. Energy tingled through me and made my leg muscles twitch and my heart beat faster. Papa Joe said the transfer of power would happen soon, and I worried it might happen in front of my family. Plus, I knew what would happen to him, and I didn't want my mom or meemaw to be around when he left this world. He had warned me the first transformation would be difficult to control and I needed to be alone so I wouldn't accidently hurt those around me. When my head began to pound, I shot up out of the chair with the intention to go for a run and release some of the overwhelming energy that flowed inside me. I froze in mid-stride when I heard a car pull into the driveway.

"Who in the world is that?" Dad said from across the room.

I stepped over to the window and peeked through the curtains. When I saw the car, my stomach lurched. "Sheriff Gilmore."

In a flash, everyone stood up.

"A visit from the law this late is never good," Meemaw said to no one in particular.

The boots of the sheriff clamored up the front porch steps. We all locked eyes with each other, and then Dad motioned for us all to sit down. He walked over to the front door and opened it before the sheriff knocked. "Evenin', Sheriff. What can I do ya for?"

"Evenin', Jared. Sorry to stop by so late, but looks like y'all weren't asleep. Need to talk to y'all for a minute."

Dad moved aside and opened the door wider. The

sheriff walked in and removed his hat. His enormous frame seemed too big for our small living room. He nodded at us all and tried his best to appear nonchalant, but a look of confusion flashed behind his eyes when he saw Papa Joe sitting in the chair closest to him. For a second, I thought he was going to comment on why Papa Joe was here, but he didn't. Instead, he turned his attention back to Dad.

"Well, I'm afraid I'm not here on a social visit, as I'm sure y'all know, so I'll just get right to it. We're lookin' into a disappearance of one of our own and wondered if you might offer some help."

"Oh Lordy, what happened? Tell me it ain't Raymond Pryor. His poor momma can't handle any more bad news. After all, she just found out about her cancer two weeks ago."

"Ms. Gertie, I didn't mean one of my deputies. I meant one of our citizens," Sheriff Gilmore said, turning his gaze over to me. "Sheryl, I'm afraid she's one of your friends. Tami Kilgore is missin'."

"Missin'?" Mom gushed, "and her with lil' Drexel just a youngin'. How long she been gone?"

I saw the shift in the sheriff's demeanor before he ever spoke. His eyes were open, wide, probing into my own. Though I wasn't a fan of Tami's, I was still taken aback by the news of her disappearance. But just because we were on the squad together and attended the same school, why would that make the sheriff come here in person this time of night to ask me? It was common knowledge throughout Junction City that we weren't exactly friends. What, was he going to stop by all twelve of us on the squad and question us personally? What's next, going door to door and informing all fifteen hundred residents of Locasia County?

No, he's here because he thinks I'm involved somehow!

That thought kept my mouth clamped shut.

"We don't have all the particulars just yet, Ms. Jolene. What we do know is that she left Kilgore's place around noon to go shoppin' for school clothes. Then she planned on headin' to cheerleadin' practice. Problem is, she never showed up at practice. Drexel got worried when she didn't come home and started callin' her cell. When she didn't answer, he and his pa went out lookin' for her. Found her car in the back lot of the high school—empty. Her phone sittin' in the driver's seat and her purse and gym bag in the passenger seat, and blood in the car and on the ground. That's when he called us. Raymond Pryor brought ol' Blue, and he picked up on her scent right quick but then lost it out past Caney Creek. Found blood on the trail...and then, nothin'. The dogs picked up on some other scent that drove them into a frenzy, and all they seem to be doin' now is runnin' around in circles. Boys are still out searchin', but the way I'm figurin' it, they ain't gonna find her alive."

My stomach dropped. Out of the corner of my eye, I saw Meemaw swayed a fraction and Mom reach her hand out to steady her. "Why is that, Sheriff?" I ventured, barely above a whisper.

"The amount of blood found is fresh...and substantial. If it's Tami's, she wouldn't survive losin' that much. No one would."

"Why, who would do such a terrible thing? Ain't nobody around here, least not that I can think of. Maybe a drifter? You know, I've heard news reports about truckers who prey on young women while drivin' to and fro. And

Lord knows lots of them come through here deliverin' supplies to the Cohestra plant ever since the tornado."

Out of the corner of my eye, I saw Dad wince. I knew exactly what he was going through his mind—the conversation with the sheriff so many years ago about Nana. How they'd found her body torn to shreds by what they had eventually concluded was a bear. After all we'd just told him, and what he witnessed with his own eyes, it all seemed to click together for him.

Sheriff Gilmore's gaze hardened. He ignored my mother's question. His face betrayed his true thoughts now. Doubt and accusations swirled behind his hooded eyes. He leaned forward, cocked his head to one side as he studied my face. "Sheryl, I understand you went out for a run earlier today out by Cohestra alone? I know y'all like to run, but I thought y'all ran at night because of the heat. Is that true, or did someone give me false information?"

My mouth was so dry, I couldn't have said a word if I wanted to. Dad bristled to my defense, his parental instincts in high gear. "Am I hearin' you right, *Sheriff?*" Dad spat out, his face a dark shade of burgundy as his anger flared. "Maybe you need to rephrase your question so it doesn't sound like you just barged into my home and accused my daughter of a crime."

"Jared, I am simply askin' questions. I've got a girl missin' and two sets of extremely upset family members wantin' answers I don't have yet. I was just hopin' maybe Sheryl happened to see Tami sometime today. Help us get a sense of her steps before she up and vanished into thin air. And the Cohestra plant is on the way toward the school. So, Sheryl," he said, turning his attention back to me, "where you out runnin' today, and did you by chance see Tami?"

It took a few seconds for my throat to unlock and my tongue to form words. "I did go for a run, but I didn't see Tami."

"You sure?" Sheriff Gilmore questioned, doubt oozing out of his voice.

This time, I nodded yes.

The sheriff chewed on that for a few seconds, his dark brown eyes burning a hole through me. He reached up and rubbed his forehead. "Then can you explain to me why she sent y'all a text sayin' she was on her way to meet ya?"

CHAPTER SIXTEEN

"As I said, I *did* go out for a run, but I didn't see Tami, so no, I can't explain that. I didn't text or call her either, I swear. I don't know what you're talkin' about. I...I'm not friends with Tami, so I..."

"Sheriff, this all can be answered with ease," Papa Joe said, his voice quiet yet with an air of authority. He rose from his spot next to Meemaw and walked over to Sheriff Gilmore. Mom, Dad, and Meemaw watched in silence, seeming to sense the power and control wielded by Papa Joe. I saw the change in his eyes from chocolate brown to vibrant sable...felt the electricity level in the house soar. I knew he was working his mind-magic on the sheriff—and I think my family did, too. The tone and timbre of his voice had the same effect on the sheriff as it had Ms. Johnson. I used the moment and bounded up the stairs to retrieve my cell phone from the bathroom. I could hear Papa Joe coo and coerce the sheriff into silence.

I snatched my phone from the bathroom counter and did a quick scroll. Sure enough, there was a text from Tami around seven, right around the time I left the bathroom and bounded downstairs. Just one and it said exactly what the sheriff mentioned. I scrolled through the others and my stomach clenched. Three texts from Barb and two from Dane. The news of Tami's vanishing act spread faster than the pox, and both wanted to know if I'd heard or not. But the last one from each of them made my heart pound since they both said they were going out to help search, and they asked if I would join them.

Oh shit.

As I flew down the stairs, I heard Papa Joe's calming voice from the living room. "Sheryl has nothing to do with Tami's disappearance, Sheriff. Someone is trying to make it appear that way, but as you will see from Sheryl's phone, there was no contact from her end with Tami."

"Look Sheriff, see? No phone calls to her or texts. The one from her to me is here, but I didn't reply back," I said, hoping my words didn't sound as rushed and fake to the sheriff's ears as they did to mine.

The sheriff's eyes glazed over as he stared into Papa Joe's, but the second he turned his gaze to me, the connection seemed to lessen somewhat. He took my phone out of my hand and scrolled through it, handing it back to me with a strange look on his face. His moves seemed robotic—forced. I wasn't sure if it was from the fact that I had no contact with Tami or the sensation of his brain no longer under his control. Maybe it was a combination of both. "Seems more investigatin' needs to be done here. Don't make no sense though. Why do you think Tami sent you the message?"

"That is a minor consequence in this matter, Sheriff.

You need to concentrate on finding her. You already stated her scent trail and the blood led into the woods. Focus on that first. Believe and know Sheryl is not involved in any way with Tami's...disappearance."

Papa Joe reinforced his words with a gentle hand on Sheriff Gilmore's shoulder. As I watched, I noticed the minute his hand touched the sheriff's body, the words reached inside his mind and took hold. With a nod of his head, the sheriff agreed. "Sorry to barge in here so late. Just tryin' to follow all leads. I see this is a dead one though. I'll be on my way now. Goodnight."

All of us remained still except Papa Joe. With his hand still on the sheriff's back, he walked him to the door and led him out into the darkness and out to his car. The four of us stood rock still, each one of us grappling with the news.

Mom was the first to break the uncomfortable silence. "Sheryl? Is Tami...I mean, is she...is this connected...?"

"I don't know why or what it means, but yes, I think it is."

"Yes, it is. He is trying to either lure you out to help save a girl he assumes is your friend, or he plans on killing her and making it look like you are involved. Either way, it does center on you."

The four of us stared at Papa Joe as he shut the front door and made his way back over to the chair. His voice was distant—tired. His gait was unsteady and slow, and when he eased his body into the cushions, he winced in pain. His mocha-colored skin looked ashy and a thin sheen of sweat coated his sunken face. The wrinkles on his brow seemed to have doubled in mere seconds, along with the strands of gray in his hair. The temperature in the cramped living room shot up—worse than the steam room at the gym. My skin prickled as sweat appeared all over me, and it almost hurt to take in a breath. The air felt like it was from a cauldron of hot magma. Each breath brought an overwhelming rush of smells, and my mind spun to process them all. Dad's cologne, Mom's skin lotion, Meemaw's shampoo, Papa Joe's musk, the dust balls under the couch, the dinner in the kitchen, the humidity-thick air from outside, full of night jasmine and gardenias. Then, the scent of the note that sat, untouched, on the small table, slammed into me with the force of a freight train. Heat snaked through my body and smothered my brain. My legs and torso began to shake as rage fueled the fire inside of me, and instinctively, I started to back away from my loved ones.

Run. Now. It's time. Follow her scent—it will lead you to him. Kill him, Sheryl. Do not let Hattak'katos win—or live. And—stay away from your mate. Do not disobey me on this. Go, Little One. Become who you were meant to be. Chi hullo li.

I love you too, Nahu'ala. Chi hullo li, Papa Joe.

Immense sorrow wracked my heart and soul at Papa Joe's words. This would be the last time I saw his face or heard his comforting voice inside my mind. No more would my furry companion snuggle with me under the covers at night, warding off my childish nightmares. No more would I be able to see through his eyes and experience the vivid imagery of his past—or my future. No more would I be the wide-eyed young girl sitting at his feet, learning the ways of my ancestors. The connection we shared would be severed—forever. My family would never be the same. I would never be the same. No life with Dane. No future outside of this place. A choice I didn't want to make but a duty I was unable to ignore.

I let out a gasp of torment as the weight of my changing

world hit me. When I reached the front door, my grief at losing Nahu'ala and my former life reached its peak. The volcanic pyre inside me exploded. The tears behind my eyes burned away as uncontrollable fury barreled through my body. The shocked gasps from my family were barely audible as the growl erupted from my burning throat. The decibel level was so loud it made the entire house shake, knocking pictures and knickknacks from the shelves across the room. My fingers clamped down on the door handle as the power surged through me. In one swift motion, I ripped the entire door from the frame, tossed it to the floor, and bounded out into the darkness, oblivious to the panicked voices of my family behind me.

I left my house as Sheryl Ilene Newcomb and wondered if I would never come back as her again—if I came back at all.

Just like my previous run, I fled through the darkness with powerful strides, my breath even and steady. White hot energy coursed through me as my feet ate up the road in front of me. Though after midnight, the world around me seemed sharp and clear. Even things on my periphery—impossible for me to see—I noticed while I navigated the quiet streets of Junction City. A surge of adrenaline pressed my muscles harder, and they responded without hesitation. Never, in my whole life, had I ever moved so fast or been full of such consuming anger and soul-crushing sadness. My bare feet seemed to make little contact with the ground with each step. Every odor of the city invaded my nostrils, but I pushed them all away until I caught the one I was looking for—Tami's.

When I passed the edge of Maple Street and made the turn toward the high school parking lot, Tami's scent slammed into me. The obnoxious odor of her wretched perfume and her personal musk was unmistakable, and it reached out and wound around me like a thick cord, snuffing out all my lamenting over my former life. My legs pumped even faster, and I covered the two mile journey toward the school at a frantic pace, my hair billowing out behind me like a silky, damp mane. I sensed it was too late and that I wouldn't find Tami alive, but I had no choice but to try.

I had to find Hattak'katos and stop him—no matter what.

Even from the distance, I heard the commotion in the parking lot and the woods as the searchers and the dogs navigated the area. Bright floodlights stationed at various spots in the parking lot cast their yellow beams into the dark forest behind the school. The sound of dogs yapping as they tried to find Tami's scent and lead their masters to her intermingled with the shouts from the people calling out Tami's name as they trudged through the dense underbrush. In my furious state, spurred on by the animal growing inside me, I had forgotten about not only the people but the dogs. If they caught a whiff of my scent...

Right when the thought hit me, my body responded and veered sharply to my right. My taut muscles contracted and my body jumped over the Shotwell's privacy fence, clearing it by almost ten feet. Less than five long strides later, flanking the backside of the school property, I ran away from the dogs and searchers. My legs took me to the opposite end of Caney Creek. The light breeze shifted and thankfully masked my scent from the dogs but brought the pungent smells of the inner forest to me. Again, I pushed all the competing aromas away and searched to find the link to Tami's. When I did, I slowed my pace down a fraction. Her scent was rancid now—tinged with the putrid aroma of death. The bitter, coppery flavor of her dead blood cells invaded my nose and mouth. My lips curled back in disgust at the stench.

I was deep in the woods. The rays of the moon bathed the forest floor in shimmering silver, making the path vivid and almost inviting for a moonlight stroll. In the distance, the noise of the search party and their canine companions started to fade as they tromped through the woods in the opposite direction. A twinge of satisfaction at my superior sense of smell over the mongrels almost made me smile, but too much was at stake for me to embrace the pettiness of it. Like a quiet fog covering the forest floor, my body was in stealth mode as I navigated the woods. As the stench of Tami's remains grew stronger, I made my feet slow down until I was at a quick trot. Something made the hairs on the back of my neck and my arms shoot straight up. I stopped moving and stood frozen in mid-stride, reaching out with all my senses to detect the reason for my internal alarm sounding. I was so deep into the woods, I no longer heard the voices of the search party or the yelps of the dogs. My eyes scanned the area and about forty yards ahead of me and to my right, I saw what was left of poor Tami. But that wasn't the reason my hackles were on high alert.

It was the silence. The woods were coated in a death shroud of nothingness. No animal chatter, no bird chirps, no small feet scurrying through the underbrush, not even a rustle of a lone leaf. Which meant only one thing.

A predator was close.

I ignored the stink of Tami's remains, tilted my head up, and took in a deep breath through my nose. My heart thundered in my chest when three distinct, familiar smells hit me. It took every ounce of effort I had to keep my lips closed and the roar of anger at bay because I was bombarded with the aromas of Barb, Dane, and the god-awful stench I'd followed the day before—the one I now understood belonged to my newly acquired enemy—Hattak'katos.

My body instantly slid down into a crouch, my back plastered against a small fir tree. The only thing that moved on me was my eyes as they searched the terrain for any signs of movement. I strained my ears, hoping to detect the slightest noise. For nearly thirty seconds, the only thing I heard was the sound of my blood pounding in my veins and my short intakes of breath. Then, the faintest sound tickled my ears and I struggled to grasp what it was. When I finally recognized it, my blood ran cold.

It was the sound of chunks of flesh being ripped from a body.

On autopilot, my body moved me closer to the disgusting sound. It originated several hundred yards in front of me, well past the corpse of Tami. Without the need to look, my feet carried me with silent footfalls, instincts allowing me to sidestep any debris that would give away my approach. Out of my peripheral vision, I cringed at the mangled, disemboweled body of Tami and continued forward, my breath held to conceal my presence. In less than one minute, my eyes focused on my quarry.

The sounds were louder now, the grunts from the effort of tearing flesh from bone unmistakable. It hadn't sensed me yet since I was still downwind. My mouth, which had been dry as the proverbial bone before, over-flowed with thick, wet saliva. How the thing didn't hear my thudding heart was simply a miracle.

The black cat in front of me was gargantuan. The head was nearly twice the size of Nahu'ala's, the fur-covered torso at least two feet longer. It had paws the size of basket-balls and a mouth big enough to swallow my head in one gulp. A few slivers of the moon's rays glinted off its back. I saw the muscles under its coat undulating as it clung onto its prey with its two front feet. In horror, I watched it lower its head again and tear an enormous chunk of leg muscle off. It flung its head and tossed the wet mess to the side almost thirty feet away. The mass landed with a heavy *thud* less than ten feet from my position in the trees. When the pile of flesh connected with the ground, my stomach rolled.

Because I recognized the odor.

It was Barb's.

In that split second, my mind ablaze with hot fury and bone-crushing sorrow, I changed. At the exact moment, the recognition Hattak'katos killed Barb and was ripping her apart, piece by piece, every fiber in my being began to vibrate. The horrid image in front of me was suddenly replaced by an intense white light. Two blazing orbs of soul-penetrating gold rushed toward me, and then I felt him.

My totem had come. The spirit, the essence, the *force*, of Nahu'ala covered me in an invisible shroud. It barreled through my body and mind, encasing me with his strength, knowledge, and wisdom of the ages and molded itself in every part. The instant the connection was made—the bonds forever ingrained inside of me—the electrical, mystical linking was complete. As the power surged through my body, I threw my head back and let the roar of what I was rip out of me. The deafening shriek reverberated through the empty forest. In the blink of an eye, I realized I was on all fours, my visual trajectory several feet higher than before—and much clearer.

There was no pain, only an overwhelming sensation of intense heat. No odd contorting of my flesh as I turned from human to beast. I felt the presence of Nahu'ala in my mind, but as a companion, a part of me, rather than an intruding entity. Though the voice of my beloved Papa Joe didn't speak to me, his guidance was felt with each movement of my limbs. Controlling my new form was no different than when I was on two legs, but it happened without a nudge or thought. The sinewy muscles of my haunches tightened, and I burst from my position in the tree line. Another loud roar shattered the stillness of the night as I landed less than three feet from Hattak'katos.

He was ready for me. He'd backed away from Barb's limp corpse and was crouched low, his rope-like tail straight in the air and his ears flat against his bulky skull. The black skin around his muzzle was pulled back, exposing his pink gums and glaring white fangs that dripped with blood. His eyes were emerald green orbs that sparkled with anger and the hunger of hate. I felt the vibrations under the pads of my paws from his deep, guttural rumble. The stench of Barb's blood and bowels paled in comparison from the horrendous odor that wafted from him. Not only did he reek of death and carnage, but the slightest hint of fear exuded from him.

Though he was much larger than I was, I felt no fear. My newfound body pulsed and vibrated, waiting to unleash the otherworldly power that flowed through it and tear the bastard into tiny shreds. I licked my lips in anticipation and responded back to his growl with one of my own. We danced in slow motion around each other, our steps silent on the soft grass. When my own snarl left my mouth, flecks of heavy spittle followed, dripping off the ends of my six-inch long fangs. Right when my body tensed to attack, he did the unthinkable—he took his eyes off of mine for a split second. They moved in a quick burst to his right. I was unable to stop my own from following. When I saw what he was looking at, I roared in agony. Because it was Dane's limp body, resting in a crumpled heap against a tree less than twenty yards away, blood oozing from a large wound on his head.

Before I realized it, I was in midair. My paws stretched out in front of me. My sheathed claws sprang forth, and I growled with delight as they found their mark. They sunk deep into the flesh of his shoulders, followed by my fangs clamping down at the base of his neck. Thick, bitter blood filled my mouth while my teeth drove deeper. His furry body jerked in response. He was much stronger than I was. Before I had a chance to tighten my grip, I realized we had rolled over several times. His heavy body pinned me to the ground, his weight crushing the air from my lungs.

Pain tore through my left flank as his mouth latched onto my side. In agony, I shook my head from side to side, unwilling to let go of the mouthful of his flesh. Suddenly, the pressure in my jaws rescinded as his nasty flesh ripped free from his body. Hot blood sprayed from the gaping wound all over my whiskers and jowls, followed by a shrill scream of pain from his lips. He rocked back and, in a flash, was off me. I pulled in a huge breath of the damp night air. I twisted my body and was upright again, ignoring the throbbing injury to my side. I hunched down again, ready to pounce, but before I could, he turned and ran. I was less than a second behind him. We bounded through the forest as I gave chase, nipping at his heels with my fangs and swiping at his rump with my paws. His speed took me by surprise, and though I tried to keep up his pace, he put distance between the two of us and was gone.

My sense of triumph at vanquishing the monster, at least temporarily, was short lived. I ducked and swung back toward the glen to Dane's side. Before my battle with Hattak'katos began, I sensed my love's blood still ran through his veins. He was still alive, and I had to get him to safety before the bloodthirsty creature came back to finish him off.

With a groan of anguish, I pushed my muscles to their limit and bounded through the woods until I was at Dane's side again. Though still unconscious, his breathing was strong and steady. A dark trickle of thick, red blood oozed out from the side of his head and had soaked into the cotton of his white T-shirt. I stuck my muzzle down closer and almost recoiled from the scent of not only Barb's but Tami's blood intermingled on his body. Dirt, leaves, and debris littered his clothes, his exposed knees and elbows full of cuts and deep scrapes. The bastard had drug Dane on the ground and covered his body with the blood of my friends! My growl of anger made my entire body shudder. I was overwhelmed with intense rage and bone-crushing love at the same time. I understood why Papa Joe had taken Nana to the Tree of Living Waters. The thought of living in a world without my mate, my beautiful Dane, tore my soul to shreds.

I suppressed the rage and leaned my head down and gently began to clean the blood from his face and neck, making sure to control the intensity of my licks as I neared the gaping cut on his head. Being this close to him, seeing him hurt because of *me*, made me want to cry, but that was impossible. Instead, my own sorrow came out as a purr while I washed the stains away from my love's injury.

Dane needed stitches, and I didn't know for sure whether Hattak'katos would return or not. My new instincts told me he wouldn't since I had inflicted some heavy damage to his body. What I did know was I had to get Dane to safety, for this wasn't his battle to fight. It was mine. And I vowed to never let him be put in danger again, no matter how much it would hurt to sever all my ties to him. If that's what it took to keep him safe, then so be it. I understood Papa Joe's warning from before to stay away from Dane because the intensity of my love for him was much greater since my transformation into beast. It clouded my judgment, and I needed to focus all of my con-centration on catching—and killing—Hattak'katos.

Dane's blood tasted like sweet nectar and rancid milk at the same time. It repulsed me and drew me to it with equal intensity. It was a part of him I was unable to experi-ence when not in this form—and one that I wouldn't want to. Though his scent, his aura, was already imprinted in my soul, his crimson life force was now part of me. The last lick was slow and long as my tongue wandered down his neck and traced the bulge of his biceps. My purring became louder and I feared being heard, so I shoved my head under his arm and tried to scoot his body onto my back. It didn't work, and he just slumped further down in the dirt.

I heard it then—the sound of the search party. The baying of the freaking dogs, their barks incessant and loud as they caught either Hattak'katos's scent, Tami's, my own, or all three. I had to leave, right then, and get Dane to safety. I couldn't leave him in the same vicinity as Barb and Tami's bodies. He was covered in their blood and would be a suspect—that is, until they realized a human being wasn't capable of the kind of damage done to them. Or even worse—next in line for death. I thought about turning back, but not only wouldn't that help, but I was unsure as to how to change back into human form. I could probably muster all my strength to lift Dane into the upright position, but there was no way I could carry his heavy weight through the woods before we got caught. And there would simply be no way to explain what we were doing out here near the corpses of two of our friends. Period.

No choice. The dogs were getting closer. I bent my head down, clamped my jaws as gently as possible around Dane's torso, lifting him off the ground. It took a few seconds to secure him so my fangs didn't pierce his skin, but I finally got him situated. I broke into an easy trot, testing myself to make sure I wasn't hurting him. As I passed by Barb's carcass, the low rumble in my chest hissed out of me when I saw what Hattak'katos had done to her.

I had to force myself not to drop him and go find the monster when I noticed he'd carved S I N into her chest with his claws. My once lovely friend was no more than a pile of shredded flesh, her wet blood all over the floor of the forest rather than inside her. The urge, the *pull*, was so strong, it felt like my brain would explode if I didn't heed it and barge through the night until I found the black beast. It wasn't until I heard Dane let out a low groan that my focus shifted back on him. Hearing my mate in pain persuaded my body to remain on its current path.

He's gonna pay for that. Oh, yes—with his life.

On silent paws I carried my love, shrouded under the

canopy of darkness. I was thankful clouds had rolled in and hidden the moon's rays. I veered off the path and waded into the shallow, murky waters of Caney Creek to mask my scent. I made my way back to Dane's house, my padded feet making no sound as I moved. My heart was heavy with sadness, but my new body was full of power and energy.

Once I deposited Dane and ensured he was safe, I had planning to do.

And a monster to kill.

A grumble so low it wouldn't have registered in the ears of humans thrummed through me as I thought, *Takes one to find one.*

CHAPTER SEVENTEEN

PART THREE – THE SHOWDOWN

"Ain't nothin' like this ever happened 'fore. Least not that I've ever heard tell of."

"I overheard Deputy Pryor talkin' to the state police on his whatchamacallit..."

"It's a CB radio, dearie. So, what did you hear?"

"Well, he said them girls was all tore up. Poor ol' Tami didn't have no face left! They only knew it was her because of her little one's name tattooed on her left shoulder, and she was in her cheerin' uniform. Well, what was left of it. And sweet lil' Barbie—not only did somethin' eat parta her, it left claw marks in her chest. Accordin' to Deputy Pryor, looked like the word *sin*."

The other two old nags at the corner booth gasped in shock at the words of Tana Skaggs, wife of the Prosecuting Attorney Jerome Skaggs. She had somehow crammed her huge ass between the edges of the tabletop and the seat, blabbing away with the sheriff's wife, Heather, and Naomi, wife of the criminal attorney, Chris Williams. Their usual gabfest foursome had been whittled down to a trio, since Nanette, Mayor Ransford's wife, was holed up at home. Barb's parents hadn't left their house in days except to attend their daughter's funeral. Nanette and the mayor were destroyed, mourning the loss of their only child. When my family and I stopped by yesterday to drop off some food and pay our respects, Mayor Ransford wouldn't even let us in the door. I heard Ms. Nanette sobbing from inside, her wails of pain stabbed my heart like a hot dagger. Mayor Ransford looked like he'd lost twenty pounds and gained ten years.

I'd known the Ransford family ever since Barb and I were old enough to talk. Countless hours had been spent at her house over the years, and though I didn't care much for Mrs. Ransford's gossipy ways, my heart broke for both of them. We left in a hurry after mumbling our condolences. I was afraid of what might happen next. My new capabilities were not fully under my control just yet. It seemed extreme emotions were the major cause of my shifting abilities. Had we stayed any longer, I feared I would change. Right in front of Mayor Ransford's bulging eyes. Then my head would be mounted on the wall as a trophy after he blew a hole through me with his ever-present shotgun.

My mind and heart were still numb after attending three funerals in the same amount of days. Tami's was difficult and tugged at the heartstrings of all in attendance. Lil' Drexel cried and cried for his momma, but his whimpers went unanswered. Barb's was horrific. Had Dane and my family not been by my side, I would never have been able to keep my emotions in check. My heart physically ached, knowing her death was on my shoulders. The last one, Papa Joe's, broke my spirit and left my senses dulled and my soul a worthless pile of mush.

I tried to ignore the Gossip Queens like I usually did, but it was an impossible task. Between the topic of their conversation, along with my newly acquired hearing, I couldn't. I refused to look their direction, afraid I wouldn't be able to hold my tongue, or my form. Out of my peripheral vision, I watched the looks of feigned shock and concern coat their faces, unable to hide their sheer delight in spreading their nasty gossip. Even though I wasn't watching them directly, my eyes took in every nuance, every movement of the old skanks. All of my concentration was on wiping the water spots off the drinking glasses and setting them in their trays. I wasn't doing a very good job at that either. I'd already busted three. A wicked smirk crossed my face at the mental image of me smashing the glasses into their flapping lips.

"Don't that beat all! Surely Raymond's mistaken? I mean, it was what, sometime after midnight when they found them? Maybe it was just his imagination after traipsin' 'round those scary woods for so long," Heather offered as she wiped away a dribble of coffee from her thin lips.

"Heather, y'all forget that I was out there, too, helpin' the men search..."

"Girl, don't even start. Y'all was servin' up water and coffee to them boys and nothin' else. Y'all wouldn't set a pinky toe on anythin' that ain't covered in carpet, tile, or hardwood."

"Heather! This ain't no time to be so rude—especially to a friend! Our town's lost so much in such a short time. We all are grievin', and petrified of what hairy beast is roamin' in our backyards, waitin' and watchin' us from the shadows. And I don't recall seein' *you* out there at all that night. At least I was tryin' to do *somethin'* to help. But now is the time that we band together and stand strong, not try to hurt each other," Tana whined, sounding genuinely hurt by her friend's remark. If I wasn't in such a foul mood, I would have laughed at the pathetic look on her face. "Let me finish my story! So I was *out* there that night..."

"We got that part, Tana," Heather shot back, motioning with her hands for Tana to hurry up and unleash some more juicy bits of horror as she stuffed a huge wad of pound cake in her face. I doubted she even tasted the lemon zest before she gulped it down. "And, by the way, I *was* helpin'. I was out at the Kilgore place, keepin' an eye on lil' Drexel. Poor Ms. Greta was so wound up, she weren't good for nothin' but wearin' holes in her shoes with all her pacin'."

"Okay, so let's just say we *all* were doin' our parts to help out? Agreed?" Tana said, watching her fellow hags nod in agreement. "Good...good. Okay, so there was a lot of yellin' and screamin', dogs barkin', and people runnin' 'round like chickens with no heads. It was crazy! Raymond was the first one back to his unit, outta breath and pale as Aunt Betty's backside in the middle of winter. I was servin' coffee off the trunk of his car. Don't think he noticed me though. He snatched up his radio and started yappin'. Told the State boys to bring in more help and started tellin' what they'd found. Asked for more dogs and such, 'cause whatever got those two girls was big. Said Barbara's body had claw marks on it that almost looked like they spelled *sin*."

"That's the craziest thing I've ever heard. Period. So what now, Tana? The bear, or wolf, or whatever critter killed them poor girls, evolved enough to write? Sheer nonsense."

"Like I said, ol' *Raymond* said that, not me. I'm just..."

Mom stormed out from the kitchen and exploded. "You're just sittin' here, talkin' about the dead, God rest their souls. Y'all sound like a bunch of crowin' ravens in an ol' maple tree at the graveyard. And y'all call yourselves women of faith and friends of poor Nanette. It's shameful, and there ain't no room for it in my diner. Our town is in *mournin'* for the loss of three invaluable residents, and y'all act like it's just another day to flap your gums and spread your venom! Cake's all gone and coffee's cold, so I think it's time for y'all to go grouse somewhere else. Ladies, don't let the door hit you on the way out."

I wanted to shout, *way to go, Mom!* from my spot behind the counter. Instead, I kept quiet. In one quick swoop, as three sets of bugged-out eyes and gaping mouths looked on, Mom cleared the table of coffee cups and plates. She never said another word, but her eyes looked as though a fire burned behind them. All three women remained silent, unaccustomed to being addressed in such a manner by *anyone*, let alone my sweeter-than-apple-pie mother, and practically fell over each other as they scrambled up from the booth. They waddled as fast as their chunky legs would let them out the front door, the bell clanging inside the quiet diner.

"For the love of all that's holy, those women's parents should be ashamed for not takin' a switch to their backsides enough when they were young. Mercy! No couth, no grace, and certainly no hearts."

I set the last glass down and walked around the counter to help Mom clean up the rest of the table. Other than the soft whir from the three ceiling fans and the hum of the large refrigerator, the diner was deathly silent. The crowing harpies had been our only customers all day. The rest of our town's inhabitants seemed to understand even though the sign on the diner said *Open*, the loss of Papa Joe would be a heavy burden for my family. Each of us hoped as we unlocked the back door and entered the stuffy kitchen at the crack of dawn earlier, no one would show up to eat. The thought of cooking or waiting tables seemed rather empty and hollow.

"Mom, here, let me," I said, taking the tray full of dirty dishes from her. She smiled softly, but it didn't make it past her lips. Her blue eyes overflowed with a myriad of emotions. The skin around them was still puffy and swollen from heavy bouts of crying. The lines on her face seemed thicker, deeper. Her skin looked as fragile as origami paper and wisps of her blonde curls had escaped her braid and stuck up every which way. She looked as though a wave of electricity had shocked her. Without uttering a word, she let me take the heavy tray from her trembling hands. She stood there, staring out the picture window and into the empty street. She looked so frail my heart ached.

Meemaw walked out from the kitchen and made a bee-line for her daughter's side. "Darlin', don't you let them get to you. We've got enough on our plates. Don't need to add their heapin' pile of ugliness to them. That's just the way some folks are. Hateful and mean."

"Meemaw's right. Ignore them. Come on," I murmured, motioning with my head toward the kitchen. "Let me go fix you a stout cup of coffee."

Mom and Meemaw's gentle footsteps followed in sync behind my own. Soon, the three Kovlin women were huddled in the kitchen and sipping hot coffee in the odd

silence. It was strange to be in the diner during the breakfast rush and not hear all the normal sounds. No calling
out of orders. No *cha-ching* from the cash register. No
plates and cups clacking together. No good mornings or
hellos shouted across the room as patrons greeted their
neighbors. No fry top sizzling while bacon and sausage
popped and sputtered. No Papa Joe humming in the back-
ground, his aged body moving faster than it should have
been capable of as he prepared mountain-high stacks of
food with uncanny ease.

It hurt my heart more than I could ever express, and I
couldn't imagine what it had done to Mom and Meemaw.
Papa Joe had been a part of their lives way longer than he
had been mine. His sudden departure, along with everything else, left each of us sort of empty. Like old corn
husks left in the fields after the summer harvest, we were
dry, alone, and shells of our former selves. Everything
seemed skewed, like we all had been magically transported
into an alternate universe or something.

Well, one of us had been, and the trip affected everyone.

"I hate to see my girls with such long faces," Dad said
from the back door. He had been as quiet as a mouse and
Mom and Meemaw jumped at the sound of his voice. Mom
busied herself by wiping her coffee from her shirt. I just
smiled since I heard him before he even put the car in park.
It was very strange having such sensitive hearing.

Yeah, like that is the only strange thing...

"You missed it, Dad. Mom told the Gossip Queens to
take a hike. Shoulda' seen their faces. Priceless."

Dad set his coffee mug and keys on the edge of the back
sink. We all watched him walk over and peek through the
opening above the grill. He winced when he noticed we

had no customers. "No women deserve to be put in their place more, that's for sure. Have they been our only payin' customers today?"

"Yes. But don't you worry none. Now that all the funerals are over, people will come back," Meemaw offered, hoping to ease Dad's financial worries.

In a huff, Mom slammed her coffee mug on the counter, and I heard the faint sound of a crack as the ceramic met the metal. "How can you worry about money at a time like this, Jared?"

"Jolene, do you really think cash flow is what's botherin' me? Seriously? After all that's happened?" A small tear slid out of the corner of Mom's eye, which she quickly brushed away.

"Stop it, you two. Squabblin' amongst each other ain't gonna help our situation none."

"We shouldn't have opened today. We just said goodbye to Papa Joe yesterday. It ain't right. We loved him! We needed more time to mourn and to soak all this other mess up," Mom said, waving her hand in my direction. Her words hit me as hard as if she'd slapped me in the face.

"Jolene..."

"Jared, if you want to stay here and sling hash for the ghosts out there, be my guest. Me? I'm goin' home. Don't have it in me today to keep my manners straight. Next customer who comes in here and says one negative word about *anythin'*, is gonna get a plate thrown at them. And that just ain't right."

Before any of us said a word, Mom turned and stomped out the back door. The three of us watched as her feet ate up the pavement, her back ramrod straight and head held high. Bearings finally back after listening to her unusual outburst, I started to go after her. Dad caught me by my arm. "Sheryl, let her go."

"But Dad..."

"Come now, darlin'. She's had a lot thrust on her in a very short time. We all have. Plus, she's a mother, and I'm sure it's eatin' her up on the inside about Barbara. Not only was she like another daughter to us..." Dad said, the last words heavy with emotion. He cleared his throat to rid himself of the pain before he continued, "...she could have been you. And that, as a parent, is the greatest fear of all. When you add all the other shockin' events, it's no wonder she's havin' a tough go of it."

I bristled and tried to control my anger. I yanked my arm free and walked to the front and locked the door. Over my shoulder, I yelled, "Oh, yes, this is the direction I wanted my life to take. I had plans! Now they're nothin' more than a blip in my memory. Because I'm stuck with this duty...no, this *curse*! Trapped in this sweaty, armpit of the South, doomed to roam and keep watch over sacred freakin' magical trees and water. Yeah, Mom ain't the only one with a lot to deal with!" I shouted as I turned the lock on the door. In my anger, I ripped the metal knob off. In a funk, I just stared at it in my shaking hands.

Dandy. Catwoman breaks everything she touches.

"Sheryl, honey..." Meemaw started.

I cut her off. I swung around and exploded. "Papa Joe is *dead* because of me! He died so he could transfer this flippin' infection. Yeah, I said 'infection' because that's what it is to me—an unwanted disease. Don't you get it, Meemaw? Your father is gone because of me! Dane is home recuperatin' from a concussion because of me, and Papa Joe said I have to stay away from him because he's a danger to me. How can that be? I'm the one who's a danger to others! And let's not forget poor Tami and Barb. Ripped to pieces and gnawed on like a stack of ribs *to get to me!* They all died because inside me lives a monster. Now, some unholy creature, some ancient evil thing, is callin' me out to a duel by goin' after the people I care about. And I've got no clue as to how to defeat him since I can't ask Papa Joe for advice anymore. Can't even pray to the Lord because He won't listen. I'm tainted with evil now. I truly am sin, so God isn't goin' to help me. I'm on my own in this battle. How am I supposed to deal with all that? How am I supposed to act normal when things are so unbelievably *abnormal?*"

Dad stared with his mouth agape from the doorway of the kitchen. Meemaw ignored my tirade and started to walk my way, her arms outstretched, ready to embrace me. I wanted nothing more than to run to her and melt inside her warm hugs. I yearned to be able to close my eyes and drift off to sleep as she whispered a sweet lullaby in my ears like she used to when I was a child.

Instead, I backed away and held my hand up to stop her. White-hot energy flowed through my limbs, the faint buzzing inside my mind a warning. My entire body began to quake and, God help me, I welcomed the sensation of the intense, raw power. I yearned to stand on four legs and let the mighty muscles contract, moving me away from the pain. To succumb to the temptation of the beast inside, urging me to disappear and let it take over. The change was coming, and I was powerless to control it. "Don't...come any closer," I whispered. My words were low, deep. "I don't know how much longer I can hold it in."

Meemaw never batted an eyelash, never hesitated or faltered. Her luminous eyes shimmered with love and kindness, not one blip of fear behind them. She reached me and wrapped her arms around me and pulled me into her chest. "Shh, girl. Breathe. Deep and easy. I'm here. We're all here, and we always will be. You aren't in this battle alone, Sheryl. And the Lord above has not forsaken you! He has endowed you with a great gift, and He will always listen to you, just like we will. Now, concentrate on love, not hate. That's it, listen to the sound of my voice and relax."

"I'm losin' my mind, Meemaw," I whimpered into her chest. "I can't believe they're gone. One minute I want to curl into a ball and cry until I dry up and blow away. The next, I'm ready to change and stalk the furry bastard to the ends of the earth and slaughter him for all the evil things he's done. No one deserves to die like Barb and Tami did, or all the people throughout the centuries the bastard is responsible for killing. No one. Except him."

"Everyone feels those things when someone they love dies, my dear. Especially when their death ain't a natural, normal way of passin'. When death comes from evil hands, it makes the wound in our heart even greater. Been happenin' since Cain slew Abel, my precious one. Man's flesh is sinful, but the soul can be reborn and made pure."

"Mine can't. I'm doomed."

Meemaw hugged me tighter. "Never you mind talkin' like that, child. Don't let the evil win you over. Submit yourself to the love...the light. Come on; let's go talk. It's high time we sit down and talk this out, like families are supposed to. Shoulda' done this sooner. We've all been selfishly wrapped inside our own minds, dealin' with a bushel full of strange happenin's. Once all the cards are on the table, so to speak, we can help you figure out what needs to happen next. Jared? It's time to close up shop and go home. We *all* need to be a part of this."

Exhausted mentally and physically, I let Meemaw lead me to the kitchen. The electrical hum inside me waned as I clung on to her words. I prayed she was right. Dad pulled himself out of his stupor and bustled about the kitchen and turned off all the equipment. Once finished, he smiled at me, his eyes full of love, compassion, and confusion. Without saying a word, he reached over and hugged us both, pulling us into a tight ball. Though I tried to fight them, the tears arrived, so I let them roll.

CHAPTER EIGHTEEN

Five hours later, vocal chords dry and worn out from talking, I watched the three most important people in my life from my spot on the couch. The air and the room had started out tinged with apprehension and dread but had turned stagnant and quiet. Dad stared out the picture window, his tired eyes focused on the vibrant blue sky. I wondered if he was wishing he could just sprout wings and soar away. Mom, who hadn't said much during my long, drawn out story, was busy studying the inside of her coffee cup. It looked like she was trying to figure out how to maneuver her body around and crawl inside so she could drift away in the caffeinated liquid. Meemaw was chewing on the edge of her thumbnail, a habit she did when nervous. At the rate she was going, her thumb would be nothing but bloody nubs in seconds.

"You know, I keep thinkin' I'm dreamin', and any moment the alarm clock will buzz and wake me up."

"I know, Dad. Believe me, I know."

Dad turned away from the window with a shrug of his shoulders. He seemed to dismiss his misgivings and accept his new reality with the movement. He put both hands on his knees with the palms down and fingers splayed wide and sighed. "But it ain't. So we can't keep treatin' it like it is. Though tough to swalla', we are all part of some-thin' magical. Truly mystic. And I won't tolerate any more negative comments from you, Sheryl, or anyone else in this house. You aren't cursed. Or infected. You're blessed, which means we all are."

"He's right, child. Blessed and given a gift from above. You were chosen by the Lord Himself to keep order in the world as guardian of sacred things. Ain't very many people who get to say that and it be true!"

The weight of my new life seemed to lighten at the words of Dad and Meemaw. I didn't say a peep in response, and neither did the two of them. All of our attention focused on Mom, waiting to hear her thoughts. The sec-onds passed like slow moving thunderclouds in the dis-tance. The wait seemed like years.

The struggle to control her emotions was intense. Her jaw was clenched tight; the muscles in her face twitched with each breath. She blinked several times and swallowed hard, forcing the tears back down inside of her. I don't think she was aware of it when her left hand wandered up to her neck. She clutched the tiny silver cross in her fingers, and as she did, I saw the change in her. Her body went from slumped dejection to stiffened resolve. She took a slow, deep breath, and it seemed to fill her deflated heart with strength. Finally, she looked up from her mug and straight at me.

"Yes, my daughter has found favor with the Lord. And

I'm sorry, Sheryl. I didn't grasp the enormity of what this means for you. I...was sort of lost in my own painful dilemmas, which ain't right. A mother's biggest fear is losin' a child and feelin' like she failed them some way. Shame and humiliation consumes mothers when they realize they wasn't there to protect their children when needed. But I don't fear that anymore. I know He watches over you in a way I've never experienced before. I knew it in my mind, but now, I feel it here." Mom let go of the cross and moved her hand over her heart. "And your meemaw is right—by extension, we are all blessed. In some small way, I understand how Mary must have felt when she realized what her son's role in this world would be. Lettin' go and lettin' God is easy to say, but difficult to put into actions sometimes."

The last heavy brick fell away from my chest. "I don't know how I would get through this without all of you."

Mom rose from her spot and motioned for the rest of us to do the same. We met in the middle for a big group hug. I drew strength from the love of my family and their willingness to accept the unacceptable. The stagnant air from before vanished, replaced with the warmth of our love for each other.

Dad pulled away first. "I'm famished. Let's head to the kitchen and sort the rest of the things out while we fix lunch. Ain't none of us able to think straight with empty gas tanks."

Mom laughed for the first time in days. "Jared, you are the livin' epitome of the expression, 'the way to a man's heart is through his stomach.'"

"I am too. I could eat a horse." All three of them stared at me for a moment, the looks on their faces hysterical. "Don't worry. I'm not the 'livin' epitome' of that expression. Geez, I was kiddin'."

"Well, excuse us, little missy. You forget we don't really understand too much about your, um, predilections, when you...oh, gosh, what do I call it? Morph?"

Loud cackles burst out of me as we entered the kitchen. I nearly ran into the doorframe from laughing so hard. "Morph? Mom, I'm not a Power Ranger!"

"I can't help it. Just popped into my head. I mean, when you were little, you used to run around the house and yell *mighty morphin' power rangers*, and they changed forms too, right?"

"Oh, yeah, she did! And didn't she have a pink costume or somethin'?" Meemaw chimed in.

My cheeks were on fire. "Okay, really? Can we forget the fact I ever watched that show and had some strange fascination with the characters? Please? By the way, the correct term is skin-walk."

Meemaw, busy gathering fruits and veggies from the fridge and arranging them on a plate at the table, interjected. "Skin-walk. I like the sound of that. Much better than shape-shiftin' or morphin'. I mean, you are walkin' in the skin of another. Sort of."

Mom rolled her eyes and began fixing sandwiches. She handed Dad the bacon and he turned on the stove and began to fry it. "I still can't believe Papa Joe was over three hundred years old! And we are all part Choctaw. Ain't none of us look it."

"Aww, come on now, Mom. All three of us may have fair complexions, but in the summer, our skin gets dark, and we don't burn. And in the winter, all of our hair darkens to a dirty blonde. We all have high cheekbones and thick hair. Guess Nana's genes were stronger in the outward features department than Papa Joe's."

"Another good thing about all of this is we can stop

thinkin' Nana's cup was half-empty. Huh, isn't that ironic? She knew all along, and we were the blind ones." Meemaw's slender fingers brushed a straggler tear as it slid down her face at her statement. I sensed the guilt she felt, we all felt, from all the years we assumed Nana was nuttier than a Christmas fruitcake.

To break the tension, I snatched a few pieces of raw bacon away from Dad and gave him a wicked smile as I shoved them into my mouth. "Yum."

"Sheryl! Yuck!"

"At least we're laughin' instead of freakin' out."

"Time of doubts and disbelief are over, my dear. We need to concentrate on what we know and work toward figurin' out what we don't. And in a hurry before another from our community dies."

"Your mom's right, Sheryl. So...any ideas who this Hat'ta..ha ta...oh, what's his name again?"

I laughed at Dad's butchering of the name. "Hat-tak'katos."

"Yeah, okay. So do you?"

I took in a heavy breath and plopped down on the kitchen chair closest to my father. "Not really. I mean, I sensed his presence in the woods the other day and, of course, fought with him in my other form, but he was in his as well. I caught the same stench and followed it to the Cohestra plant a few days ago. I didn't know it then, but it was the same, foul smellin' odor. All I knew at the time was the scent revved me up into a wicked frenzy."

"What do you mean?" Meemaw queried.

"I...I don't know how to explain it, Meemaw. Really. Not with words. It was like I tasted, felt, and smelled anger. It took complete and total control of me and my body. It was just one giant, overpowerin' urge to follow the smell and kill him when I found him. It pushed everythin' else out of the way."

Meemaw lowered herself into the chair next to me, her warm hand covering my own. "Sheryl, do you have all the same abilities as Papa Joe? I mean, can you control other's minds like he did to Ms. Johnson and Sheriff Gilmore?"

I stuttered and averted my eyes from hers. "No clue. I've...never tried." I hung my head in shame at my lack of knowledge of all my new gifts. After I deposited Dane's unconscious body on his back porch three days ago, I watched from the woods until his mother found him and drove him to the hospital. I didn't remember much after that until I woke up in my bed. It was almost twenty-four hours later. I had been covered in dirt from head to toe and felt like a grain silo had fallen over on me. Every muscle ached, and my head felt like I'd been on a five day drunk. Then, dealing with Papa Joe's death and all the fallout from Barb and Tami's left me little time to deal with much else.

"What about changin' into a different creature? Like how Papa Joe turned into Tinker? Can you do that?" Meemaw pressed.

Frustrated for some strange reason by Meemaw's questions, I jerked my arm away and stood up. I sighed heavily and looked out the window in the direction of Dane's house. A stab of pain ripped through me when I thought about him. God, I missed him. The pull to see him unnerved me. "I don't know that either. It's only been a few days, and the first night is a blur. I can't really remember much—just glimpses of feelin's, sensations. Splashes of images. Ones I don't want to ever recall." I turned around and faced my family. All three of their worried faces stared at me as they waited on pins and needles for my next words. For a brief second, I envisioned myself standing naked at the front of class, giving a speech on an unfamiliar subject—like foreign policy or Greek literature—to a room full of dumbfounded third graders. "Why do you ask, Meemaw? What are you thinkin'?"

A glint of mischief backlit her blue eyes. Her smile was warm, genuine, and made me feel like a complete and utter ass for my previous thoughts. "Your enemy is expectin' you to hunt him, or at least search for him, as a big cat, right?"

"I suppose..." I offered.

"Then don't give him what he wants, dear. Do your sleuthin' under the cover of somethin' much smaller. Stealthier. It will be harder to pick up on your scent if the trail isn't as large, don't you think?"

I smiled at my Meemaw's devious mind and moved across the floor to hug her neck. "I love the way your mind works, Meemaw."

"Try it, honey. Your mind trick. Let me be the guinea pig, so to speak."

My jaw dropped as I stared at my Dad. He was *serious!*

"Don't look at me like I'm crazy. It's just, well, if you have the ability, shouldn't you test it out on the most stubborn person you know first? I mean, if you can make me believe somethin' or change my mind about somethin', then..."

"Then there will be no mistaken it's a gift from above, all right. Lord knows I've been prayin' for years for him to..."

Dad laughed. "Stop right there, Jolene. Let's keep this civil, shall we?" Mom held her hands up in mock surrender. "Start off with somethin' small, honey."

I moved away from Meemaw and the rest of them to

the doorway. I wouldn't have admitted it out loud, but I worried what would happen when I tried using my abilities. What if, once I tapped into the particular corner of my mind that controlled my body's new skills, I was unable to stop? What if I went from, *Hey, I can control your thoughts!* to *Oops, I just turned into a huge beast and destroyed the house?*

"Come on, baby. It's okay. Concentrate." Meemaw's gentle voice pulled me out of my worried thoughts. I squared my shoulders and focused my eyes on Dad's. I closed my ears to the sounds of the sizzling bacon, the hypnotic *tick tock, tick tock* of the grandfather clock in the hallway. I ignored the collective breath my family was holding and their rapid heartbeats I felt thrum through me. I pushed all other thoughts aside and hung on to just one mundane, trivial item and zeroed in on it. In my mind, I repeated it over and over.

Tell Mom how beautiful she looks in her new pink shirt. Tell Mom how beautiful she looks in her new pink shirt. Tell Mom how beautiful she looks in her new pink shirt.

After the third repetition, an electrical surge shot through my mind and I nearly gasped when it left my body. It shimmered and moved like languid waves of heat above the blacktop in the summer. It crossed the expanse of the kitchen and disappeared when it reached Dad's chest. For a second, I stood frozen, fearing what it would do once it barreled its way inside his body. I wanted to break my gaze with Dad and see if Mom or Meemaw saw the clear burst of energy as well, but I didn't.

Dad's dark blue eyes, surrounded by thick black lashes and full of playful mischief, glazed over. He blinked once, gave an odd nod of his head, and then he looked over at my mom. He spoke in a halting, monotone voice, "Jolene, you look so beautiful in your new pink shirt."

Mom eyed him with curiosity and a coy wink at first as her hands pressed down the wrinkled edges of her vibrant blue T-shirt. "Very funny, Jared."

Dad looked confused. "Givin' my wife a compliment on her new shirt is funny?"

"No, it's just...hmm. You meant my blue shirt, which, by the way, isn't new."

Dad's eyebrows furrowed in irritation. "Jolene, we ain't got time for no games. Sheryl needs to work on her...wait, did you already?"

Meemaw and I both grinned from ear to ear, answering Dad's question. Meemaw picked up her blue coffee mug from the table and held it up. "Jared, what color is this?"

"Blue."

"And what color is Mom's shirt?" I asked, pointing at her.

"Pink."

"Oh, my...it worked!" I yelped, jumping around the kitchen like my feet were stepping on needles. "I did it!"

"Well, I'll be. If I didn't know any better, I'd swear this was a joke. 'Cause your Mom's shirt is pink!"

I flung my arms around Dad's neck and squeezed tight. In his shoulder, I muffled, "Did it hurt?"

"Did what hurt?"

I pulled back and gave him a good once-over. "When it, the energy wave, the force, hit you?"

"I have no idea what you're talkin' about, darlin'."

"Mom? Meemaw? Did you see it? When it left me?"

Both of them shook their heads no.

Dad clapped his hands together and smiled. "Okay, ladies. Enough standin' around waitin'. Let's see what else our little gal here can do."

"I think we should wait until its dark before she tries

the other, Jared. Don't want no pryin' eyes peekin' through the windows now, do we? I still can't grasp it all, and tryin' to explain it to someone else would be impossible."

CHAPTER NINETEEN

I tried to rest. It was a wasted plan. Nervous energy hummed through my mind and body like a car engine pushed to the red line. My fingers hovered over the thick scar on my right flank. I cringed at the knobby indentations from the closed wound. Thinking about how fast the skin healed made me feel weird, like I wasn't a member of the human race any longer. A quiet chuckle left my lips, for I wasn't completely human anymore. I was a real-life *Catwoman*, a freak of nature with numerous abilities, including healing at an accelerated rate. My thumb traced the numb spot, and the sensation brought back the emotions of the night in the woods. It made my head swim in the dark visions I witnessed down by Caney Creek. I jerked my hand away and forced it to remain still in my lap.

My gaze settled at my desk, where my silent computer sat. Earlier, I shut the system down before the urge to throw it out the window overtook me and I succumbed to the pressure. The second I logged on, the screen over-loaded me with notifications. Emails, instant messages, pokes, tweets, you name it—the vibrant screen displayed them all. I thought things would quiet down when I shut the system down but was sorely mistaken. Junction City's underground teen chat app, known as *ChatnSnap*, created by Albert Crittendon, our local geek guru, was installed on the cell phone of everyone under the age of twenty-five in Locasia County, including me. My phone had been inundated with chat notifications from friends and squad mates, all jockeying for my attention. Most wanted to dis-cuss the deaths of Barb and Tami, but some asked me how Dane was doing. The messages were full of pathetic, shal-low questions about how the squad would change now that two slots were open. Things like when we should schedule new tryouts so we could get back on track...the newbies up to speed on the moves. Savannah Richardson even asked our thoughts on how we should announce the tryouts without upsetting the families of Barb and Tami. Should a memorial service for our teammates be held at the school, and if so, when should it be scheduled? Savan-nah insisted we just *had* to do something, otherwise we wouldn't be ready for football season. The ones that really made my blood boil were the thinly veiled questions about how Dane had been hurt. Savannah casually typed, *"Hadn't he gone with Barb to go search for Tami? How come Barb was shredded to pieces, but Dane wasn't?"*

Ugh. It was enough to make me want to puke.

I ignored them all. How could I not? I mean, really. Yes, this was the digital age, and my age group lived and died by their electronic addiction, but text messages about a very sensitive subject matter seemed so *wrong*, so *imper-sonal*. Characters on a screen didn't even come close to truly reflect the feelings inside one's heart. Then again, the hearts of the senders seemed cold as ice, concerned only with trivial, surface-level crap. It seemed to me they were sent to entice more mellow-dramatic, bullshit responses from the recipients. Not one person even hinted at getting together, *in person,* to discuss the matter or to collectively grieve for our dead friends. No one mentioned a word about all of this when we attended the funerals. Nor was there any discussion about the well-known fact that had already burned its way through the town courtesy of the Gossip Queens: a very large animal was responsible for Tami and Barb's deaths, not Dane—or any other human for that matter. Not one. Any other time, I wouldn't have blinked an eye because I had been just as shallow, uncaring about the real truths, the real issues, but now, my perceptions on things had shifted.

These are the people I'm protecting? Why?

It had been twenty minutes since I'd called to check on Dane. Ms. Emma said he was taking a shower, and although she told me she'd have him call me back, I knew she wouldn't. The distant, annoyed tone in her voice spoke volumes. She wouldn't pass along the fact I'd called him. Again. It was the tenth time in two days. Ms. Emma was in full parental protective mode, and who could blame her? Two of his friends died, and he showed up, unconscious and bleeding in their backyard on the same night. Plus, if Dane had been awake and had seen the enormous cat attack him and Barb, and told his mother what he'd witnessed, she probably assumed he was either lying or was suffering from paranoid delusions.

Whether Ms. Emma informed him of my calls or not, I knew my sweet Dane hadn't tried to call me because he probably thought I needed some space to deal with everything. He knew how close I was to Papa Joe and Barb. The entire town did. On the outside, I may have seemed like an effervescent, social diva, but Dane understood me. He'd seen me retreat inside the walls of my own mind when I was upset. But that was the old me. The new me craved his touch, needed to see his face and hold him just one more time. Five minutes to explain to him why the kiss would be our last and the intense, heated lovemaking on his living room floor a few days ago was the final hurrah. I needed a few minutes alone to tell him I wished him well and loved him so much, but he needed to find someone else to share his life with.

I sighed and stared up at the picture of Dane on my nightstand and felt my heart break. I knew I couldn't do that either. He wouldn't just let me walk away without a real, plausible explanation. He'd want to know why, and telling him the truth was out of the question. So I'd have to break it off between the two of us by lying to him. Force myself to stand and look into those beautiful eyes and say the words *"I don't love you anymore, Dane. It's over."* Hurt him by ripping his heart out, stomping it into the ground, and then spitting on top of it. I would console my own wounded heart with the fact it was better for him to experience the metaphorical version rather than actually having it happen to him. He'd come close to dying because of his association with me, and I wouldn't let it happen again. Being a part of my life made him a target now, just like everyone else I loved.

Nahu'ala's words of warning about Dane made sense to me now. Dane posed a great threat to me because I loved him so much, and my feelings toward him competed with my new duties. God, how in the world did Papa Joe stand being around Nana for all those years without succumbing to the yearnings, the gut-wrenching, overwhelming desire to be with her? How did he have the intestinal fortitude to watch her from afar as she lived her life alone, only spending time with her on Sundays? No wonder Nana was a bit off in the mental department. She had to do the same thing. Not only did she experience great sorrow and loss of a love that could never be, but then she died and came back, and knew the man she loved was some otherworldly being who could never return her love. Not because he didn't want to but because of his duty to protect and guard the Tree. How intense and painful the struggle to watch Nana marry another must have been for Papa Joe! Then again, they did end up together at least once during her marriage, which ended up producing Meemaw. Guess both of them, in a moment of weakness, succumbed to their yearnings.

I felt a lump of hot, salty tears form in my throat and pushed them back down. No way would I do that to him. I was barely able to stand what my new reality had done to my family. Adding Dane to the mix would surely push me over the edge into insanity. No, it would be better for him to believe our little high school romance was just that, a high school romance, and let it be snuffed out so he could move on. After all, wasn't that the usual way for teenage sweethearts to end? Weren't we supposed to grow up and apart, spread our wings and fly off to new territories? My parents were among the limited few who broke the tradition, got married, had a family, and stayed happily married. The odds were favored in the other direction. I sighed. Yes, Dane needed to find a new life, a new woman to love him and one he could love back. A woman who could offer her love to him without any worries or fears of having to take her love for him away.

God, how I wanted the woman to be me.

Though all these thoughts were difficult to wrestle with, I had to make the hard choice. I had a new destiny, a new duty to uphold. I felt a twinge of shame at my personal feelings when compared to the unbelievable suffering others before me had experienced. People had been murdered, families decimated, everything they loved destroyed because of Hattak'katos and his insatiable quest for the location. For water that didn't grant immortality, but merely extended human life by many years. An ancient sibling rivalry had resulted in the near annihilation of an entire race. For nothing but a few extended years on the planet and the money holding that little treasure would put in the pocket of whomever held the rights to the water.

Pathetic.

The sun was long gone and the moon was proudly spreading its silvery rays through my bedroom window. The ceiling fan above me was on full blast, the sleek, black blades pushing the heavy air in small circles. I glanced around and chuckled at the vast array of animal print items I owned...and the twisted irony. My ridiculous obsession with all things cat related was a long standing joke around the Newcomb household and with all my friends. No one ever lacked an idea for a gift because all they had to do was find something covered in faux cat print. Purses, shoes, T-shirts, underwear, notebooks, a lamp shade cover, and even my comforter sported various types of big cat patterns. Cheetah, tiger, lion, and jaguar prints were splashed all over my room. I even had one large, framed oil painting of a black panther with shimmering green eyes on the wall next to my closet. It was a beautiful rendition of the namesake for Junction City's school mascot, painted by one of Meemaw's bridge club friends for me when I made the cheerleading team. Now, it just made me furious. The resemblance to my enemy was uncanny, and I had to fight the urge to rip it to shreds.

Guess the fake skins aren't necessary anymore now that I have my own. Except I'm all white.

I looked at my phone and stifled a groan when I noticed it was after eleven p.m. Mom and Dad had crashed in front of the television earlier. The stress of the last few days weighed down their eyelids as they snuggled next to each other, seeking familiar comfort. They tried to stay awake so they could watch me attempt to change into a small cat, but once they settled into the soft folds of the couch, exhaustion overtook them. Meemaw ushered me upstairs with a silent nod of her head but stopped me in the hall-way. She insisted I try to sleep before I attempted a transi-tion. I had given her a weak smile. I nodded in agreement and watched her trudge off to the bathroom to take a shower.

The shower was still running, and I could hear her humming an unfamiliar tune. If she stayed any longer under the hot water, her skin would be so dry it would crack when she walked. I had promised Meemaw I wouldn't change until she was out of the bathroom. She'd almost seemed like a giddy school girl when she asked me about it earlier. I had laughed and told her I wasn't one hundred percent sure I knew *how* to shift on command, much less into a smaller cat rather than a ginormous pan-ther. I warned her it might be like a car stuck in neutral, engine revved up but going nowhere.

I couldn't stand to think about Dane any longer, so I forced my thoughts to concentrate on the day I followed the scent of my enemy. It had stopped at the Cohestra plant and had covered every inch of the car with the Illinois plate. My guess was that the car was a rental, which meant anyone could be driving it. There had been a lot of out of town visitors ever since the tornado ravaged Cohestra's main building. The vehicle could belong to an insurance adjustor, company investors, a new employee, or even Dane's dad. The only thing I knew for sure was the scent. Once I caught it again, I wouldn't stop until I destroyed the unholy beast. I let a loud huff of breath out as I recalled my conversation with Nahu'ala about my enemy. He had assured me that Hattak'katos did not possess the ability to control the minds of others, but he did have the capacity to sway emotions in the direction he wanted them to go. He could plant the seeds inside the minds of the weak or the hateful, just as he did so many years ago. It was a blessing and a curse at the same time, according to Nahu'ala.

If Hattak'katos had the ability to control the thoughts of others, the world would be in bigger trouble than it already was. The flip side, however, was it left Nahu'ala incapable of seeking out through his mind to find and destroy him. Nahu'ala told me that although he had his suspicions about the human identity of our enemy since he could recognize the smell, he wouldn't share it with me. I would be required to use my own instincts, my own internal knowledge, to lead me to the truth, and the only way to know for sure was to follow the smell.

The water shut off, and I listened to Meemaw dry herself off and get dressed. The new ability to hear things I couldn't before was strange at best, downright creepy at worst. Earlier, I had to put headphones on because the sounds of a family of mice in the walls scurrying around nearly drove me crazy.

Within seconds, Meemaw was walking down the hallway toward my room. I could tell she was barefooted, and though her steps would barely have registered to the ears of others, mine picked up the sounds as a loud thump. I stood up, slipped my shoes off, and opened my window. I tugged at the replica of Dane's basketball workout jersey he gave me last year for Christmas and pulled on my shorts. The soft tap of Meemaw's knuckles on the door made my skin begin to vibrate since I knew it was almost time to get the show rolling. "Door's open."

"It was so quiet in here, I was afraid you might have crashed too. I see I was wrong. So are you ready?"

"I've been ready. Someone decided to take the world's longest shower and made me wait for an eternity."

Meemaw ignored my jab and moved over to the edge of my bed, patting the comforter for me to sit next to her. "Sit a spell, baby girl. I got some things to say before you venture out in the dark and start your recon mission." My old bed creaked when I sat down next to her. As usual, she smelled like a warm summer day, a sweet mixture of cinnamon and jasmine. She put her damp arm around me and smiled. "You just remember this is a gift from God. He's chosen you, and He don't make mistakes. It's us silly humans who screw things up in the world. I may not understand all of this just yet, heck, even you may not. But after what you shared with us, you need to stand strong. What that monster wants ain't rightfully his. I've done some serious prayin' these last few days. I understand enough to know that ol' Hattak'katos ain't gonna give up. Don't let our ancestors down. Don't let their shed blood be forgotten. Don't let the Lord down. Stand strong for Him. Embrace your gift. And don't give the Devil a chance to worm his way inside your mind. You know he'll try. He will seek out your weaknesses to use against you."

"I know. I won't let him. I promise."

"Wrong answer, baby. You didn't choose this as your duty. It was bestowed upon you. And you won't be able to get through this on your own either. You are goin' to have to rely on your faith in the good Lord above to give you strength. He's the only one who can withstand the sharp barbs of the Devil. Now, you just remember these things I've told you when bearin' this burden gets too heavy, okay?"

"Yes, ma'am."

"On a personal note, I want to share two other things with you."

Curious, I cocked my head and let a small smile appear, "That wasn't personal enough?"

"I just love that smart mouth of yours." Meemaw smiled back at me, her eyes misting over with a light shimmer of tears. "And no, not personal enough. Number one is I want to thank you for easin' my mind about Nana and myself. Because of you, I can rest assured my mother wasn't loony and that I ain't either. My visions, dreams, premonitions—call them what you like—well, I thought my cheese had done slid off my cracker a few times. Worried myself into a tizzy durin' my late teens and early twenties, thinkin' my mind was about to crack. This whole town believed Nana was bonkers, and I was, oh, what did Lucinda always say? Oh, yeah, that my rocker dipped sideways sometimes. It don't much matter to me now, and I don't care if no one else knows we weren't crazier than a basket of wet cats. At least *we* know."

The pesky lump of tears was back in my throat. Afraid they would jump out, I simply nodded in agreement.

"Two, it's been a great joy watchin' you grow into a young woman, and I didn't think I could have been any prouder of you than what I was before. Now, I know that's not true. I'm, well, just so honored to call you granddaughter. I love you, Sheryl."

Meemaw wiped her tears away and gave me a quick, warm kiss on my forehead. She then pushed me to my feet before we both ended up bawling like two baby calves. I was already on an emotional roller coaster, so I just thanked her by giving her a bear hug. She returned the embrace for a few seconds, and then pulled away. "Enough of my jawin' and all this mushy crap. Show me what ya got, sweet pea. Concentrate on makin' your body small so that old Hataaka-hairball can't smell you."

"Meemaw! I can't do this if you're goin' to keep my emotions tiltin' one direction to the next! How am I supposed to concentrate when I can't decide if I should cry or laugh?" I eked out through my tears of sadness and laughter. "That was hysterical. I'm gonna call him that when I see him next. Or, well, guess I can't really talk in my other form, but I'll surely be thinkin' it!"

"You know what they say about the medicinal properties of laughter. Now, stop dilly dallyin' and get to...um," she snapped her fingers, trying to remember the correct term. "Skin-walkin'."

"I love you, Meemaw. So much."

"I love you too, sugar. Now, get to switchin' before the sun comes up! You've got some prowlin' to do!"

I moved away and stood next to the open window. I shook my head and closed my eyes and mind off to everything around me. I focused my thoughts on the rusty stench of the spilled blood of my friends, remembered the horrors of the words carved into Barb's lily white skin. I saw the stillness of Tami's dead eyes, frozen in terror as they stared into the night sky. I picked up the stale scent of the nasty beast from when he'd been in our house. I licked my lips and recalled the sensual yet sickening taste of Dane's blood on my thick tongue, the weight of his body as it hung like a limp spaghetti noodle in my enormous jaws. I knew from the change before it was intense emotion that caused me to turn, so I let my anger take hold. I visualized it as a long, thick, red piece of leather as it wormed through me. I mentally grabbed the edges and clung on, like I did as a child with the reins when I rode a horse, careful to control the fury from running amok. As my anger grew, so did the heat inside my body. It bubbled and churned like a pot of boiling water on the stove. I sought out imprinted memories of Tinker—his body size, structure—and tried to steer the anger and compress it down to fit in the smaller version of the beast inside me.

The struggle was intense, and I felt my body begin to tremble. In my mind, I called out to Nahu'ala, *"Please, help me. I need you to help me."*

"I am here, Little One. Always. We are one."

I heard myself choke back a sob of grief at the sound of Papa Joe's voice in my mind, and in that moment, I felt myself change. In a split second, the warmth vanished, and my body quit shaking. I felt the floor quake as Meemaw connected hard with the bed, and I heard her exclaim, "Dear Jesus, God in Heaven! In all my days! You did it! You did it!" but the location of her voice was all wrong. I opened my eyes and discovered it was because I was on the floor, on all fours, and Meemaw looked like a giant.

With a few steps, I stretched my small torso and wriggled in and out of her trembling legs, rubbing my head against her calf. Her hand shook as it reached out and touched my arched back. A low purr rumbled through me, and I responded to her gentle fingers by licking her bare skin with my rough tongue.

"Is it...are you...Sheryl?" Meemaw stuttered.

I replied with a dainty "*Meow*" and watched Meemaw's face light up, her smile bigger than I'd ever seen it before. Then, without a sound, I leapt off the floor and up to the windowsill, swishing my fluffy white tail. I glanced back once and saw the shimmer of tears streak down Meemaw's flushed face. Then I turned back and jumped on the roof and disappeared into the night.

CHAPTER TWENTY

Junction City, with all its familiar places and smells, took on a completely different aura when viewed from less than a foot off the ground. The scents filtered through my hypersensitive olfactory system, and I was bombarded with information each particular one held. I wrinkled my nose at the stench of the neighborhood dogs behind their fences, and had I been able, I would have laughed at the annoying barks from the baying mutts while I strode by. Into the dark night I moved, lithely trotting on silent paws. Unlike when I was in my full state, this time, I didn't feel the sense of raw power or intense rage flowing through me. My only guess as to why was because I was no bigger than any other ordinary housecat.

In other words, I was vulnerable.

With one last look at Meemaw's face as she watched in awe from my open window, I broke out into a full run. I zigzagged through the quiet street, making sure to stay in the shadows and away from the bright street lamps. Hell, the yapping hounds were enough, and I didn't need any more help announcing my presence to the world.

It was close to midnight, yet the blacktop was still warm under the pads of my paws. Dirt mixed with the oil from the street and adhered to the tufts of fur between my toes. I ignored the strange sensation and focused on the road, making sure to look twice before I crossed. My lips curved over my teeth in my feline version of a smile at the thought. Even when on four feet, the admonition drilled into the head of every child to *look both ways twice before crossing* still rang true.

Once I crossed Center Street, I crouched next to the stinky tires of old Mr. Howell's ancient Ford truck and listened to the sounds of the night. My ears flicked from front to back and picked up Mr. Howell's TV set, tuned to some comedy show, judging by the annoying laugh track. Three doors down, I heard the nasal symphony of Steven Marshall and his wife Annette. She was going to be my biology teacher starting next week. I wondered if I would be able to sit in class and keep a straight face, knowing she bellowed like a walrus when she slept.

Movement to my right caught my attention, and I saw Rosemary Hinkle, Junction City's local *Mrs. Robinson*, walk to her kitchen from her bedroom and fix a glass of water. She paused by the light of the fridge. No, she didn't pause, she *posed*. Her full rump in the air and back arched seductively, her heavy breasts flopping against her arm. She was as naked as the day she was born and the curtains were wide open. I looked to my left at Dale Standfield's house, and sure enough, he was watching her, his tongue nearly hanging from his mouth as he massaged his crotch. For once, the rumors spread by the Gossip Queens were right on the money. I shuddered, feeling a bit sick to my stomach at watching a boy I had a crush on in the fourth grade drool over a woman twice his age. Yuck.

Some things were better left hidden in the darkness.

I turned away from the spectacle. There were a few other sounds of humanity, but not much. No cars, no sounds of people talking, no *chug chug chug* from the silos at the Cohestra plant. Basically, the town of Junction City rolled up the carpet of life at midnight and tucked it away until sunrise.

Well, *most* of the town.

I raised my miniature nose and sniffed, sensing a summer storm was heading our way. Though the sky was cloudless at the moment, I felt the electrical shift in the air and knew within two hours, a downpour would hit. That short window didn't give me much time to snoop around. I straightened my legs and started to cross the street to head toward Dane's when the hackles on my neck stood erect. On instinct, my ears flattened and my tail bristled. The scent molecules were faint, scattered across the heavy air, but unmistakable. Without thinking, my body shot forward, guided by my nose. Within seconds, I came to the intersection of Center and Spruce and stopped.

Right in front of Ms. Johnson's house.

The small, three bedroom house was dark, the curtains drawn tight. Her yard needed to be mowed, and two unopened newspapers sat in silence in the empty carport. The old stench of my enemy was mixed with new death in the humid night air. I jumped the metal fence and stood on Ms. Johnson's back patio. My eyes focused on the fresh mound of upturned dirt, and I knew without investigating any further what was buried beneath it. Had Ms. Johnson dug the hole for the mongrel? No, I saw the vacant look in her eyes when she left the diner. She wasn't in any shape to do anything but skedaddle out of town and maybe pack a few bags. Plus, she'd been under Papa Joe's mind manipulation, and he'd convinced her there was no dog in her bedroom, so how would it have been possible for her to come home and bury something she couldn't see?

A light breeze shifted the direction of the heavy air, and the smell I missed more than anything in the world hit me. It was Papa Joe's musky aroma. Though no longer fresh, it was there. On instinct, I followed the trail. When I reached the back door, I noticed the smell was stronger. Full clarity hit me. Papa Joe had been here and disposed of the thing.

He thought of everything and everyone, even near the end of his time here. God love him.

With a growl of disgust and sadness, I left and headed toward Dane's house. I knew it was selfish and not part of the work I was supposed to be doing, but I had to see him. I needed to know he was okay, and in my current form, I could at least tell him the truth in my own mind while near him. It wouldn't really be closure for him, but it would be for me.

As I cut through the side streets toward the Witherspoon manse at the edge of town, my thoughts on the love of my life, I wasn't paying enough attention to my surroundings. On autopilot, I made my way through the quiet town until the stench smacked me back to the present. I froze and noticed I was less than a mile from Dane's house, and the smell of my enemy was strong and fresh. I crouched and scanned the area, looking with my sharp eyes for any signs of movement. But I saw nothing. I tamped down the growl of fury inside my chest, knowing any sound would give my position away if Hattak'katos was near. I lowered my nose and sniffed the ground, opening my mouth a bit to catch every molecule. Even though I recognized the scent trail was about twenty-four hours old, my senses were still on high alert.

Because the trail led straight to Dane's house.

Without thinking, I bolted. My small, furry feet kicked up dust and debris as I raced down the road toward Dane's. I forced my body to remain its current size, knowing if I changed and arrived in my *other* form and Hattak'katos was there, things would take a serious nosedive. I couldn't risk a fight with my enemy when people I loved were close enough they could sustain damage from the epic battle between two gigantic creatures. As my paws ate up the ground, I willed myself to remember this was a reconnaissance mission, not a full out assault.

If he's hurt one hair on Dane's or Ms. Emma's head...

I stopped at the edge of the Witherspoon property line and scoped it out. Though the front porch light was on and the landscape was dotted with garden lights, the rest of the house was dark. I ducked under the fence and crept through the thick, damp grass to the back of the property. The smell adhered to the driveway and waned as I made my way to the backyard. Moving away from the disgusting odor allowed my instinct to kill relax a bit. I paused next to the wooden trellis covered in vibrant red roses and listened. My heart slowed down when I heard the rhythmic breathing of Dane and Ms. Emma from their rooms upstairs. My heart settled back down and the fur on my back relaxed when the sounds of bugs and other nocturnal creatures greeted my ears. If Hattak'katos was near, the natural inhabitants around the Witherspoon place would fall silent.

Though I had climbed the sturdy trellis several times

in the dark during the last year, I had never accomplished the task with such ease or silence. My claws were like little spikes that dug into the soft wood, and within seconds, I was sitting on the windowsill, watching my sleeping lover.

From across the room, my eyes caressed the body of my sleeping mate. His head was cocked to one side, and his raven hair splayed out across the pillow like shimmering black gold. Seeing him made my new reality so much harder to bear. A low mew of sorrow left my lungs when I noticed last year's yearbook rested on his chest, opened to a page that had my junior picture. The knowledge that I would never wake up again next to his body, smell his scent on me, marry, have children, grow old together, tore a hole in my chest. No college in Memphis. No trips to Greenville to pick out my wedding dress or a walk down the aisle on the arm of my nervous father. Thoughts of the life I would not be able to live swelled inside me, and the pain was unbearable.

No, I wouldn't ruin my life or the lives of those I loved. I could end all of it and destroy this unholy curse, by killing Hattak'katos. If what Nahu'ala said was true, which I had no reason to doubt, the curse could only be passed on from one generation to the next through the lineage of the carrier. So if I could find out who Hattak'katos was in his physical state and determine if he ever fathered any offspring, I stood a fighting chance to stop the madness. If, indeed, the hairy fleabag spawned a band of little hairballs, I would just wipe the entire group out. Then there wouldn't be anyone or anything for me to protect the Tree from. It would be breaking the rules I was to follow by not engaging the enemy unless the Tree was in danger, but so be it. After all, Papa Joe broke the rules when he took Nana to the waters, and no harm came from that. So if I could stop Hattak'katos and ensure the Tree's safety forever, what could go wrong?

Renewed hope welled up inside of me. The muscles in my back haunches tightened, and I leapt from the windowsill onto Dane's bed without a sound. With tentative footsteps, I crept up to where his beautiful head rested and rubbed my head against his strong chin. He moaned and turned his body away from me, so I buried my paws in the silky waves of his hair. I stuck my nose in the mound of blackness and inhaled his aroma. Drunk off of my love for him and the intense, new ways my body could connect with him, I had to force myself to back away and remember why I had come here. It wasn't to ravage Dane's delicious body (which I *really* wanted to do at the moment). It was to make sure Dane and Ms. Emma were safe.

I jumped off the bed and padded over to the bedroom door. It was cracked just a hair, so I poked my head out and sniffed the air. The scent of Hattak'katos barely registered. He hadn't been in Dane's room, thank Heaven, but he *had* been somewhere in the house. From the location of the scent molecules, I surmised it had been downstairs. The hallway was clear, so I trotted off and down to Ms. Emma's room. When I peeked inside her open door, she was sound asleep on top of the covers, a thin sheen of sweat glistening on her head, arms, and legs. A conversation I'd had with Dane several weeks before popped into my mind. Dane had told me his mom was going through *the change,* and he was tired of the house feeling like a freezer. Said Ms. Emma was having trouble with heat surges and kept the thermostat down to sixty. I watched her chest rise and fall for a minute just to make sure her breathing was normal before I turned around and walked over to the top of the stairs. When I did, the smell became stronger.

It was coming from the kitchen.

I went through every room in the lower level, sniffing and investigating, and saved the kitchen for last. The beast hadn't been in any other room except the foyer, the hallway, and the kitchen. When my feet stepped on the cold tile floor, the scent nearly knocked me over. Unable to stop myself, I jumped onto the counter and made a beeline for the two empty coffee cups and the large bouquet of fresh flowers next to them. My lips curled back, and I couldn't stop the snarl in response to the stench from the cup to my right.

He'd been here. Inside the house!

Whoever Hattak'katos was in his human form, he wasn't a stranger. Dane didn't drink coffee, but Ms. Emma did, and it seemed she felt comfortable enough with the bastard to let him inside her house and have a drink with him. I didn't need to get any closer to understand the flowers had been brought in by the same hands, for the rotten smell of my enemy masked the aroma of the lilies and roses.

Then, it hit me. Like a freight train barreling through my mind, the answers to all my questions slammed into my head. I jumped off the countertop and sped back up the stairs to Dane's room. I forced myself not to look in his direction, for I knew the distraction of his body under the covers would overpower me. In one long jump, I cleared half the room and was out the window without making a lick of noise. Seconds later, I was down the trellis and loping through the front yard.

I ran faster than ever, my paws pounding the warm pavement. The Witherspoon spread was less than two miles from my destination, and I reached the driveway in record time. The trail Hattak'katos left was so strong it was almost like a shimmering light. The horrid smell whipped me into a frenzy. Just as I cut across the street and darted under the construction tape, the voice of Nahu'ala thundered in my mind.

Go home! Now is not the time! Something is wrong.

Unlike before, when the commanding voice of Nahu'ala resounded in my head, I didn't cower or feel overcome with the urge to comply with his orders. I was beyond rational thought, my senses to kill and maim controlled me now. When I saw the same vehicle in the back parking lot with the Illinois license plates, surrounded by the appalling stench, I was beyond livid. I was less than thirty feet from the construction fiasco at the main building when searing heat scorched through me. In mid-stride, I went from small housecat to magnificent beast. The unstable ground and remaining debris that had yet to be cleaned up by the construction crews shook when my massive paws struck the ground.

I chuffed and snorted, my low growls calling Hattak'katos out from inside the building. He didn't answer, so in a few swift strikes with my paw, I destroyed his car. The front, back, and side windows shattered when my heavy paw made contact with the roof. The second swipe took the driver door clean off the hinges, and the third one caused all four tires to explode when I jumped and landed on the roof. In the distance, I heard the baleful sounds of hounds yapping from the noise, but I didn't care. I wanted Hattak'katos's blood to fill my mouth with its coppery taste; I needed to feel chunks of his flesh rip from his body. The urge to clamp my jaws around his soft throat and crush his airway turned me into a snarling, growling, drooling maniac.

I jumped off the demolished sedan and in two short

steps was in front of the entrance to what was left of the main building. He'd been there within the last hour; the scent was that fresh. Determined to drag his furry torso outside and destroy it like I'd done to his car, I started to lower my head and use it as a battering ram through the makeshift entryway but stopped when another smell invaded my nostrils. A flash of white caught my attention. I shook the anger from my mind and forced my trembling body to hold still while I read it.

The game has begun. Guess where to look next? Make sure to play in human form,

or you and your loved ones will regret it.

The smear of red at the edge of the paper sent shock-waves of fury through me. It was Meemaw's blood. I roared with anger, the sound so loud the glass from some of the newly installed windows in the front of the main building shattered. The enormity of the words crushed my soul, for I knew Hattak'katos was at my house, and my family was in grave danger.

I had no choice but to obey and play his game if I wanted to save their lives. The painful truth exploded through my mind and was followed by the change in my body. Back on two feet, I ran through the quiet of the night toward my house, my mind numbed with dread over what I would find once I arrived.

TWENTY-ONE

Just like earlier at Dane's, I stood still at the edge of the driveway and scanned the area around my house, trying to control my breathing. The place was dark. The entire street was quiet. Not even the dogs barked when I ran by. I choked back an angry sob at the fresh stench of Hattak'katos as I walked up to the front door, which was wide open. When the rhythmic sounds of life from my parents in the living room hit me, I almost collapsed from joy. Careful to sidestep the sections of the porch I knew creaked when stepped upon, I crept up and stopped at the doorway and peeked in. Mom and Dad were sound asleep on the couch, blissfully unaware of the horror that awaited them upon waking.

I slipped inside and shut the door behind me without making a sound. I paused and contemplated waking them but decided not to involve them. I gave them both a good once over to make sure they weren't injured. My pulsed quickened at the knowledge they were fine. No, I wouldn't subject them to what was about to happen. This was my fight—my burden to bear—not theirs.

I turned and made my way up to the second floor, mindful of the spots of Meemaw's blood. My heartbeat increased in intensity each time I saw a new droplet of red. Though it wasn't a large amount, which meant the injury was superficial, it was still her blood. Spilled by a monster who shouldn't exist and wouldn't any longer after I was through with him.

The scent trail led straight to my room, which is where Meemaw had been as she watched me change. Anger flooded my mind when it dawned on me the hairy bastard must have been hiding, watching, waiting for me to leave so he could snatch her. Sure enough, a large smudge of vibrant red was on the windowsill and had begun to trickle down the wall. He must have snuck up behind her and knocked her down. My body shook from anger at the thought.

Please, God, let her still be alive.

I spun in a quick circle and took in every spot in my room, looking for the next clue, but I knew I wouldn't find it. I could tell from the scent trail he'd only walked in and right back out. The nasty stench hadn't adhered to anything else, never veered from the straight path into my room and then back down the stairs. I paced around and tried to think. He wanted, no, he *craved*, to know the location of the Tree. Hattak'katos had killed thousands, if not hundreds of thousands of people—almost wiped out an entire race to find it. It was his wicked life's quest. He was trying to distract me from my purpose, my new destiny, by toying with my emotions. Maybe he thought he could break me. Kill my friends, kidnap my meemaw, thinking it would be too much for me to handle, and I would cave and show him the way.

Be strong, Little One. He will stop at nothing to learn the secret. Nothing.

My knees buckled as a wave of dizziness slammed inside my mind. I collapsed in the middle of my bedroom floor in a crumpled heap. The minute Nahu'ala spoke inside my head, I knew Meemaw was facing more than just being a kidnap victim.

She was bait.

Hattak'katos would lead me to her body in hopes I would be overcome with grief and take her, just as Papa Joe had done with Nana, to the Tree for healing. I had to figure out where he took her and get to her before it was too late.

Think, Sheryl! Where would he take her?

My head thumped from the overload of information and stress. Too many thoughts and images fluttered around. It was like I was in a ticker tape parade in Times Square. In frustration, I shot up from the floor and stared out the window, my sharp eyes scanning the quiet town for any signs of movement. When my phone rang, time seemed to stand still.

Because it was Dane's ringtone.

My mouth felt like I'd stuffed it with a wad of cotton, and my body froze as I stared at the phone in the middle of my bed. The sweet, tinkling chimes of the bells I'd assigned to Dane beckoned me to answer, but somehow, I knew when I did, my world would be destroyed.

God, please. Let him be calling to tell me about a nightmare he had. Let him be horny and looking for a midnight romp in the sack. Let him have had an argument with Ms. Emma and want to talk about it. Anything, anything, other than what I know it is. Please?

My limbs thawed and in one quick move, I was across the floor and on my bed. I snatched the phone up before the fifth ring.

"Dane?" I whispered.

"Dane is...indisposed at the moment. He asked me to relay a message to you, and don't worry, you won't need to take notes. It's quite simple to remember. Ready?"

The deep voice drummed inside my head. His sarcastic, mocking tone almost drove me to madness. I wanted to reach through the phone line and grab him around his neck, silencing his wicked vocal chords forever. Though I'd never heard it before, I knew who it was, and why he was calling.

"Yes," I grunted, my body tense, every muscle on edge.

"You'll find us all by following *his* blood. Oh, and remember the rules. Come in human form. Change, and they're as dead as a sack of meat. Mmm, and I'm sure just as tasty."

I never had a chance to respond because my hand crushed the phone into tiny pieces. Sharp slivers from the screen embedded under my palm, but I didn't care. It took every bit of strength I could gather to keep myself on two feet, instead of four, and my screeching growl of torment to remain inside me.

Leaping out of the open window and onto the roof, I jumped and rolled in the soft grass. An invisible clock was ticking away precious seconds in my mind, counting down the time left I had to find Meemaw and Dane before Hattak'katos took their lives. As I ran through the streets of Junction City, it dawned on me I heard no sounds. No bugs, no nocturnal creatures. Nothing but the faint sounds of traffic from the freeway miles away. Even the nightlife recognized all hell was about to break loose in

Locasia County and scurried off to hide from the brewing battle.

In the distance, I saw a crackle of lightning skitter across the black sky. The storm was close, and judging by the electrical surges in the air, it was going to be a wicked one because it wasn't a *natural* storm. It had been conjured. But the thunderstorm would pale in comparison to the storm I was about to bring down, right on top of the furry bastard's head.

Within minutes, I was close to Dane's house. I didn't need to stop, for the scent of his sweet blood was like a living entity I could almost see. When it hit my nostrils, I had to literally wrap my arms around my chest to hold my form. Hot waves of anger bubbled and churned inside me. Forcing my body to comply and not change was too much. I stopped and bent down, throwing up in the ditch. While I heaved onto the dry grass, I could hear Nahu'ala whispering inside my head, encouraging me to stand strong and not give up. With my final retch, I silenced his voice, determined to listen to my own instincts, rather than his.

Once finished, I stood up and wiped the back of my hand across my damp lips. My mind was alone, free from the sound of Nahu'ala. At that moment, I made the conscious decision to absorb every nuance, every inch and responsibility of my new life. I felt the melding of my mind with his and we became one. I was no longer Sheryl Ilene Newcomb. I was Nahu'ala, guardian and protector of the Tree of Living Waters. My role—my destiny—was to protect it. Nothing more, nothing less.

A new plan began to take shape as I stared at the road in front of me. To accomplish it would require help, even though I knew I wasn't to involve outsiders. I knew where the final showdown would take place, with whom, and why.

So, instead of following the scent trail of Dane's blood, I ran to the house of the one and only man who I knew could, and would, help me. I prayed I had enough time, and the strength, to reach inside his mind and bend him to my will before it was too late.

TWENTY-TWO

Thirty minutes later, I stood in front of the crumbled entrance to the main building at Cohestra. The safety lights blinked in the distance, casting eerie shadows across the empty parking lot and building. The note from earlier had been removed. What replaced it was a dark stain of Dane's bloody handprint on the porous wood. Though the building had sustained heavy damage from the tornado, sections of it were still intact. I pushed the dilapidated door aside and stepped into what once was the lobby. My heightened vision made it seem like the overhead lights were on, as I navigated my way through the debris and twisted pieces of metal and sheetrock toward the water packing plant in the back.

With nimble moves, I picked my way through the mess. The aromas of Dane and Meemaw were intermixed with the stench of blood and of Hattak'katos. He was close. I could feel the negative, evil energy surround me. It permeated the air like a thick cloud, making my eyes water and forcing me to hold my breath before madness overcame me.

I made it to the center of the plant, the place where the water treatment and distribution center had once been. It had some damage to the ceiling and the walls, but the main floor was untouched. Two massive pieces of steel about twenty feet high, each in the shape of bullets, stood like silver statues at opposite ends of the room. My throat clamped shut and I couldn't breathe when I saw Dane and Meemaw. Dane was to my right and Meemaw to my left, both crudely tied to each water cylinder with thick rope around their waists.

Had I not been able to recognize them from their scents, determining who they were would have been difficult. Dane's face was gone, his skin stripped down to the bare bone of his skull. He'd been scalped, his once beautiful head of hair missing and his once white shirt was red, covered in bright red crimson and gray brain matter. Chunks of flesh from his torso, arms, and legs rested in a mushy pile next to his feet. I closed my eyes from the horrific image and listened for the sound of his heartbeat, knowing I would hear none. I let out a low, whimpering growl.

I opened my eyes and swung my gaze to my left. My throat opened and a huge *whoosh* of air left my lungs in the form of a tormented roar. Meemaw still had her face and hair, but every other inch of her exposed arms and legs had been shredded from her body. Her shirt had been ripped off and in her chest the letters S I N had been clawed into her skin. Two pools of crimson, each about the size of basketballs, had formed underneath where her arms dangled at her sides. The sound of her blood dripping as it left her fingertips made my vision blur as tormented wails growled from my soul. My hopes to save her were dashed when I realized she wasn't breathing either. They were both too far gone to be saved, even by the Tree or the hand of God himself.

Oh, God, their deaths were my fault!

"Well, seems you can follow some directions well since you arrived in your weaker form. Sorry about the mess. Couldn't control myself. You shouldn't have made me wait. Patience is not one of my virtues."

The voice was from the ceiling, and I looked up just in time to see a body jump from its perch from the railing on the second floor. His feet landed on the concrete with a soft *thud*, his body crouched low to absorb the impact. He stood up, his dark brown eyes never leaving my own, and smiled. It was a sick, warped grin that I wanted to rip off of his face. As I stared at his familiar countenance, etching every line of his face, each curve of his body, every strand of long, thick ebony hair in my memory, I fought with all my might to control my anger. "I see you decided to take over Dane Witherspoon *the fourth*. Knowin' your history as I do, I'm not surprised you killed your own child," I responded, seething with fury at the man standing in front of me. "Your son may look like you, but thank God, he never acted like you."

His smile grew bigger as he replied, "I believe you mean *used to* look like me. You know...past tense since he's dead. And don't refer to him as my child. That word embodies a relationship. Feelings. Neither of which I had with him. He was just a potential vessel, and one I decided not to use. He was too weak...too kind-hearted. You seemed surprised by my actions, which I find rather odd. You know I've killed many."

With moves not perceptible to the human eye, I saw

him begin to shift to his right. The predatory circling had begun, and I welcomed it. Hungered for it. He had wounded me, tore my heart to shreds, but I would strike back with a mortal blow. "No, you aren't capable of real emotions. You kill without thought, without mercy, without reason. Not just strangers either. Family. Your ancestors. *Your people,* Hattak'katos. For this? For access to water tinged with the grace and power of Heaven? I already know the waters don't contain eternal life. That's only from God Almighty. It just has the power to extend life, but those who drink it will eventually pass. So why all this? Why the insatiable desire to control it? It's not like you and I don't possess the ability to live for hundreds of years on our own. But that isn't enough for you, is it? You've jumped from body to body, from generation to generation. How vain of you to constantly seek out youth through your own flesh and blood. The gifts given to you weren't enough, were they?"

"Ah, you truly have become Nahu'ala, haven't you? I hear it in your words and see it behind your eyes. Am I wrong?" Hattak'katos purred.

"No, brother, you aren't wrong. I just wanted to hear you admit from your lips your cowardice. My prayer is that when you hear the depth of your greed, the descent of your madness, you will finally be free of your curse and take ownership of the immense sorrow you've caused."

He threw his head back and laughed, heavy and deep. His thick, raven hair bounced in harmony, his features eerily similar to Dane's. The disgusting sound reverberated off the walls of the building and caused some of the teetering debris to fall from the ceiling and crash to the floor around us.

"Cursed? *Cursed?* Is that how you view our abilities,

brother? Come now, it's just the two of us. Tell the truth, for I won't judge you. Are you saying you don't enjoy what we can do? We can walk the line between animal and man, enjoy the pleasures of our animalistic desires in both human form and when on all fours. Tell me you didn't enjoy copulating with your mate, Beulah, in the woods, free from all inhibitions? Tell me the feel of the power running through your body and the capacity to control the thoughts of others, to bend them to your will, doesn't make you feel like a god? Tell me the taste of flesh and blood doesn't excite you in ways nothing else can? We *are* gods, brother. The water will prolong our reign and then, we will truly be blessed. And you are right. My quest to control it hasn't been for monetary gain. I couldn't care less about the pathetic humans. I want the ability to wield the power. Join me, Nahu'ala. Cast aside your misplaced loyalties and ancient moral codes for these feeble humans and embrace who and what you are, my brother. Together, we could rule the world!"

"It has always been greed and power that controlled you, Hattak'katos. Power to control things you weren't meant to, and covetous greed for things never meant to be yours. Those two wicked desires have overtaken your heart and your mind. Turned you into a monstrous beast with no morals, no values, and no ability to love or feel compassion. You orchestrated the near annihilation of our *people*, Hattak'katos. You have killed thousands of innocents in your attempt to take something that never belonged to you! We were to work in tandem to keep the Tree a sacred, holy place. God sought our race out because we stayed true to His ways. We worshiped Him as Creator and loved and respected the world He made for us. But your heart was already full of hate when your totem came.

Look what it turned you into. A cold-hearted, vicious killer."

His feet began to move faster, his body making a slow descent into a crouch. I could feel his anger bubble to the surface, along with my own. I mimicked his movements, my eyes focused on his. Madness and fury pulsed behind them, and I knew my own reflected the same. "I should have killed you that night beside the river long ago, *brother*," he spat, the words hurled like vocal daggers. "You have been nothing but a thorn in my paw...an annoying gnat in my face. I should have known better than to think I could lure you to reveal the location. Guess I misjudged your loyalty to those pathetic hunks of flesh, didn't I? You didn't come to save your mate so long ago, so your off-spring and *mine* matter even less."

My response was low and angry. "Your lusts overshadowed your ability to plan, Hattak'katos. Had they still been alive when I arrived, I might not have been able to control the urge to save them, and may have taken them to the Tree. So don't blame me for your inability to control your hunger."

"You are a fool, Nahu'ala. A stupid, old fool. You've been in the human realm too long. It's made you weak, soft. Which will make ending your life as easy as swatting a fly."

"You've never been more wrong, *brother*," I hissed back.

The second the words left my mouth, I heard the sound I'd been waiting for behind me as my body changed forms. It was the unmistakable grind of metal on metal of a pump-action shotgun. Hattak'katos heard it too, but had already changed as well. The two of us stood, nose to nose, in the middle of the plant floor, the loud snarls and growls of anger filled the space, and more debris began to fall from above us and crash to the floor.

The monster who had once been my brother made the fatal mistake of taking his gaze off my own for a split second to look in the direction where the sound emanated from. In that small blip in the vast ocean of time, all the pain our people endured, all the death, destruction, sorrow, torture, and bloodshed, congealed into one throbbing mass of rage. The loss of Nana, Barbara, Dane, Meemaw, and others piled on top of it—the last spark before the pyre of my rage erupted into a fiery inferno. When I opened my mouth, the growl was so loud it sounded like a stadium full of women had just screamed all at once. I bared my teeth and lunged.

My fangs sank into the warm flesh under his burly neck, my claws embedded in the strong muscle of each shoulder blade. The force of my attack knocked him to the ground, his shrieks of pain muffled from my grip on his vocal chords. He spat, hissed, and tried to knock me away with painful swipes of his paws into my back, but I ignored him. Chunks of my fur and flesh were ripped away, but I welcomed the pain. I had him in a death grip and nothing would make me release his flesh from my jaws.

We rolled over and over on the cold concrete, knocking more debris from the shaky ceiling and second level. A large piece of metal ceiling landed on my back with such force I felt my bones in my back haunches crack, and my grip around his neck waivered for a brief second as I took in a lungful of dusty air. He sensed the advantage and with one mighty jerk, braced his back legs against the wall and pushed with his front paws at the same time with all the strength he possessed. I felt my body fly backward and knew I was heading toward the metal cylinder where

Dane was tied. I tried to shift the trajectory of my torso so I wouldn't crash into his corpse, but I overcompensated. Before I could veer further to the right, my head slammed into the control valve next to the metal tank. The cold steel sank deep into my eye socket, the pain so intense it took my breath away. When I pulled myself free, I collapsed from the pain.

"Die, you unholy beast! Die!"

The sound of the familiar voice rang out, followed by the bellow of the shotgun blast. My ears rang when Drexel Kilgore fired, pumped once, then fired again. From my spot on the floor, I watched the hairy, black torso of Hattak'katos shudder as chunks of his flesh were blown off his right flank and shoulder. He roared in pain as his body crashed to the floor, the blood spatter covering a full ten feet around him.

God, help me end this.

I summoned every screaming nerve to obey my command to move and stood up. My legs wobbled as I made my way across the debris and blood strewn floor over to the quivering body of Hattak'katos. His breath came in heavy gurgles from not only the damage I'd done earlier, but the gunshots as well. His enormous feet pawed at the air, a sad attempt to deflect my attack.

With ears back and teeth bared, I shot my head forward and ripped out his throat. Hot blood squirted from his artery, and his gurgles ceased as I yanked his windpipe from his torso, then spit it back on the floor next to him. He jerked twice as his eyes rolled back in his head and his paws fell to the ground. Blood poured from his wounds and covered the floor and my feet in seconds. I heard the last *lub-dub* of his heart and felt his life force leave his body. When it did, he was no longer in animal form.

I rocked back on my hind feet, ignoring the pain in my hips, and brought both my heavy paws down on top of his fragile human skull. His head exploded under my weight, shooting out blood and gore in all directions. When I stepped back to examine my work, I chuffed in glee.

The battle was over. This time, Abel slew Cain.

"Is it dead?" Drexel Kilgore yelled from the other side of the building. His voice was full of anger and awe at the same time. Without moving to face him, I nodded my head. "Good! Now, come on. We got to get outta here before the whole place falls down on us."

I didn't know how much longer I could stay conscious and on my feet, but there was no way I was going to leave the body of Dane and my meemaw. I wasn't sure how well the connection and control I had over Drexel would work when I was in this form, but I needed to find out. I swung my gaze and locked eyes with the old man and spoke in his mind. *Help me free them and take them out of here.*

Drexel didn't move for a full ten seconds, but then seemed to find his legs. He crossed the plant floor in long, purposeful strides, making sure to steer clear of not only the dead corpse of my former brother, but also from me. I limped behind him, my thick claws making a strange sound against the cold concrete. In seconds, he was next to Meemaw and the sharp knife he produced from his back pocket sliced through the old rope with ease. I crouched down right next to her feet and tried to ignore the rank stench of her death. *Place her on my back, and then climb on as well. Hold her so she doesn't fall off.*

Drexel complied, and I moved with slow, tender steps through the mess of the plant and out to the soft grass next to the front parking lot. He jumped off my back and eased my meemaw down on the grass. I started to head back inside to get Dane, but just then, a bright bolt of lightning hit a tree less than twenty yards from the back of the plant. It was followed by a loud clap of thunder that shook the entire area. Under my feet, I felt the movement before I heard the sounds of the interior of the plant collapsing in.

I bolted and ran back inside, desperate to free Dane before the entire place was a pile of rubble. Pieces of metal showered around me, peppering my back and head. I made it to Dane's corpse just as a twelve foot section of the second floor railing crashed near us. I latched on to the rope, bit through it, gathered Dane's remains in my mouth, and started to head back to the front.

I was overcome with physical and mental pain at the taste of his blood in my mouth. Sorrow distorted my thoughts long enough that I never heard the sound of the steel girder above me creak and whine until it was too late. The tail end of it smashed into my right hip, knocking me to the ground. Dane's body went flying out of my jaws, bouncing like a broken toy in front of me. Sickened by the sight, I roared in pain and dug my claws into the concrete, pulling myself across the floor on my belly. It took several seconds to reach Dane, but once I did, I scooped him up in my jaws and willed my body to obey my commands.

Several minutes later, my torso trembling from pain and exhaustion, I reached the threshold of the main entrance. I could hear sirens in the distance and feel the cooling rain pepper my fur. Drexel was suddenly by my side. "Come on, honey. Let go. I've got him," his gentle voice urged. I unclasped my mouth and waited until I felt the weight of Dane's body leave before letting my head collapse on my bleeding paws. "Sheryl, you must change back. Hurry. You can't let others see you like this."

He was right; I knew he was. But my mind, body, and

spirit were destroyed. I didn't have the strength or stamina to move any more. I couldn't feel my back legs or see out of one eye. Consumed with grief and sorrow of so much death and destruction, my mind began to shut down. As the sirens neared, I felt a warm hand touch my snout.

"You said if things got bad, you wanted me to say the word Talulah, and it would give you strength. So, Sheryl, Talulah. Come on, Talulah!"

Just as the ambulance and fire truck turned in the drive to the Cohestra plant, the entire building behind me collapsed. I could smell the acrid stench of fire as flames roared to life. I paid it no attention and just focused on the name I had commanded Drexel Kilgore to repeat if things went sour.

Talulah. Talulah. Talulah.

When I realized I could feel pebbles press into the skin on my bare cheek, I knew I'd succeeded in changing. Drexel squatted down and whispered in my ear. "Your secret's safe with me."

I heard the doors to the ambulance and police cars open and four sets of heavy footsteps running our direction. With my last bit of strength, I reached into the mind of Drexel and the others heading in our direction. *I'm fine. Do not take me to the hospital. Call my mother. Now.* Then I reached up and grabbed Drexel's hand and whispered only in his mind.

And you will remember nothing about my visit or what you've seen. You just heard yelling and stopped to help. You were out tracking the bear that killed Tami and heard a commotion.

TWENTY-THREE

PART FOUR – NEW BEGINNINGS

The pencil in my hand snapped as the emotional weight of my memories hit me. I looked down at my feet and noticed it was the fifth one I'd broken during the last three hours I'd been writing. Remembering that day had drained me.

I smiled when I heard footsteps in the hallway and answered my mother before she had a chance to knock on my door. I rubbed my stomach to quiet the growl of hunger. "Come on in," I said, setting down the shattered remains of the pencil, then scooping up the others at my feet. My fingers were tired and needed a break, and the food she brought smelled heavenly.

"Wow, you've been a busy gal. How many pages you think you've written?" Mom asked as she set down the tray in front of me, full of baked chicken and fresh vegetables from our garden.

"I'm not sure but enough that my fingers refuse to do any more writing today. Thanks for the food, Mom."

"No thanks needed, precious. You must be feelin' better today. I see some color is back in your checks. A nice, healthy pink glow."

I replied with a smile I didn't feel on the inside and took a huge bite of the crispy chicken. With a slight nod of my head to the chair across from me, I motioned for her to sit. As she did, I saw her cast a quick glance at the stacks of paper on the table, a heavy dose of curiosity and revulsion behind her brilliant blue eyes. I could tell she was desperate to ask, but instead, steered the conversation in a different direction. "Your dad called earlier to tell me some interestin' news. Said the whole town is gabbin' about it."

I swallowed the mouthful of chicken and followed it with a long gulp of cold tea. "Oh yeah? I hope it's somethin' other than what happened three months ago."

"Sort of. Well, the first thing is that ol' Drexel Kilgore shot and killed a huge black bear on his property yesterday. He then called the sheriff to come out and showed him the carcass. The sheriff came by the diner earlier today to tell your dad. Said he thought we would like to know the town is safe again from the beast that killed Barb and Tami. Apparently, ol' Drexel's been huntin' for the monster ever since Tami passed."

I stopped chewing on the chicken leg for a minute and contemplated telling Mom the reason for Mr. Kilgore's quest wasn't actually his idea but decided not to. I sort of felt bad, knowing an innocent creature of the woods had to die to keep my secret safe. "Huh, well that should quell the fears of the town."

Mom gave me a strange look and continued. "Your dad also said Drexel came in today for lunch, joined by Mayor Ransford. Their topic of discussion was about the Cohestra plant and what to do about it. Apparently, Drexel put in an offer to buy it from Ms. Emma, and she accepted. And the mayor is fit to be tied about the purchase."

I took a deep breath to suppress the pang of guilt in my heart at the mention of Ms. Emma. Though we hadn't spoken since Dane's funeral, since she'd basically gone into seclusion afterward, it didn't surprise me she was going to sell the place. The entire town had been shocked when she produced Pops Witherspoon's Last Will and Testament. It left everything he owned, including the Cohestra plant, to my Dane, and in the event of his death, to Ms. Emma. The old man had completely cut out his monstrous son. "I don't understand. Why would that upset the mayor? Or anyone else? Drexel's offer is a *good* thing. People will be able to go back to work."

"At the mill, yes. But Drexel isn't going to revive the water plant. He wants to tear down the entire structure and rebuild...expand the services of the mill. That's it."

I couldn't stop the sarcasm from leaking into my voice. "And that decision is bad, why?"

"Sheryl, honey, *we* know it's a good thing, but others don't. The mayor thinks it will destroy the economy of the town, and a lot of people agree with him. After all, it's been three months, and those who worked on the water side of the plant are antsy to get their regular paychecks back in their pockets. And, accordin' to what your dad overheard durin' the heated conversation between Drexel and the mayor, some of the townsfolk think it's a cop-out, tryin' to whitewash what happened there. Guess they think rebuildin' the water plant will somehow erase the memories of the murders. They seem to believe goin' back and workin' on the same soil will lessen the pain, or somethin' along those lines."

I bristled. "They are wrong. *Nothin'* will ever make it

better. Period. Doesn't matter whether they raze it to the ground or rebuild it to twice its original size, it won't change the fact that innocent blood was shed there. Besides, the entire Delta region blossomed and boomed over the years from the production of *crops*, not the bottlin' of water. That was only a recent development and one that's caused nothin' but heartache and pain. So the mayor and the other fools who believe like him can all just suck it up and be happy the mill will be up and runnin' full steam soon. I guarantee you, Drexel won't let one employee go. He'll find a place for them. No mouths in Locasia will go hungry, at least not because of lack of work."

Mom reached across the table and patted my hand with a reassuring touch. "Calm down, Sheryl. You don't have to convince me. I'm on your side, remember?"

"I'm sorry. Didn't mean to get so riled up. So if Ms. Emma took the deal, do you think she'll be leavin' town, too?"

"I don't know, honey. She's grievin', which means she could change her mind at the drop of a hat. If I had to venture a guess, I'd put my money on her stayin'. After all, her roots are here, and her only child's restin' here. If it were me, I'd stay close, just to keep the good memories alive. But that's just what *I* would do. It never bodes well when one tries to anticipate the reactions of others."

I forced down the lump of tears in my throat. "I wish she'd talk to me. I have somethin' I need to tell her. Do you think she'll ever speak to me again?"

"When her heart has mended enough, she will. I'm sure seein' your face will just make the pain of losin' her son fresh again. I bet you once the final batch of debris is removed from Cohestra, and she never has to lay eyes on the spot where her son died, she'll be receptive to a visit from you."

"I can't imagine why she'd stay. She's had to endure a lot of whispers and tongue waggin' for years now."

Mom dismissed my words with a twitch of her hand. "Honey, we could be livin' in paradise and people would *still* find things in the lives of others to spread gossip about. But this, well, it's a lot to absorb. Even though the *whole* truth isn't known, what people have been led to believe is so shockin', it will never really leave their minds. I mean, the printin' press couldn't spit out the news articles fast enough when the investigation concluded. This town ain't seen this much sorrow in *decades*. Ol' Pops Witherspoon dies. Then his son, who skedaddled out of town years ago when he knocked up a *colored* gal, shows back up, then flies into a killin' rage when he realizes he's been left high and dry in his estranged father's will and owns nothin'. Tried to get his grubby paws on what he thought was his inheritance by goin' after his own son, and you and Meemaw gettin' caught in the middle durin' your nightly run. And ol' Drexel, out and about with his shotgun, searchin' for the hairy beast responsible for killin' his kin, happens by and shoots a Witherspoon. Lord-a-mercy, the story was so intense the national news even picked it up. I swear, Mississippi ain't never in the news for anythin' good. I just wish we could tell them..."

Mom stopped when her voice cracked. Fresh pain and sorrow made my stomach lurch as the chicken tried to digest. This time, it was my hand that reached out for her. "I'm so sorry about Meemaw. I tried...I was too late."

Tears filled her eyes, but she blinked them back before they spilled down her cheeks. "Sheryl, we've already been over this. You did everythin' you could to save them, even gettin' to ol' Drexel as backup. You were smart enough to know you couldn't handle the situation alone, and I think your instincts knew what the outcome would be the second you realized that monster took them. As much as I miss her, and as much as you pine for Dane, you did what Papa Joe and the Lord entrusted you to do, which was keep the location of the Tree of Living Waters safe. You place the blame for the deaths of your friends and our loved ones right where it belongs. On the head of that hairy beast."

I let out my pain in a low growl and saw her flinch just a fraction. "He doesn't have a head anymore. I crushed it after I ripped his throat out."

Mom took a deep breath and leaned back against the chair. Though we had danced around the subject and I'd told her and Dad the basics of what happened at the plant, I had yet to tell either of them *everything*. Movement in my stomach convinced me it was time. "I'm ready to answer your questions if you're prepared to hear the answers."

It took a few seconds for her to formulate a response. I wondered if she was sending up a silent prayer to the Lord for strength to withstand what my answers would be. Finally, her jaw relaxed and she sat up a bit straighter. "I'm ready. Okay, so this is probably goin' to sound silly, but, um, how are you supposed to protect the Tree if you don't change into your *other* form? I mean, I don't think you have changed since that night, right? After all your injuries, you can still skin-walk, can't you?"

I almost laughed, thinking she was teasing me, until I noticed the look of real concern behind her eyes. "It's not that I can't change. I just don't need to right now. I'm givin' my body a chance to heal... among other things. Don't worry though. The location of the Tree is safe. Promise."

Taken aback, she queried, "How can you be so sure it's safe? What if Hattak'katos had other children and they have the same sick, twisted desire to find the spot?"

I softened my voice to try to calm her fears. "Mom, he had no other children."

Mom threw her arms up in exasperation. "How do you know that, Sheryl? He lived out of state for *years*! He could have sired an entire herd!"

I suppressed a chuckle at her use of the word *herd*. "But he didn't. You see, we do have some ingrained rules, edicts if you will, that can't be broken, no matter how much we want to break them. One of them is we only have one mate during our time here—never again for the rest of our lives. The desires or urges to be with another never happen, and even if they did, we couldn't *do* anythin'. Certain body parts wouldn't, um, *function*. When Dane IV met Emma Carter, they were mated, and that is a one-time only event. Same with Papa Joe and Nana. Papa Joe called it a safety valve. Something God put in place to ensure only one person would be born in each lineage to be able to shift. Besides, when I touched Hattak'katos's skin when he was in human form, I was able to, hmm, how should I put it? I couldn't exactly read his mind, but I *absorbed* his thoughts and memories. I knew the second my paws connected with his flesh Dane was his only offspring."

Confusion spread across Mom's face as she tried to understand my words. "Well, what a relief that there won't be others for you to fight! But wait. Are you sayin' that me...or Meemaw...could have been?"

"If things would have happened differently with Hattak'katos, yes. Either of you could have been the one to skin-walk. The ability is inside you, but the essence of

Nahu'ala was never transferred to you to complete the bond and the change."

Mom shook her head like she was trying to remove her perplexed thoughts. "Help me out here. Dane Witherspoon the *fourth* was Hattak'katos, right?"

"Yes, but not until he mated with Ms. Emma. Before then, his grandfather, Dane II, was. And before him, Dane Witherspoon."

"Wait, Pops Witherspoon wasn't ever Hattak'katos?"

"No. The power skipped him, just like it did with you and Meemaw. When Hattak'katos still resided in Dane II, he stayed until his grandson hit puberty. He sensed the evil in his heart and left the old body for Dane IV. Pops was well aware of the family's lineage and feared his own son when he sensed the transformation happened. He was afraid the hunger for power and the greedy soul of his child would be too hard to control, so he sent him away. It was just an added bonus it happened near the same time Ms. Emma turned up pregnant. Of course, Hattak'katos agreed to leave for other reasons...not because his father ordered him to split town. He left because he wanted to work on gettin' all the land. He knew the Kilgore clan would never sell it to him, so he finished high school and college in Chicago and took a job in Washington, D.C. He was workin' on a deal for the government to take over Drexel Kilgore's land. It would have given him free access to Caney Creek and no one would have batted an eye if he came down here to head up the farm."

"I don't understand. Why didn't Papa Joe just kill Dane II, when he had the chance? The old geezer lived a long time!"

"Papa Joe was just followin' another guideline. No blood can be shed unless the Tree was in danger. Even though Papa Joe knew Dane II, embodied the soul of Hattak'katos, he wasn't allowed to harm him. He wasn't actively confrontin' Papa Joe to force him to reveal the location. Hattak'katos was the weaker of the two. His powers and abilities weren't as strong as Nahu'ala's. So like all evil vermin, he used trickery and deceit to get what he wanted. His plan was to stay put in Locasia County and keep searchin' on his own for the location by buyin' up all the muddy land in the Delta. That's why the family started the water bottlin' business at the plant. It was a sham company, set up to give the clan a reason to purchase the swampy land."

"Pardon me for my mouth hangin' agape, but all of this is so hard to put together."

"I know, Mom. It's hard for me too. I mean, when I think about him waitin' in the shadows, knowin' Papa Joe's body was old and Nahu'ala would need to transfer his power to me, I feel sick to my stomach. That's why he tried to get to me the night Nahu'ala saved me when I was nine. His visit that night was twofold. If Hattak'katos could turn me to his side, he could find the location. After all, I was just a small child. He thought I could be easily manipulated. If that didn't work, he planned on killin' me because he knew the lineage ended with me. If I was dead, he would be free to search the Delta without worry, and then simply pass on to either my Dane—or *his* offspring—when he felt the need for a newer body."

Mom bristled. "Well, that ol' hairy creature thought wrong! He had no clue how strong us Kovlin women are!"

This time, I did chuckle. "Estrogen always trumps testosterone."

"Ain't that the truth! No man, not even one with fangs, claws, and fur, can stand up to a pissed off woman!"

For a few blessed minutes, we laughed. Hard. The bright afternoon sun showered my bedroom with its golden rays. The beams licked across my mother's headful of newly gray hair, making it look like a white halo encircled her head. Hearing her sweet laughter inside the four walls of my bedroom reminded me of my childhood, and a twinge of sadness swept through me. Life at the Newcomb house would never, ever be the same.

Mom's giggles trailed away, and a shadow of concern spread across her face. "So if I am undertandin' all this right, since your enemy is dead and his bloodline has ended, then you won't ever need to change again, right?" As she spoke, she became more animated. "Yeah, you can go on and live a normal life, Sheryl! Finish high school...go to college like you planned! I know you said you couldn't be with another again, which means your Dad and I won't be grandparents, but that's okay! There isn't anythin' holdin' you, or any of us, here now. Right?"

The second her words left her mouth, I felt the movement in my stomach again. This time, it was a hard, jarring poke. On instinct, my hand went to my stomach and gave it a gentle pat.

I had to tell her.

"My duty holds me here, Mom. You and Dad don't have to stay just because of me. I know you two have talked about retirin' and movin' down to Florida. Families are spread out far and wide these days, and there is no reason why we should be any different. But I'm bound to remain in Locasia."

Mom's face fell. She looked crushed. "Why, Sheryl? If the danger is gone, why must you stay?"

"As I said earlier, I absorbed the thoughts and memories of Hattak'katos right before I killed him. Believe it or not, he knew somethin' even I didn't know until I touched him. It was the reason he killed my Dane, and what will keep me bound to the Mississippi Delta until the day I die."

Mom swallowed hard, her voice cracked with pain when she spoke. "What...what did you see?"

I couldn't bring the words up from my throat. Instead, I rose and moved over in front of my petrified mother, knelt down, and took her shaking hands and placed them on my stomach. I saw her flinch in shock when she felt the movement. Her eyes bulged and tears sprang out and raced down her cheeks as full clarity set in. Her shoulders jerked as silent sobs wracked her body. She took her hands away and pulled my head to her lap and began stroking my hair, her body slowly rocking me back and forth just as she did when I was a child.

For a few minutes, we clung to each other like we were both the other's life vest before we drowned from the tidal waves of what the news meant. I ended our embrace when I heard Dad's truck a few blocks away. "Dad's almost home. Better pull ourselves together before we tell him he's goin' to be a grandpa."

Mom wiped her tear-stained face on her shirt. She stood up and tried to press out the wrinkles in it with her hands. "I just have one more question. Do I have time to ask?"

"Yes, about two minutes."

"Why, if Hattak'katos knew you were pregnant with Dane's child, did he kill Dane?"

I let out a deep, painful sigh and rubbed my belly. "Because only one heir can be in the lineage at a time. My Dane was the next in line. Now, he isn't."

"I don't understand."

"It means, our child carries *both* lines. Which means he or she could turn either way. This...has never happened before. Ever. Hattak'katos saw an opening to gain access through me, and he took it."

"That's why you are writin' all this down, right?! For your child! To make sure they understand where they came from...and why!"

I nodded in agreement. "I'm just like every other mother from the dawn of time. Waitin' for their little one to arrive and hopin' and prayin' they raise them right so they'll make the right choices and decisions when grown. I won't let Hattak'katos win. I won't. His evil spirit won't inhabit our child."

Hot, fresh tears rolled down my cheeks at the thought. I expected my mother's reaction to be the same, but to my surprise, it wasn't. She straightened her shoulders, stood ramrod straight, placed her right hand on my belly, and locked her vibrant blue eyes with my own. "The Kovlin women are strong, and we don't back down from a challenge...or run away in fear. There is much love between us all, and by the grace of God above, we will stand by your side and help you teach the truth to our grandchild. We won't let the wrong choice be made."

I sputtered, "Mom, we haven't even told Dad yet. Aren't you puttin' words into his mouth? What if he doesn't share your opinion?"

Mom looped her arm in mine and ushered me toward the bedroom door as we heard Dad pull up in the driveway. She smiled at me and gave me a conspiratorial wink. "He doesn't stand a chance between the two of us. Besides, after we tell Ms. Emma she is goin' to be a grandma, it will be three against one. Ain't no man in the world ever stood a shot against those odds." We both laughed as we made our way down the stairs. Just as the door opened and Dad tromped in, Mom whispered, "So...got any names picked out yet?"

I thought back to when I sat in Drexel Kilgore's living room, reaching into his mind to inform him he would make a trip to the Cohestra plant ten minutes after I left, shotgun in tow, and to shoot the black beast when he had a clean shot. The last instruction I gave him was to say the name *Talulah* if he noticed I was struggling to survive. The name of my spirit mother was a strong force and kept me in this world.

"If she's a girl, Talulah. Loosely translated, it means *Leaping Water* in Choctaw. If he's a boy, then Dane Jared Newcomb."

Mom pulled me closer and whispered, "Perfect choices, baby girl. Perfect."

We paused at the bottom of the stairs as Dad looked at the two disheveled women in front of him. He'd been around females long enough to sense something was amiss. He tried to break the tension he felt with an attempt at humor. "If you two are havin' a conversation about womanly things, I can always head back to the diner. Because if one of you is about to ask me to head to Wilson's Sundries to grab a box of feminine products, I'm outta here."

Mom and I both burst out laughing. She let go of my arm and moved next to Dad, grabbing his elbow and leading him to the couch. The smile on her face would have lit up the living room had it been dark. "Oh, we were discussin' womanly things, but a trip to buy feminine products isn't necessary. Won't be for another, what Sheryl, six months at least?"

Dad's face was unreadable as I sat down next to him.

His watery blue eyes searched my own and I just nodded in agreement. I then took his hand and placed it on my belly. A wide smile of understanding crossed his face when he felt the dainty kick. He pulled me close and enveloped me in a bear hug. I felt Mom's arms wrap around us both, completing the family circle.

I knew then, at least for the time being, as Nana used to say, my world was right as rain. Our love would trump the hate from my enemy's lineage. Love for my parents, Dane, Meemaw, Papa Joe, Nana, my people, and mankind, would win out. Darkness didn't stand a chance. We wouldn't let it. I would raise the baby surrounded by love so strong, my child would never even consider turning into something evil.

I couldn't stop the low, rhythmic purr of contentment as it vibrated deep from within my chest, the love of my family filling me with peace.

God, the purr of happiness was so much better than the growl of anger.

About the Author

To learn more about Ashley and her other works, please visit her website www.ashleyfontainne.com

Sneak peek of "Blood Ties - Book One of The Magnolia Series"

BLOOD TIES

THE BONDS ARE PERMANENT...

THE MAGNOLIA SERIES - BOOK ONE

ASHLEY FONTAINNE
LILLIAN HANSEN

Chapter One

It took all of his concentration to keep his foot steady on the accelerator and the truck hovering at the speed limit. He clenched his jaw hard. The sound of his teeth grinding filled up the entire cab. He was still pissed off he was out doing this in the middle of the frigging night. He knew his eyes were bloodshot. Lack of sleep and staring at the dark highway for the last three hours made them feel like he'd poured salt into them.

"You ain't your own man, Lucas Hill. Your ass is owned by another. Just his bitch to jump when he snaps those meaty fingers and points," he grumbled to himself.

He swirled another mint around in his mouth, hoping it hid the smell of the three beers he had earlier. He didn't even want to think what would happen if he got pulled over. With his luck, it would be for something like speeding, not waiting the full three seconds at a stop sign, or not using his turn signal before changing lanes. He blinked twice and made sure to keep the truck in between the white lines. All or any of the minor screw ups would put him in the middle of a shit storm for sure. He had no desire to make headline news like other runners from committing some stupid traffic infraction. Jail time for drug running was stout enough, but he shuddered at the thought of what his sentence would be if some nosy pig poked his face inside the cooler and got the shock of his cop life viewing its contents.

A shiver of panic travelled down his spine, and he gripped the steering wheel of the inconspicuous black Dodge truck with a bit more force. While chewing on the well-worn spot on his bottom lip, he double-checked the side and rearview mirrors. Nope, he was safe. No blue lights behind him and no strange vehicles following either. Normal, sane people who lived normal, sane lives weren't out at three o'clock in the morning. He let go of his crushed lip when the nasty rust taste hit him.

"Damn, another piece of my flesh offered to him. Damn!" he muttered after he swallowed the droplets of his own blood.

Lucas didn't fear much in this world, especially not the frigging police or even a stint behind bars. He could handle both with ease. And it wasn't like he sought out trouble; it just seemed to come to him. Like a damned homing pigeon or boomerang—it kept landing right on his lap, no matter how hard he tried to stay on the straight and narrow. His last six-month stint in Lafayette County, Tennessee, had been a walk in the park. A brawl with the bouncer at *Gigi's Strip-n-Tip* landed him in the slammer after he got too friendly with a damned stripper. What a joke. How were you *not* supposed to touch all that flesh when it was in your face? When it was all said and done, he was convicted of battery after a dust-up with the bouncer. Lucas had some bruises, but the bouncer suffered a broken nose and was missing two front teeth.

Time spent in county lock-ups was a breeze compared to doing hard time like his old man was doing down in Tucker. The sorry excuse of a father would die behind the concrete walls of the maximum security prison.

His minor run-ins with the fat, slow, and lazy cops of the Southeast were as easy to handle as banging a virgin. Slip in, slip out, and leave a slight stain of blood behind as a reminder you were there. He didn't fear the police, the court system, the frigging President of the United States.

Not even God himself. There was only one person who set his guts on fire and turned his blood cold. The cold-hearted devil with black eyes and no heart ruled his life—and the lives of others—with an iron fist. Lucas feared the man enough not to even think his name inside his head, much less speak it out loud. If he made some asinine mistake tonight, and the contents of the cooler in the passenger floorboard were discovered, Lucas was a dead man.

No doubt. Dead, dead, *deadski.* Then someone else would be delivering *his* organs in the middle of the night to some sick, rich douchebag with enough cash to pay for new body parts on the black market.

He squinted as he fought to see through the dirty windshield, looking for the blue *Hospital* sign. He couldn't believe he checked everything else on the frigging truck *but* the washer fluid levels. If he knew who the dick was who prepped the truck, he'd introduce himself the proper way—with a fist to his face. Christ, he needed to get a grip on his nerves. After all, this was his twentieth delivery and every time prior, the goods were dropped off without a hitch. Still, he knew he couldn't let his guard down or focus his attention on anything else until after the package was in the hands of the buyers.

And the Devil was off his ass.

This was all Ray-Ray's fault. Dumb bastard. He wanted to kick his own ass for becoming friends with the little prick. What the hell had he been thinking? The moment he met Ray-Ray in tenth grade, he knew the dude was trouble with a capital *T.* But Ray-Ray had access to the life he had wanted to live—girls, drugs, and hot cars. His mom struggled to put food on the table every day and keep the lights on in their small apartment. Clothes were bought at second-hand stores, and it was a rarity if they fit. Or lasted longer than a few weeks.

His piece of shit, no-good father hadn't been around since Lucas was a sperm stain on his mom's panties. Coward ran off the second his mom told him she was knocked up. The old geezer never coughed up a red cent to help support the fruit of his filthy loins. When he was a young buck, he hated his old man for it. Now that he had grown up some and spent some of his own life behind bars, he understood—at least a little. Can't pay for a child when you have no income or way of making any. Plain and simple.

His less-than-stellar home compared to the fancy, upscale one Ray-Ray lived drew Lucas in like the old moth to a flame. And like all moths, he got burned. But if Ray-Ray hadn't gotten his brains blasted out of his head two days ago by his ex-old-lady's jealous boyfriend, Lucas would've given him an earful about the situation he'd left him stuck in. He wanted to go two years back in time and drink about three more Jack-n-Cokes so he would have passed out on Ray-Ray's couch. If he had, he would never have ridden with him to "make a delivery for some quick cash" as Ray-Ray called it.

"Five hundred bucks? For just ridin' shotgun? What you deliverin', Ray-Ray? Gold dust?"

"Nah, man. Just a one-of-a-kind piece for my uncle. That's all you need to know. You just watch our tail, got it?" Ray-Ray had said as he smiled at Lucas, half-drunk in the passenger seat.

And then Ray-Ray sealed his fate by telling the Devil about him. Lucas had been the one who noticed something wasn't right about the set up when Ray-Ray was about to pull and drop off the package. No sooner had they driven past the designated point, the cops swarmed the parking lot like a horde of locusts. Ray-Ray and Lucas watched the entire scene from across the street at the Waffle House after they hid the truck in the back parking lot. They tried to act casual when they sat down, but both of their hands shook with fear.

The Devil had been so impressed with Lucas's skills, considering he had been drinking, that the job as runner was pulled from Ray-Ray. Lucas was forced to watch as the Devil had his henchmen beat Ray-Ray unconscious as punishment for including a stranger in the run and the loss of the expensive package. The broken bones, bruises, and burns inflicted served as a reminder to never deviate from the Devil's careful plans. Neither of them said a word of protest when their sentences were handed down. Lucas's street instincts lit up like a Christmas tree when around the Devil. After witnessing what the man was capable of doing to his own flesh and blood, Lucas knew better than to question his orders.

So did Ray-Ray. The two friends never spoke again about the day both of their lives changed as they stood on the dirty carpet inside the Devil's lair. He thought about that for a second—nope, their friendship ended when they walked out from the smoke-filled office of the man. And now, at twenty-five, Lucas was stuck in a job he didn't want and no escape route was in sight.

When he first started, he assumed he was trafficking drugs. But on his second delivery, he made the mistake of lifting the lid of the cooler to see what type of drugs he was transporting. When he saw the heart and lungs tucked inside the slushy mess of ice, he puked for twenty minutes. After that fun experience, he made sure never to open the lid again. His mom's warnings about hanging out with the wrong crowd from his youth slammed into his thoughts. He was glad she was dead and hadn't seen what her only son was doing for a living.

Though Lucas hated shuttling the cold body parts—and it gave him the willies just to think about it—he had grown quite fond of the cash his deliveries put in his pocket. Ten thousand dollars a pop. Unfortunately, his wallet was running on fumes after being behind bars for so many months. When he was released from jail, he went back home and tried to find a legitimate job. He hoped his time away would have given the Devil a good reason to find another runner, but it didn't work. It was the beginning of his third week out of the joint, and he had celebrated his newfound freedom and the lack of contact from the Devil with a few beers while watching a basketball game on television. But his brief taste of freedom ended with a phone call around midnight.

He pulled his head out of the memory. He needed to concentrate on the task at hand. No mistakes. He noticed the moon was hidden by a thick blanket of rain clouds. The streetlights were a joke. He wondered why in the hell would someone want to live in the backwoods, redneck city. For Christ's sake, the streetlights were no better than a flashlight with a low battery. He wished the sky would open up and let the rain out, but then he wondered if the frigging wipers worked.

A bright, flashing yellow sign ahead on his right beckoned him to *Fill your tank and your belly!* He glanced at his watch and then down at his gas gauge. He had plenty of time to stop and refuel, and he needed to hit the head. Thinking about his boss made the beer and coffee run through him. As he pulled in off the main highway, the faint neon of green from the old dashboard cast an eerie glow on the white cooler. He swallowed his disgust and fear, looking away from the thing before he really *did* freak out.

Once he pulled up to the pump and cut the engine, he yanked off his jacket and tossed it over the container. He reached over and pulled on the black ball cap down low over his forehead. The brown wig attached underneath made his neck itch but he ignored the urge to take it off. The two, crisp twenty dollar bills sat on top of the instruction letter that had been taped to the underside of the driver's seat. The surgical glove slid with ease over his left hand and then he picked up the cash. Before he stepped out of the truck to go inside to prepay for the gas, he scanned the area. No other cars...no one lurking in the shadows.

No paper trail was to be left behind. No cell phones, GPS, or anything electronic were to be used during the delivery process. Even the old Dodge didn't have the fancy tracking equipment of the newer vehicles available. A different disguise was to be used each time and was provided, along with the cash for gas and instructions, under the front seat. The rust-bucket was always parked in the same spot each time—at the back end of the funeral home, hidden behind the storage shed under an old tarp.

As he stepped out of the truck and into the sweltering heat of the Tennessee evening, he shot a final glance over to the floorboard and made sure the cooler was hidden. Satisfied, he held the twenties in his gloved hand and the ignition key in the other. He pushed the lock down and headed into the store.

As his boots crunched the pavement under his feet, Lucas couldn't shake the sensation that Ray-Ray *was* with him. Well, at least part of him. After all, it wasn't like Ray-Ray's uncle to let any body part go to waste.

Forcing his emotions to remain in check, he walked inside. There had been an additional note tonight. A handwritten one that had made his head spin when he read it.

Glad you are back. Stop getting into trouble and keep your nose clean. I'm watching you and don't want to hear any more news about my favorite courier locked up behind bars. Because if it happens again, there won't be enough of you left to fill a baggie. Got it?

Lucas got it. Message received loud and clear. As he walked to the counter and paid for his gas, he thought about the line from a movie in his youth. *You ever dance with the devil in the pale moonlight?*

Yes, yes he had. And he wanted nothing more than to get off the dance floor and never waltz again. But the Devil owned his dance card. Lucas was so dizzy from all the spinning, he knew he was stuck in the tight embrace of the macabre leader's arms.